b l u e m

No Good From A Corpse

LEIGH DOUGLASS BRACKETT was born in Los Angeles in 1915. Her first love was science fiction and she was a great fan in her youth of Edgar Rice Burroughs' Tarzan and John Carter Martian stories. Her first story, 'Martian Quest', was published in *Astounding Science Fiction* in 1940, but her first novel was *No Good From A Corpse* (1944), a tough-minded and realistic thriller in the Raymond Chandler tradition which few at the time realised was written by a woman.

On the strength of the novel, she was brought to Hollywood where she worked with William Faulkner and Jules Furthman on the script of Howard Hawks' film version of Chandler's *The Big Sleep*. She became one of Hawks' favoured screenwriters, responsible in later years for the screenplays of *Rio Bravo* (1959), *Hatari!* (1961), *El Dorado* (1967) and *Rio Lobo* (1970), curiously all films about male bonding. Other notable screen credits include another Chandler adaptation, Robert Altman's *The Long Goodbye* (1973), and the second *Star Wars* movie, *The Empire Strikes Back* (1979).

Her only other crime books are *The Tiger Among Us* (1957), a harrowing precursor of the vigilante yarn, *Silent Partner* (1969) and *Stranger at Home* (1946) which she ghost-wrote for actor George Sanders.

She is better remembered for countless short stories and fourteen volumes of science fiction which include classics like *The Sword of Rhiannon* (1953), *The Big Jump* (1955) and *The Long Tomorrow* (1955). Equally at ease in diverse popular genres, Leigh Brackett was also awarded the Spur Award for the best Western for *Follow the Free Wind* (1963).

Happily married to science fiction writer Edmond Hamilton from 1946 to his death in 1977, she survived him barely a year and died in 1978.

Series Editor: Maxim Jakubowski

b l u e   m u r d e r

Leigh Brackett
No Good From A Corpse
The Tiger Among Us

Gil Brewer
13 French Street and *The Red Scarf*

David Goodis
The Burglar

Davis Grubb
The Night of the Hunter

Dolores Hitchens
Sleep with Slander
Sleep with Strangers

Geoffrey Homes
Build My Gallows High

William P. McGivern
The Big Heat

Newton Thornburg
Cutter and Bone

Joel Townsley Rogers
The Red Right Hand

Charles Williams
The Diamond Bikini

Cornell Woolrich
Rear Window and Other Stories
(Introduction by Richard Rayner)

blue murder

NO GOOD FROM A CORPSE

Leigh Brackett

SIMON & SCHUSTER

LONDON • SYDNEY • NEW YORK • TOKYO • TORONTO

First published in 1944
First published as a Blue Murder paperback by
Simon & Schuster Limited 1989

Simon & Schuster Ltd
West Garden Place
Kendal Street
London W2 2AQ

Simon & Schuster of Australia Pty Ltd
Sydney

British Library Cataloguing-in-Publication Data available

ISBN 0–671–65284 2

Phototypeset by Selectmove Ltd in Ehrhardt Roman 10.5/12pt
Printed and bound in Great Britain by
Richard Clay Ltd, Bungay, Suffolk

It is better to live,
Even to live miserably;
The halt can ride on horseback;
The one-handed, drive cattle;
The deaf, fight and be useful;
To be blind is better
Than to be burnt;
No one gets good from a corpse.

HÁVAMÁL

CHAPTER ONE

EDMOND CLIVE saw her almost as soon as he came into the tunnel from the San Francisco train. She was standing beyond the gate, watching for him, and somehow in all that seething press of uniforms and eager women, she was quite alone.

Clive smiled and tried to shove a little faster through the mob. Then her gray eyes found him. Suddenly there was no mob, no station, no noise, nothing. Nothing but the two of them, alone in a silent place with the look in Laurel Dane's gray eyes.

Clive's step slowed. He saw her smile. He answered and went on, but the lift was gone out of him.

She was wearing a white raincoat with the hood thrown back. There were raindrops caught in her soft black hair, but the drops in her thick lashes never came out of a Los Angeles sky. Her arms went around him, tight.

He kissed her.

'Hello, tramp.'

'Hello. Oh, Ed, I'm so glad to have you back!'

He looked down at her. Cream-white skin, her face that had no beauty of feature and yet was beautiful because it was so alive and glowing, her red mouth, full and curved and a little sullen. He found it, as always, hard to breathe. He bent his head again.

They stood for a long time, the noise and the crowd flowing around them and leaving them untouched. Her lips were faintly bitter under his, with the taste of tears that had run down and caught in the corners of them.

'The car's outside, Ed.'

They walked toward the door. She held his hand, like a child.

Clive said, 'Johnny didn't come down?'

'No. And you're to go straight to the office. He's got a client waiting. A very expensive and very urgent client.'

Clive groaned.

1

Laurel said acidly, 'Female.'

'Oh, well! That's different.'

His wide, mischievous grin did a lot for his face. It was a sinewy, angular face that had known its way around for a long time, and there were those who said that Ed Clive could look tougher than the people he sent up. But his dark eyes were alert and friendly, his smile was nice, and most women decided he had a certain sinister fascination. They caught themselves wishing secretly that their own men didn't look quite so *good*. . . .

He made himself comfortable in the coupé.

'You drive, baby. I'm an old man, and I'm tired.'

'The age I'll grant, but the rest is just plain laziness.'

Clive shook his head. 'Hookworm.' His eyes were closed. The rain on the metal top sounded like a regiment of small boys bouncing golf balls.

'Drive slowly, dear, and be careful of skidding.'

Laurel pulled his hat down over his face and drove off through swirling streets toward Hollywood.

After a while she said, 'I've been reading all about the case. The Los Angeles papers played it up big. They just loved watching a native son make the Frisco cops look silly.'

'I hope they used a good picture of me.'

'With that mug, darling, there's no such thing. You're not happy about it, are you?'

'The case or the face?'

'You know damn well what I mean.'

Clive's mouth was suddenly bitter. 'I caught me a killer, all right. She's twenty-three; she had red hair and the bluest eyes I ever saw. Sure, I'm happy.'

'Twenty-three,' echoed Laurel. 'And she killed him for love.'

The car quivered sharply. Clive looked up. Her hands were rigid on the wheel.

'Love can be a terrible thing, Ed . . .'

He waited. When she didn't go on with it, he said gently, 'You want to tell me now, or later?'

She sighed. 'I suppose you've known all along, haven't you? I mean, that I have one of those things they call a Past.'

'Uh-huh. And I also had an idea that you had an idea that the Past might suddenly sneak up and become the President again.'

'I'm afraid it has ... No, not now, Ed. I have a rehearsal I'm late for already; you're tired and you have business waiting. Come down to the club tonight. Early.' Suddenly she laughed. 'I've got a surprise for you, Ed.'

'Yeah? I'll bet I can guess.'

'Try.'

'I'll bet it's a man.'

'Mm-hm.'

Clive relaxed, tilting his hat over his eyes again. 'How do you make a noise like jealousy?'

'You'll make a noise like something when you meet him, Ed!'

'Not any more, baby. I've got calluses.'

'You wait!' Presently she burst out, 'Oh damn it, Ed! Why do you stay around me if you don't love me? Why do you want to be so ...'

Clive said quietly, 'I thought we had that all settled.'

'No.' Her voice was throaty with tears. 'No, it isn't settled. It's ... Oh, Ed, I wish I were different. I wish you were different. I wish the whole thing ...'

'Sure.' He patted her thigh. 'Sure.' He let his hand stay there, feeling the lithe play of the muscles as she drove. His mouth twitched, once, as though something hurt him.

They didn't speak again until Laurel stopped the car and said tiredly, 'Well, here I am. You can drive yourself back to your office.'

Clive sat up. They were on Ivar just below Hollywood Boulevard. Across the sidewalk were the pseudo-airliner doors of the Skyway Club. The rain had slacked off.

There was a chrome-and-gray custom job parked in front of them. Clive frowned at it, but he didn't say anything. He took Laurel inside.

The foyer was small but opulent, with the airliner motif carried throughout. Queenie, one of the bouncers, was standing in front of the closed inner doors, talking to a tall, well-built man in a trench coat and a snap-brim felt.

'Can't help it,' Queenie said. 'Boss's orders. Not even the President could get in during rehearsal.'

The man in the trench coat said something under his breath and turned around. He had a blond mustache above a sensual

3

mouth. His skin was tanned, like Clive's. His eyes were very blue, very bright, and very angry.

Clive said, 'I thought that was your car outside. When did you start haunting the Skyway Club, Farrar?'

Farrar ignored him. He said to Laurel, 'That's a fine way to treat people! Honey, tell this big ape who I am.'

Clive knew she already had. He got in when he wanted to.

'I'm sorry, Mr. Farrar. It's a house rule. We can't take anybody in to rehearsal.' Laurel smiled.

'Well, if you put it that way – ' Farrar smiled back, making it personal – 'I suppose I can't get sore.' He examined Clive. 'I'm disappointed. I thought you'd be wearing your crown of laurels.'

'I was afraid it would sprout in the rain.'

'Just as cute as ever,' said Farrar. 'All right, Laurel. I'll be around again.'

He went out. Queenie said, 'The ork's waitin', Miss Dane.'

'Be right there.'

Queenie went inside, letting through the sound of a man's voice crooning 'As Time Goes By.' Clive jerked his head at the way Farrar had gone.

'Is that your surprise man?'

'Farrar? Heavens, no!'

'What's he doing here?'

'Oh, he came in for dinner one night around three weeks ago – just after you left for Frisco. He fell for me, I guess. He's been making a pest of himself ever since.'

Clive said, 'That guy is not used to being called a pest by the female sex.'

'So I gathered. Well, I just don't like his type.'

'You better keep on not liking it. Kenneth Farrar is supposed to be just another honest private dick, but between the two of us he's one of the smartest blackmailers on the Coast.'

A brief look of fear crossed Laurel's face. Then she shrugged. 'I can handle him all right.' She came close to him. 'Promise me, Ed? You will come early tonight. There's so much I have to tell you, and not all of it about me.'

'What does that mean?'

'I'll explain tonight. Just promise me, darling. Please.'

4

'Sure.' He laughed and kissed her. She put her arms around him tightly, the way she had in the station. He felt her shiver.

'I'm scared, Ed,' she whispered. 'I'm scared.'

'I can send someone over to keep an eye on you.'

'Oh, no. It isn't like that. Maybe it isn't anything at all, except that I've got a guilty conscience. Anyway, I'd be all right here.' She pushed away from him, smiling. 'I've got to run, or Jimmy will scalp me. Try and get some sleep, Ed. You look worn out.'

'Getting old,' he said cheerfully. 'So long, kid.' He started to go, and then suddenly Laurel said:

'Ed . . .'

'Yes?'

She was looking around at the place as though she had never seen it before, or as though she wanted to be able to remember it if she never saw it again.

'Ed, I've been awfully happy here, with you.'

She was gone before he could say anything. The swinging doors let through the sound of the man's voice and bit it off again.

Clive walked slowly out of the Skyway Club.

CHAPTER TWO

THERE WERE five people in Edmond Clive's office. Three men, one of whom, a big black-haired fellow, was slumped in a dark corner with his head in his hands; two women, and a silence that Clive's entrance did not break but only deepened.

The office was not too large. It was paneled in Philippine mahogany and contained an expensive leather couch, matching armchairs, filing cabinets, and a desk. Wide windows looked out on the intersection of Vine Street and Hollywood Boulevard a block away.

Jonathan Ladd Jones got up from behind the desk. He was a little man with a large head and a face like a healthy, sunburned frog. His eyes might have belonged to a spaniel, only for a certain wicked brightness.

Clive said, 'Hello, Johnny.' He included the whole room in his smile. He took off his hat and coat. Johnny said, 'Hello, Ed.' Aside from that, no one spoke. Four pairs of eyes followed the course of Clive's five feet and eight inches of well-tailored symmetry across to the desk and into the chair that was still warm from Johnny Jones's small bottom.

'Now,' said Clive, 'what can I do for you?'

The man in the corner took his head out of his hands and said uncertainly, 'Eddie . . .'

Clive's face became perfectly blank. Cords tightened in his cheeks and around his mouth, standing out sharply. He started to get up.

One of the women rose. She said, 'Mick didn't want to come. I made him. I'm Jane Hammond, Mr. Clive – Mick's wife. Everything I have, everything I might have, depends on your help.'

Clive sat down again. After that first glance he avoided seeing Mick Hammond.

'I'm sorry,' he said. 'I imagine you understand . . .'

'Listen to me, Mr. Clive!' Her gloved hands crushed the big suede bag she held. She wore blue, expensively plain, and she had perfect legs. Clive was beginning to notice that she was beautiful, in a clear, golden, highbred way. She was also tired, inexpressibly so, in a way that had nothing to do with her body.

'I've waited a very long time to see you,' she said. 'I can't tell you how important it is.'

Clive lighted a cigarette. He was politely impersonal now, but his hands jerked. 'I never handle divorce cases.'

The young man sitting nearest the desk laughed loudly. 'Divorce! That's good, that is! Divorce!' He resembled Jane Hammond. He was probably younger, but he was already getting saggy and bleared, and there was no iron in his face. He began to grow red with the force of his amusement.

The girl over on the couch said, 'Richard. Shut up.'

She said it with an old, accustomed venom. She was curled up like a child on the seat, so that nothing much of her showed except that she wore a crimson coat and had light brown hair. Her head hung forward so that her face was hidden.

She said, 'We've argued about coming here until I'm sick of it. Now we are here, let's get it over with. For good.'

Jane Hammond said, 'My sister, Vivien Alcott. And my brother, Richard.'

Richard Alcott stopped laughing, breathing as though he had been exerting himself. Clive nodded briefly at both of them. Alcott acknowledged it. Vivien ignored him.

Jane Hammond came to the desk. 'You don't understand, Mr. Clive. I'm trying to prevent a divorce – or something . . . something more permanent. I know how things are between you and Mick. But all that was years ago. It's different now. And from what Mick has told me of you I believe you're a big enough person to realize . . .'

'Forgive and forget,' said Alcott. 'Kiss the bastard and make up. Don't let her fool you, Clive. Jane's a persuasive talker. Any woman is, when she's in love.' The way he said 'love' had a peculiarly nasty implication.

'I am in love with Mick,' Jane said quietly. 'And he has changed.'

'Oh, yes,' said Alcott. 'He's changed, all right. I can tell you how much he's changed. He's got himself a fancy bitch . . .'

'Richard!' Hammond rose abruptly. He steadied himself with a heavy blackthorn stick. Clive realized for the first time that he was lame. He had not until then remembered the year-old newspaper stories of an automobile accident in which Hammond had been badly injured.

Clive kept his attention centred carefully on his blotter.

'I don't like this, Eddie,' said Hammond. 'I didn't want it this way. Eddie . . .' He stopped, and then went on hoarsely, 'If you'd just let me talk to you . . . God, I don't blame you! But if you'd only give me a chance . . . It isn't me that's important now. It's Jane.'

'Jane, Jane, Jane.' Vivien Alcott drawled the name mockingly. 'Be honest, Mick. You're scared. You're so scared you'd crawl to anybody for help.' She laughed. 'Jane! Yes – you love Jane so much, and that's why you have to spend your nights . . .'

This time it was Jane who said, 'Vivien, stop it.' She turned to Clive. She was pale but stonily composed. 'I knew it would be like this. I didn't want them to come.'

7

'No,' said Alcott. 'You didn't, did you? Clive, she thinks one of us is sending her those letters. That's how she treats her family, since she married that bastard. She wanted to come down here alone with him and talk us into trouble.'

'I would say,' Clive told him, 'that you were doing a better job of that than anyone else could.' He reached for a card and began to write.

'Does that mean you're going to take the case? You're going to help that dirty rat after all he's done?' Alcott got up. His face was suffused. Clive saw that he was slightly drunk. 'All right,' said Alcott. 'Go ahead. Pull him out of this mess. Mick gets away with everything. But someday it'll catch up with him. Someday they'll find that bastard stuffed down a drain, where he belongs. And I'll tell you this much, to make the job easier for you. Everybody Mick Hammond has ever known has a reason to hate his guts. Even you!'

He went out, slamming the door hard after him. Vivien laughed.

Clive stood up and held out the card to Jane Hammond. 'This man is a good operative and completely reliable. I can recommend him for whatever you may have in mind.'

She made no move to take it. 'You can't refuse even to listen.'

'I'm sorry.'

'I forced Mick to come here with me because I knew that if you could see and talk to him you'd understand.'

'This man will do as much for you as I could.'

'I don't believe that.'

Clive said impatiently, 'Mrs. Hammond! I'm not the only private investigator in the country.'

'You're the only one I know, and trust.'

Clive frowned. He studied her with sudden intentness, and then said again, sincerely, 'I'm sorry.'

She sighed and bent her head. Clive put the card in her hand and turned away. He stood looking out at the rain, smoking nervously.

'Eddie,' said Mick Hammond, 'there's something I ought to tell you.'

Clive said, 'Johnny, will you show these people out, please.'

8

Jonathan Ladd Jones went to the door. He had been perched in a corner listening. His expression now was peculiar – partly malicious excitement, partly apprehension.

Hammond said again, 'Eddie . . .'

'Yes, Mick,' said Vivien Alcott. 'Go ahead. Tell him. He's in the mood for dirty stories. He'll enjoy it.'

Hammond made a sound in his throat. His wife caught his arm.

'Come on, Mick,' she said gently. 'Mr. Clive seems to be quite sure he knows everything as it is.'

Johnny bowed them out. Clive thought they were gone, and then Vivien Alcott's voice said:

'Mr. Clive.'

She was standing in the doorway. The dreary light touched her broad cheekbones and the sulky line of her lips. It caught in her eyes, so that Clive couldn't see what color they were, only that they were not large and had a faint tilt to them like the eyes of a cat. They were disconcertingly intent.

'I knew you'd turn them down,' she said. 'The bitch. The sweet bitch! My brother was right. She tried to sneak away, because she's afraid one of us is sending the letters. I'm glad you turned her down!'

She studied him for a moment and then laughed. 'You should have listened to what Mick had to say. I hope you kill him when you find out!'

She went away. Johnny shut the door.

'Oi!' he said. 'Such a family! For Chrissake, Ed, what was all that, anyhow? I never knew you knew any Michael Hammond.'

Clive poured himself a stiff shot from the office bottle, rattling it against the glass.

'Long time ago, Johnny.'

'Uh-huh. Okay. Well – uh – going home now?'

'Yeah. I haven't slept in three weeks, and I'm beginning to get punchy.' He pulled his coat on.

'That was a swell job, Ed.'

'Thanks. Oh, Johnny, about Laurel. I know about Farrar, but is there anything else?'

Johnny looked uncomfortable but stimulated. 'Well . . .'

'I know there's a man. Take it from there.'

9

'That was it, that just went out. Mick Hammond. He's been home with her four times.'

Clive stared at him. A sullen flush crawled up over his cheekbones.

'I'm beginning to get it. Two strings to his bow, huh? If the wife doesn't work, he's still got Laurel. Well I'll be . . .'

He went on from there. Johnny sat down behind the desk. 'Wow!' he said, when Clive had quieted again. 'Don't ever turn that loose on me, Ed. Uh – look, pal. It's none of my business, but if you put that guy on ice I'll be out of a job . . .'

Clive laughed. 'I'll cling to that thought when I need something to steady me. I started to ask you if there was anything Laurel ought to be scared about.'

'Not a thing, unless she's scared of Farrar.'

'Sure of that?'

'Sure I'm sure. Listen, I'm the second greatest private dick in the country . . .'

'So sorry.' He opened the door. 'So long, genius!'

The office was on the second floor. As Clive reached the lower hall, which was dark even in sunny weather and showed nothing but closed doors, somebody stepped out of the shadows.

'Wait!' It was Richard Alcott. He gripped Clive's sleeve, breathing whisky fumes in his face.

'Listen,' he said. 'I'll pay you not to take that case.'

Clive jerked his arm free. He started away, and Alcott grabbed him again.

'Listen, Clive, I'm talking to you. I'll pay you plenty. They've got it coming to them. You don't want to help that bastard after what he did to your Marian.'

Clive turned quickly and hit him in the stomach. Alcott doubled up on the tiles.

Clive said furiously, 'Why couldn't that son of a bitch keep his mouth shut!'

He went on out of the building.

It had stopped raining when he reached his apartment hotel. A thin kid in a blue uniform came out for his bags.

'Gee, Mr. Clive,' he said, 'you sure showed up those cops all right! I'll bet there isn't anybody in the country any smarter than you.'

Clive laughed. 'Go easy, Chuck! You'll have me so I can't wear a hat any more.' He gave the car a slap. 'You can put the baby to bed for me.'

Chuck was overjoyed. He loved cars, but drove so poorly that he seldom had the chance.

The clerk, the switchboard girl, and the elevator boy all had a greeting for Clive. He kidded them, secretly enjoying the fuss, and went on upstairs. Chuck put the bags in the bedroom. Clive flipped him a folded bill.

'Gee, thanks! Gee, you're a swell guy!' Chuck's eyes shone. Young eyes, clean like a new sheet. Clive laughed, without humor.

'Don't trust it, kid,' he said. 'Don't trust anything, and you won't get hurt.' He wondered if his own eyes had ever looked like that.

It was pouring rain again and Clive was in the shower when the phone rang. He cursed and went dripping across the carpet, wiping his hands on a towel. His body was lean and tanned, put together with tough, wiry neatness. There was dark hair on his chest and forearms.

'Edmond Clive speaking.'

It took him a minute to realize what the person on the other end was doing. He, or she, was whispering. Slowly, distinctly, but without a trace of honest voice.

'You're over draft age, Clive, but you're still young. You wouldn't want to die so young.'

Clive's eyelids narrowed. 'What is this?'

'Just a suggestion. Nosy guys get hurt, is all.'

'Yeah?'

'Yeah.' There was a terrible, callous indifference about the whispering. 'I'm talking about Laurel Dane. She's on a spot, pal, and nobody can get her off it. I don't want to have to bother with you. That's why I'm telling you. But if you're stubborn . . . it's a free country, pal, and you can die any time you want.' The receiver clicked.

Clive put the phone down carefully, and then raised his hand and inspected it. It was shaking. In spite of the sizzling radiator, the room had grown very cold.

11

CHAPTER THREE

EDMOND CLIVE walked to the Skyway Club. The storm had cleared momentarily, and he wanted the exercise. The cold wind felt good.

Hollywood Boulevard looked like a strip of polished jet in the glow of dimmed-out store fronts and street lamps half covered with conical black caps. There was a surprising amount of traffic. Ivar, however, was deserted. Halfway along it the blacked-out neons of the Skyway Club gave an eerie feeling of desolation, as though Clive were the last man walking on a dead world.

The hat-check girl squealed at him as soon as he came in the door. 'Well, Mr. Clive! When did you get back in town?'

She had a Pekingese face with too much make-up on it, bleached hair, and long blood-red nails.

'Hiya, Sugar.' Clive surrendered his hat and coat. 'Been behaving?'

'You know how it is.'

'I can guess.'

He was wearing a dinner jacket, and the severe black and white did things to him. Sugar liked what it did. She handed him his check, leaning farther over the counter than there was any real need for.

'I read all about it in the papers,' she said. 'My, you're wonderful. Just like a detective in the movies.'

'Oh, sure,' said Clive. 'Only handsomer.' Sugar was breathing hard through her mouth. She wasn't thinking about the San Francisco case, much. Her satin uniform was tight all the way down.

He reached over quickly and slapped it where it was tightest. 'Sorry, Sugar. Don't you ever get tired trying?'

She jerked away from him. 'You son of a bitch!'

Clive grinned. 'You should see my pedigree. Five champions.' He left her fuming and went into the main rooms.

There was a shallow chrome-railed balcony, and then the floor. Chandeliers in the shape of miniature planes shed an intimate glow. The orchestra was soft and good, and quite a few couples were dancing. Laurel Dane was not on yet.

Samuels, the maître, had once run a speakeasy in Saint Paul. He still looked like a speakeasy owner in spite of his impeccable tailoring.

Clive said cheerfully, 'Hi, Sammy.'

'Hi.' Sammy was not cheerful. 'Now look, Mr. Clive. None of this is my business, except one thing. I don't want trouble in my place.'

'Why, Sammy. Have you ever known me to make trouble?'

'That I have, pal! And more than any four other guys I ever knew. You're a good customer, and I like you. But you get rough, I'll have to send the boys around.'

'You do that, Sammy, and no hard feelings.'

Samuels went away, rubbing his hard blue jowls. Clive got out a cigarette and stood smoking. He looked over the crowd but found nothing to interest him except one gorgeous redhead. Presently he started down the steps.

Off to the right on the balcony, the door marked *Gentlemen* opened and Kenneth Farrar came out. Clive went back up the steps.

Farrar was extremely blond, bronzed, and attractive in his dinner clothes. He nodded to Clive, smiling with his mouth only.

Clive moved slightly, so that the post of the chrome railing was out of his way. In the distance he saw Samuels passing the high-sign to the bouncer brigade.

'Farrar,' he said pleasantly, 'stay away from Laurel.'

Farrar examined him without haste. 'I've always wondered what God looked like.'

'Now you know. And by the way, chum, how's the blackmail business?'

Farrar's neck reddened above his white collar. 'Are you looking for trouble, Clive?'

'Are you?'

'You've got nothing to back up that statement. Nobody has. Nobody ever will have. And your own record isn't so goddam pure.'

'No. So you ought to know I don't need anything on you. You get in my way, sonny, and I'll frame you right into San Quentin.'

Farrar smiled. He had magnificent teeth. 'Your way, Clive – or your bed?'

Clive hit him.

The bouncers might have come up out of the carpet. There were four of them, and they were big tough boys who knew their business. Neither Clive nor Farrar struggled much.

'I'll remember that,' Farrar said.

Clive nodded. 'Sure. We'll both remember it.'

Farrar shook himself free. He went down the steps and out between the tables, toward the swinging doors marked *The Cockpit*, where the bar was.

Samuels came up. He said, 'If you're not gonna behave . . .'

Clive looked at the four big men. He laughed. 'You keep those nursemaids around and baby won't even play with his rattle.'

'All right,' said Samuels. 'But I'm watching you.'

The orchestra struck a chord. People left the dance floor, and the lights began to dim. Clive glanced across at his table, a small one by the performers' entrance, close to the stage. It was empty. There was a 'reserved' sign on it.

'Be seeing you, Sammy,' he said.

As he went away one of the bouncers announced in a hoarse whisper, 'He's clean, boss.'

Clive grinned.

He sat down at the table. The band leader, a personality boy with very curly hair and a white coat, was announcing Laurel. The lights deepened to indigo. A spot lanced downward, centering on the curtained doorway.

Laurel Dane came in. She wore soft gray that clung and floated, and was shot with folds of flame color. Her flesh looked silver, her lips a warm scarlet. She walked across toward the stage, gracefully acknowledging the applause.

She found Clive and smiled at him. He could see a shimmer of tears in her eyes. He raised his hand.

14

Laurel sang 'Blues in the Night.' The throbbing wail suited her and her voice. People liked her. She came down off the stage flushed with pleasure and looking as though she didn't have a care in the world. Clive got up and took her hand.

'I think we'd better go back to your dressing room, Laurel.'

'You sound queer, Ed. What's wrong?'

'I'm going to have to spoil your surprise. Hammond was in my office today.'

'Oh. I didn't know he was going to see you. He said he was afraid because of the threats . . . Well?'

'Well, what?'

'Oh,' said Laurel softly. 'You refused him. Oh, Ed, how could you look at him and be so mean?'

'He's got right around you, hasn't he? There's a lot you need to know about that guy.'

'But I know it all, Ed! He's told me everything. And he needs help so badly.'

'He's apt to get it some day, for good.' Clive beckoned to a waiter. 'Tell the man who comes to this table – if he comes – that Miss Dane is waiting in her dressing room.'

'Ed,' said Laurel, 'you're not going to start trouble, are you?'

'Should I?'

'I know you when your mouth gets like that. Ed, listen to me . . .'

She stopped. Clive was staring over her head, at a tall man coming toward them, leaning on a heavy blackthorn stick.

Laurel took hold of Clive's wrists. 'Let me talk to you before you say anything.' She shook him. 'Ed, listen to me!'

Veins began to stand out on Clive's forehead. Hammond stopped some distance away.

Clive said mildly, 'I'm not sore at you, Laurel. Let me go.'

'I can't until I've made you understand!'

'I'm not going to touch him. Let me go!'

She took her hands away and clasped them between her breasts. 'Everybody's looking at us. Ed, won't you come back to my room and let me tell you . . .'

Clive drew a long breath. 'Laurel,' he said, 'I'm not blaming you. Mick is a genius at things like this. I don't know what he's told you . . .'

'He's in trouble. Terrible trouble.'

15

'So he wants my help and he's using you to get it.'

'That's not true. If you'd only listen . . .'

Clive wasn't paying any attention to her. Hammond let his head and shoulders crumple forward – a strangely old gesture for a man no older than Clive. He turned away.

Laurel said shrilly, 'You wait, Mick.' She put her hands up on Clive's chest. 'Listen to me, Ed. I know all about you and Mick. But all that's different now.'

'My God,' said Clive. 'He teaches all his women the same song.'

Samuels and his four big men were drifting up between the tables. There were dancers on the floor, but they weren't dancing. The music sounded loud and empty.

Laurel said, 'You watch what you're saying, Ed.'

Clive lost what was left of his temper. 'Quit pawing me! Listen, you fool. I've known that bastard since we were in kindergarten. He'll lie to or with any woman in the state to get what he wants. And he can always get what he wants.'

Laurel's palm cracked like a shot against his cheek.

'You son of a bitch, you can't talk to me like that! You know so damned much! You know everything. You couldn't possibly be wrong . . .'

He backhanded her across the shoulder, hard enough to knock her against the table and out of his way. He walked onto the dance floor. Samuels and the bouncers closed in.

Samuels said, 'Now, Laurel . . .'

'You shut up! She was standing straight again, holding her hand over her shoulder. Hammond stayed where he was, looking dazed. Laurel yelled, 'Ed! Ed Clive!'

Clive went on. Nobody tried to stop him.

Laurel scooped up the sugar bowl from the table and threw it.

It hit Clive between the shoulders and then bounced to the floor and split open. Sugar-cubes rolled like dice. Clive turned around.

Two pairs of large hairy hands reached out for him. He swung at the nearest face and was stopped halfway. He was held expertly, so that he couldn't even kick. Laurel came up to him.

'God damn you,' she whispered. 'I said you stay and listen!'

Clive stared at her. He was sweating, breathing harshly as though he had run a long way.

16

'You make me sick,' said Laurel. Her voice had no inflection, and no shrillness. 'Who do you think you are – God? You can't accuse me of something and then not even listen. You can't walk out on people like a nasty-tempered brat.' She began to cry, without changing expression. 'I've been waiting for three weeks. I've been praying for you to come home. People need you, Ed Clive. You can't walk out on people when they need you.'

Clive's face twitched. Suddenly he began to laugh. It was clear, healthy laughter. Samuels and the strong men looked stunned.

'Of course not, baby.' There was not even any bitterness in Clive's voice. 'That's what I'm here for, just to be around when people need me.' He waited courteously for the men to free him.

He put his arm around Laurel and started toward the curtained doorway. Over his shoulder, as though nothing had happened, he said, 'Come along, Mick. The lady's buying the drinks.'

Michael Hammond ran a hand across his eyes and followed. Clive noticed that for all his limp he managed to be damnably graceful.

No one spoke on the way to Laurel's dressing room. She lay heavily against Clive's shoulder, mastering her sobs. She looked up at him when he opened the door. His face was relaxed and pleasant.

'Sometimes I'm afraid of you,' she said.

He smiled. He motioned Hammond inside and closed the door. Laurel sat down by the dressing table.

Clive said, 'May we have a drink, Laurel?'

She nodded. Clive crossed the room. It was small, with a worn carpet on the floor. There was a couch with a chintz cover, a slipper chair, and an open closet with a lot of Laurel's clothes in it. One window with a heavy wire screen gave onto the alley behind the Skyway Club. It was open, because the heat from the kitchen made the place stuffy.

There was a bottle of bourbon on the table. Clive got three glasses from the bathroom cupboard and filled them.

'I wish you'd get some Scotch, Laurel,' he said. 'I don't like bourbon.'

Hammond had sunk down on the couch, holding his head in his hands. Clive saw that his thick black hair was beginning to streak at the temples. He passed the drinks and sat down in the slipper chair.

'And now,' he said, 'let us talk.'

The whisky had brought some life back into Laurel. 'Ed, I don't trust you when you're polite.'

He smiled faintly. 'After all this row, isn't anybody going to say anything?'

Hammond straightened up. For the first time Clive looked him in the face. He had always been handsome. Now he was beautiful, with the fine-drawn, unearthly beauty that suffering brings to some people. His eyes were tired beyond anything Clive had ever seen, except the tiredness in the eyes of Hammond's wife.

'Don't be angry with Laurel about me, Eddie,' said Hammond. 'There's nothing between us. She just kept me from going crazy, that's all.' He paused helplessly. 'I don't know how to begin. I suppose I had no right to come to you, but a man in a bad enough spot will try anything. Like the helldiver we saved from drowning during that storm. Remember? It didn't even peck us.'

'I remember.'

Hammond looked down at the floor, at nothing. 'I've been through hell, Eddie. Nothing's the same any more. Somehow I've got to make you believe that.'

'You always were a good talker, Mick.' Clive lighted a cigarette with quick, nervous hands. 'Go on.'

Hammond said again, 'I don't know how to begin.'

Laurel got up, smiling wickedly at Clive. 'Suppose you start with us, Mick. That ought to put him in a good mood.' She went across into the bathroom, her silver slippers sparkling on the dingy rug. She turned on the cold water, bent over the washbowl, and began splashing her face.

Hammond took his blackthorn stick and held it across his knees, trying to hide the fact that his hands were shaking. There was a long ragged gash in the wood. It had been covered with stain and polish, but the light showed it up like a scar on a man's face. Very slowly, as though he were not thinking about it, Hammond turned the stick so that the gash was hidden.

'I was afraid to come to your office, Eddie,' he said. 'I'm being watched. I've been warned not to try to get help.'

'Can't you be watched here as well as anywhere?'

'I have been. If you were to look out the front entrance now you'd probably see Richard sitting in his car, waiting for me to come out with Laurel. But that doesn't matter. It's expected of me. I've spent a long time building up a reputation.'

'Yeah. How did it happen you were in my office today, then?'

'Jane did that. You see we're about at the end of our rope . . . I guess we both decided that anything was better than just waiting. Jane tried to keep it from Richard and Vivien, but in our family you can't do that. We argued and fought until none of it mattered much anyway, and Jane convinced me we'd have a better chance if I were there so you could talk to me . . . I'm sorry about what happened.'

'In other words, you and your wife went about getting help separately, each of you trying to keep it dark.'

'Yes. Well, I called your apartment, Eddie. They told me you were out of town. They weren't going to tell me anything more except your office address, but . . .'

'But you convinced the switchboard girl it was a matter of life or death, and she told you where I hang out nights.' Clive often had calls relayed to the Skyway Club. 'Isn't there anything you can't do with women?'

Hammond let that go. 'I couldn't hang around your apartment any more than I could your office. So I came here. I was going to come every night until you got back. I hadn't had much sleep, and I got the shakes. I don't like doing it in public. I crawled out into the back hallway here and Laurel found me. She pulled me round and I went to sleep on her couch.'

Hammond's head dropped forward so that Clive could see only the top of it. He had forgotten that view of Mick. A kid with black hair, baiting fishhooks or bending over to watch a red crab scuttle around a wet rock.

Hammond said, 'Perhaps you know how Laurel is. You tell her things you wouldn't tell anyone else. She let me come home with her because there's no rest where I live. She slept on the couch in the living room, with the bedroom door closed.' Something like anger hardened his face briefly. 'She kept me from going crazy. She promised to help me, with you. And that's all there is to it.'

Laurel came out of the bathroom. She went down on her knees in front of Ed Clive, her head tilted back, smiling. Her lips were red even without rouge. He could see the tight pale skin between her breasts and the motion of her breathing.

She said, 'Aren't you ashamed?'

'I know you too well, darling, to be ashamed.' He bent over and kissed her. Her flesh was cold from the water. He shivered suddenly, drawing back. 'Better go put your face on, baby.'

She pouted at him and went and did things with lipstick and a comb. Somebody knocked on the door. She called, 'I'm coming,' patted her dress down, and started out. Then she paused with her hand on the knob, looking at Clive.

He grinned. 'Run along, hussy, and make with the music. What's Sammy paying you for?'

She shook back her cloudy black hair. 'It's all right,' she said. 'Everything's all right.' She went out.

Clive rose, pacing the room restlessly. 'Go ahead, Mick. What's your jam?'

'Then you will . . .?'

'I haven't said that. Go ahead and talk.'

'All right . . . God knows I don't have to tell you what a heel I was. Growing up on those sand dunes, wearing ragged overalls, never having enough to eat . . . I wanted success, and women were the easiest way. I don't think I ever thought about the ethics of it. They wanted something, and I wanted something, and nobody got hurt.'

Clive said, with cold anger, 'Except Marian.'

Hammond nodded slowly. 'Except Marian. Anyway, I got where I wanted to go. I talked a rich widow into getting me a job in a department store she half owned. I did work there, Eddie. I had to, because I knew she wouldn't keep me after she got wise to me. I even got promoted. The other partner was satisfied, so I stayed. I was all set. All I needed was a rich wife, with a spot in the social register. I found her. Her name was Jane Alcott, she came from Boston, and she didn't know much about me. I married her a little less than three years ago.'

He got out a gold case, braced his wrists on his knees, and managed to get a cigarette between his lips. His hands were shaking badly. He dropped the case. Clive put it back in his pocket and held a lighter for him.

'Got it kind of bad, haven't you?'

20

'Kind of.' Hammond closed his eyes, dragging the smoke down. 'I didn't change after I married Jane. I went on parties, and I gambled, and if there was a pretty girl around I knew it. I never gave her grounds for divorce, but a woman doesn't like that sort of thing! We quarreled incessantly, and yet she stuck with me, Eddie – even with her brother and sister nagging all the time to get rid of me. You know why? Pride, of course, partly. But she really loved me. That's funny, isn't it?'

He clenched his hands together between his knees, trying to stop their trembling.

'Then about a year ago I fought with Jane at a party. Richard, my brother-in-law, was engaged to a girl named Anne Lofting, and they were there, too. Richard left Anne to talk business with some big money and she was sore about it. We were both a little tight, and – well, we went off in the car together.

'We consoled each other for a while, down on the Coast highway. Then she got mad at me and made me drive her to where she could get a cab. I started home. I picked a winding road to speed on, went off the shoulder and down a steep bank and wound up in a gully. Nobody saw it happen. I was pinned under the car. It was dark there in the canyon, and still. There was a thin fog and it was cold and the car weighed more than Mount Whitney. Pain, Eddie – I couldn't even faint. I just had to lie there, and think.'

There was a long silence. It was raining hard outside in the alley. Someone slammed the kitchen door. The sound of Laurel's voice came very faintly from the hall.

Hammond went on slowly. 'I realized that I'd never thought before in my life. I did some more thinking in the hospital. I'd have died without Jane. She stood by me even when she knew I was crocked for good. What is it, Eddie, that makes a woman love a man like me?'

Clive didn't answer. He stood by the window, listening to the rush and slam of the rain. It was very dark beyond the screen.

'I know what the Bible says about leopards and Ethiopians, but it isn't always true. I started to try and make it up to Jane – only it was too late. Someone has checked up on my past, Eddie. Everything I ever did. About six months ago Jane began getting

21

letters telling her about me. They come at irregular intervals, and of course they're not signed. But they're accurate.

'It isn't blackmail. Money is never mentioned. But the letters hold it over us that some day they'll be sent to other people. My boss, our friends, the newspapers. Jane knows I've changed, and she wants to help. But that constant threat . . .

'I can't stand losing her, Eddie. That's why I wanted your help. Whoever writes the letters warns us not to try and find out who it is. But you've got to find out, Eddie! Unless you think I haven't any right to Jane, and I ought to kill myself.'

Clive turned. Hammond was crying, not making any fuss about it, and shivering like a dog that's cold, or frightened.

Clive said quietly, 'All right, Mick. I'll do what I can.'

He moved, one step. He didn't have any warning. The beat of the rain on the alley paving covered any footsteps. Even the gun was silenced. All he knew was that something came out of nowhere behind him and slammed him forward on his face.

He tasted dust on the carpet. He tried to get up and was a little surprised that he could. Mick Hammond was standing erect, like a marble image. The slug had ripped the couch beside him.

Clive snarled, 'Get down!' and went for the light switch. There were no more shots. In the darkness he found the table and jerked the drawer open and got the little gun that Laurel kept there. There was blood pouring down his left side and arm. He cursed and went out into the hall.

There was nobody there. From the front of the club came a crescendo of music and a burst of applause. Things rattled comfortably in the kitchen. Someone was whistling 'Blues in the Night' and missing the tune badly. The door to the alley was closed.

There was a light switch. Clive turned it and then opened the door, standing flat in the corner beside it. A snarling, fretful gust of wind blew rain against his face. There was a smell of wet bricks and the gurgle of water down a storm drain. The alley was deserted.

Clive shut the door and turned the light on again. He leaned his right elbow against the wall, letting the hand with the gun in it droop. He was white around the lips. There was a lot of blood running down his arm. He watched it drip off his fingers and thought Sammy would be sore as hell about the carpet.

Someone screamed.

Laurel Dane had come down the hall. She looked at the gun and the blood and said, 'Ed,' very quietly, and folded up like a marionette when the strings are dropped. Mick Hammond came out of the dressing room.

'How do you like that?' said Clive. His cheek muscles twitched. 'I get shot, and she does the fainting!'

CHAPTER FOUR

SAMUELS CAME down the hall in Laurel's wake. He looked at her, and then at Hammond, and then at Clive.

'Will you get to hell off my rug,' he said.

He picked Laurel up, shoved past Hammond, and put her down on the couch. Clive went in after him. He was reasonably steady. Samuels closed the door and glared.

'Did you kill anybody?'

Clive grinned. 'He didn't wait long enough.' He dropped the little gun back in the table drawer. 'Some guy just took a shot at me through the window.'

Samuels closed it and pulled the shade. 'Get in the bathroom, will you, and bleed in the washbowl.'

Clive went in. Hammond was there, wringing out a cold towel for Laurel.

'Worrying about his carpets, the son of a bitch,' Clive muttered. 'What about my clothes?' He held his hand over the bowl. Hammond limped out with the towel. He still hadn't said anything. Samuels came in and pulled off Clive's coat and shirt. Clive cursed him.

Samuels' hard, practiced eye appraised the damage. 'Slug

23

went right through between your arm and your side. Forty-five, I'd say. Just a couple of grooves. Another two inches and you'd have slept in the morgue tonight.' He looked in the washbowl. 'For a guy your build you got a lot of blood. Just stay put, buddy, till I get back.'

'You and your lousy carpets!'

Clive inspected the wounds. They were ragged, but not deep. The blood was already beginning to clot. He looked like something out of a slaughter house.

Laurel began to make noises as though she were coming round. Clive pulled the bathroom door to. He called out, 'How you doing, baby?'

'Ed! Ed, darling, are you all right?'

'Just a scratch, hon. Stay in there till I get cleaned up, will you? You shouldn't see me with my shirtie off.'

She laughed. 'Take him a drink, Mick, and then get me one.'

Presently Hammond held a glass in through the door. His face was bone-white and his eyes were like glass in the light. He was out on his feet from sheer exhaustion.

'I'm glad you're all right, Eddie. Did you mean . . .'

'Sure, Mick. We'll talk some in the morning.'

Hammond smiled, the smile of a tired small boy whose father has just promised him that everything will be all right. He went away. Clive shook his head irritably and drank his bourbon.

Samuels came back and did things with towels and disinfectant and gauze.

Clive said admiringly, 'You act like you've done this before.'

Samuels scowled at him. 'I have. And I can throw lead as well as I can clean up after it. Christ, the way you guys use my premises!'

Clive laughed, getting gingerly into his ruined shirt. 'Relax, chum. I have no intention of using your premises to get killed on.' He eased into his coat and began fooling halfheartedly with his tie. 'By the way, was Farrar heeled tonight?'

'No. You guys want to play rough, you go somewhere else, see?' He started out. 'Better go home and get some sleep,' he said to Laurel. 'My God, the boy friends you pick! You oughta be singing in a shooting gallery.' He glared at the ripped couch.

'Any more like this, and you will be!' He slammed the door behind him.

Laurel got up and pulled a fur-trimmed coat out of the closet. All the vitality was gone from her. Her lips were like a smear of blood on white porcelain.

She said, 'Let's go home.'

Clive's face was expressionless. He watched Mick Hammond help her on with her coat.

'Want to play angel, Mick, and drive me home?'

Hammond said, 'Of course.'

Clive turned the knob. Laurel said, 'Wait, darling. Your tie.' She fixed it for him. 'There. You look fine, Ed.'

She didn't look fine. The way she looked frightened him. Hammond limped out, still graceful. Laurel turned off the light.

'Darn it,' she said suddenly. 'Forgot my compact.' She went back inside, swinging the door to behind her. Clive heard the table drawer pulled out softly and pushed in again. She came out, smiled, and walked on down the hall. The weight in her coat pocket was not a compact.

On the way out Clive stopped to phone. Jonathan Ladd Jones was not at home, nor in any of the dens of iniquity he frequented. Clive cursed him fluently.

He and Hammond retrieved their coats from the checking booth. Sugar saw the blood on Clive's cuff, and her eyes got round and shiny. Clive grinned at her.

'She bit me,' he said. 'You know how women are with me.' He put his arm around Laurel. Sugar hated him.

It was still pouring outside. Hammond said, 'My car is right over there.'

'See your brother-in-law?'

'No.'

They made a dash for the car – a long, swanky black-and-chrome job. Hammond slid under the wheel. Clive got in the back seat with Laurel. She was silent and depressed, and everyone seemed to have caught her mood.

Laurel's apartment house was a block or two north of the Boulevard, not far from Clive's. There was no hotel service, so there was no one in the lobby to see them go in. The elevator was automatic. They rode up in it, without speaking, to the third floor. Laurel opened her door, turned around, and gave them a sunny smile.

'Well, good night, children.'

Clive said pleasantly, 'Good night, Laurel.' He put his arms around her. She relaxed. Her eyes closed, and her lips were hungry. He lifted her off her feet and went with her through the door.

Laurel said, 'Damn you!' and kicked him on the shins. He cursed and put her down and she went for the gun in her pocket. 'I'll make you get out! I won't let you stay here!'

Clive's hand got there first. She whimpered and clamped down on his wrist. Her nails hurt. He put the heel of his right hand under her chin and shoved. Laurel fell backward onto an overstuffed couch. Clive winced and grabbed his shoulder.

'Don't play so rough,' he said. 'You want me to start bleeding again?' He dropped the gun in his own pocket.

'I want you to get out of here, Ed. Will you go, for God's sake!'

'Shut up, darling.' Mick Hammond was still standing in the doorway. Clive pulled him in and shut the door and made sure the bolt was turned all the way.

He took off Hammond's hat and topcoat, his dinner jacket, and tie. He opened his shirt and laid the blackthorn stick on a table. Then he pointed to the bedroom.

'Go on in there and get some sleep before you fall down.'

Hammond went straight across the room. Without the stick his limp was not graceful. Clive watched him. For a moment his expression was almost tender.

Hammond closed the door behind him.

Laurel had found a cigarette, and her gray eyes were steady again. Her hair was lovely even when it was tumbled.

She said quietly, 'I suppose I can't make you go away.'

'That's fine thing! After all this time I consent to spend the night with you, and you try to throw me out. Don't you love me any more?'

'Love you? You son of a bitch, I hate you!'

Clive nodded. 'That's why,' he said mildly, 'you're willing to face death alone rather than risk my life.'

She looked up at him, as though there were no place else in the universe to look. There was a light in her that blinded him.

He sat down and pulled her over into his arms and kissed her – the hollow between her breasts, the curve of her throat, and then her lips. Their arms around each other were tight and rough.

After a while Clive raised his head, and she caught a sobbing breath.

'Oh, Ed, why did it have to be like this?'

'Because you're you and I'm me. Because I should have stayed away from you, and didn't have guts enough to do it.'

He rose, moving away from her. 'I've known you for two years. I lost my immortal soul to you, and I couldn't help that. But up to a point I could help what I did about it. How many men have you been in love with during those two years?'

'I know of at least one woman you . . .'

'Sure! I've been drunk a couple of times, too. The hell with it!'

There was silence.

Presently Laurel said dully, 'I'm no good Ed. I never have been.'

'That's not true.' He was startlingly quiet. 'You can no more help falling in love than a pelican can help diving for fish. Every new man to you is like a new toy to a kid. I just couldn't play it that way.'

'I always came back to you.'

'Yeah. Sure. You came back because you couldn't get me. You had me hooked but you couldn't get me, and that was something you had to find out about. Don't you suppose I knew that was the only way to hold you?'

'You're being cruel, Ed.'

'My God, do you think I didn't want you, on any kind of terms? Do you think I didn't lie in bed nights . . .' He broke off, and then went on, 'I've seen things happen to a lot of guys who were fool enough to try and own the wrong woman, Laurel. I'd have had to own you.' There was nothing now in his face but a somber weariness. 'I haven't any right to talk. I guess I haven't done you any good, either.'

She whispered, 'I wouldn't have wanted to live without knowing you.' She went to him. 'I'm leaving town in the morning, Ed.'

'I was waiting for that.'

'You're happy about Mick, though. I'm glad I met Mick, because now I know a lot of things about you that I've always wanted to know – what kind of a little boy you were, and why you're so full of contradictions.'

He smiled. 'I didn't know you were one of those curious women.'

'We're always curious about the people we love. Mick told me about Marian. Did you love her very much, Ed?'

'I was seventeen then.'

'And she and Mick were your whole world. You even thought it was right that they should love each other. And then Mick threw her over, the way he did . . .'

'My God, he must have talked!'

'He had to. To get it off his conscience.'

Clive turned away.

Laurel said softly, 'But it wasn't all Mick, was it? Something else happened about Marian, something even Mick doesn't know about. Something that killed you inside.'

Clive laughed suddenly. 'Hey, we're not doing this right! Wait till I send out for a couple of beers and a guy to play "Hearts and Flowers."'

She made a face at him. 'All right, so I'm being sloppy! Well, I'm a woman and I've got a right to be when I feel like it.' She came to him, close but not touching him. 'I wish I were the right woman, Ed. You don't give yourself to everybody, and when you do it's for keeps. I wish I were like that. But I'm not. I tried it once, and it – it didn't work.'

She sighed and leaned back against the table, studying the bright toes of her slippers.

'I'm kind of a fool, I guess. Life's so full, and tomorrow's a long way off, and things just take care of themselves. And then all of a sudden they don't, and I get scared, like a silly kid. You were right, Ed. I wanted to get you. You're the only man I ever met that I couldn't have if I wanted him. And I loved you. You made me furious, you made me unhappy, but I couldn't get you out of my mind. I'd have married you if you'd asked me.

'And then tonight I saw you standing there ... I hadn't thought about your getting hurt. I was scared, and I wanted your shoulder to lean on, but I hadn't realized that I was putting you in danger.'

She raised her head. 'I don't want you any more, Ed. Not that way. I know why you wouldn't take me, and I'm glad you didn't. I'm glad I'm going away, so it'll be easier for us both to break off.' Her dark lashes dropped, and her lips were sullen with tears. 'You're so damned stubborn and you play for keeps, but you're straight. You're the straightest man I ever knew. That's why I want you to go away and let me fight this alone. It's my fight. I did it. And I don't want you hurt again, Ed. Can you understand that, you stiff-necked stone image? I don't want you hurt on account of me!'

'I understand.' Clive put his hand under her chin and tilted her head back. He kissed her, a lingering, gentle caress. Then, suddenly, he laughed.

'Sorry, darling, but I've already made a blood offering on this altar. About two gallons of it, in fact.'

He found Highland Cream in a cellarette and poured two drinks. He gave one to Laurel and then sat down on the big couch, crossing his legs comfortably.

'Now, then. Tell papa all about it.'

Laurel shrugged. 'There's really nothing to tell. Somebody searched my apartment a couple of days ago, that's all. They didn't take anything.'

'Okay,' Clive said. 'We'll make a game out of it. Let's see. ... Once upon a time you met a guy and married him. You were pretty young then, and didn't know much. You probably loved him like hell. And then, after a while, someone else came along. Or several someones. Maybe your husband was the kind who plays for keeps, too. Maybe he just didn't like being run out on. Anyway, he threatened to beat your brains out, and you thought he was tough enough to do it. So you bought a one-way ticket and used it, quick.'

Laurel stared at him. 'My God. But I don't keep a diary . . .'

Clive laughed. 'I'm a very smart detective, precious. You should read my publicity.' He finished his drink. 'Look, honey. Girls without Pasts don't keep guns in their dressing rooms. They don't watch every man that goes by to see if maybe he's somebody they'd rather dodge. They don't get the flaming horrors in their eyes when they see a man that looks enough like somebody to be that somebody, almost.'

He leaned forward. 'Laurel Dane isn't your real name. Ten to one your hair is red instead of black. You couldn't have married me if I had asked you because you are married, and you can't get a divorce because your husband would find you. Am I right?'

Laurel shivered. She rose and walked away from him, her hands at her temples. 'Don't say any more, Ed. I don't like even to talk about it.' After a moment she said, 'Yes, I was married. I was in New Orleans. His name was Dion Beauvais, he was a gambler, he was black and beautiful and wild, and I loved him – like hell. But he wanted to own me, too, Ed, and I . . . Ed, have you ever been afraid, really afraid – of dying?'

'Have you seen him? Has he threatened you?'

'No. I'm not even positive that he's here. Maybe it's just my guilty conscience.'

'Got a picture of him, Laurel? Or – what is your name?'

'Sue,' she said. 'Sue Tanner.'

'Let's keep it Laurel. It was Laurel I fell in love with.'

'I wish I'd never known Sue Tanner . . .'

She unlocked a drawer in the desk and brought him a photograph, one of those things that people have taken at weddings. The man was just as she had said. Clive had never seen him before.

'What kind of a voice does he have, Laurel?'

'What a funny question!'

'I'm just curious.'

'A lovely voice. All music – and steel.'

Clive drew her closer to him. The girl in the picture was strange, stranger than if he had not known her at all.

'I did have red hair, Ed.'

He was suddenly overcome with dislike for the picture. He threw it down and put both hands in her hair, lifting her mouth to his. 'Let's leave it black, Laurel. I like it that way . . . and this hasn't changed . . .'

Her lips moved under his. 'I'm going away in the morning, Ed. Whether Di's here or not I'd have to go.'

'It's your own life, Laurel. I can't tell you how to live it. But I'll do anything I can to help you.'

'I'm going away. I've stayed too long in one place.' She gave him a quick, tight hug and stood up. 'I've got to get some sleep now or I'll look worse than Mick.' She began kicking off her silver shoes.

Clive went into the bedroom to get a pillow and some blankets. He was careful about it, but he could have walked around shouting as far as Mick Hammond was concerned. Clive had never seen anything but a corpse as dead to the world as he was. He pulled the satin quilt up around Hammond's shoulders and anchored it with one of Hammond's hands. The rhythm of his breathing never changed. Clive went out with the blankets, trailing a faint scent of lavender behind him.

He helped Laurel fix the couch. She had her dress off, and the pale gray satin slip molded her like a glossy skin. She nestled down and closed her eyes.

'Ed, I'm not really such an awful tramp. Is it wrong to have fun and like to have people like me?'

'That depends, honey. Some guys take it seriously.'

'I wish you'd go home, Ed.'

'I wish you'd go to sleep.'

She put out her hand. 'Kiss me good night.' He bent over. Her mouth was warm and sleepy. 'I'm glad you're here,' she said. 'I'm so glad you're here.'

Clive rumpled her hair. 'Go to sleep, will you?'

She did, with the ease of a tired kitten. Clive stood for a while, looking down at her . . .

He turned away abruptly, taking the little gun out of his pocket, and went through the apartment. There was nothing and no one that didn't belong there. The wall outside the windows was without fire escapes, pipes, or foothold of any kind. He went out onto the concrete service porch.

Laurel shared it with another apartment, which was dark and apparently empty. From somewhere below in the lighted

31

stair well came a whisper of music and the ghost of a woman's laughter. The back door had a glass panel in it. Clive scowled at that, made sure of the lock and the extra bolt, and returned to the living room, where he switched off the lights and raised the blinds.

It was still raining. A little weak glow filtered in from the street lamps. Clive went to the telephone, standing so that he could be in shadow and still watch the black opening of the kitchen door. The dial rattled like machine-gun fire but did not disturb Laurel.

Jonathan Ladd Jones had not come home.

Clive whispered, 'God damn it!' He weighed the little gun in his hand and thought about the men he had seen shot with .25's who had not minded it enough to let it slow them down. He managed to see the dial on his wrist watch. It was only twelve-thirty-four. He didn't believe it, but his watch hadn't stopped.

He rubbed his face and tried not to yawn. He was beginning to feel the sleep he'd been missing for three weeks. He dialed another number.

'George? Clive speaking. Is Johnny there?' The wire brought him sounds of people being happy in a loudish way. A jukebox was screaming 'Murder, He Says!' George came back presently and said, 'He ain't here.'

'Phone around for him, will you? It's important. Have him call this number, or call me back yourself if you can't find him.'

George said, 'Sure.' They hung up. Clive waited fifteen minutes and grabbed the phone on the first ring. Jonathan Ladd Jones was still missing.

Clive said, 'Well, thanks anyway. 'Bye.' He yawned again and pressed his shoulder, which was hurting him. He had had nothing to eat since breakfast. He decided that there was nothing definite about anybody gunning for Laurel tonight, and if anyone was going to he could wait while Clive got food and some strong black coffee.

He picked up Mick's dinner jacket to hang over the un-curtained window and then paused in the kitchen doorway, listening. It was pitch dark, except for a dull glimmer from the

32

stair well away at the back. There was no sound anywhere but Laurel's even breathing. He started forward.

Somebody put a key in the lock of the front door and turned it, and pushed it against the bolt. Clive swung around. The bolt rattled again. Clive smiled. He took one catlike step toward it.

Something came out of the shadows behind him and connected with his skull just back of the right ear. There was a tremendous explosion without any noise to it. He fell a long way, into a place that was black and cold and utterly quiet. He had a dream while he was down there. Someone was slapping his face, sharply but without passion. He tried to move away, but he was held. He cursed thickly and opened his eyes, but the darkness was still there.

A voice spoke out of it. It was not really a voice, but a whisper. It said, 'I just wanted you to know, pal. Laurel's off her spot, now – for good.'

It laughed. A heavy object slammed against Clive's jaw. The silence closed in again, completely.

After a long, long time there was another sound. It was far off, but painfully insistent. Now, when Clive raised his eyelids he could see the pale square of the icebox looming above him, and the bigger, paler square of the open door.

It came to him what the sound was. The telephone. He ought to answer it. No particular reason. It was just a thing you did. He rolled over on his face and started to get up.

Somebody hit him in the head with a red-hot axe. They kept on hitting him. He couldn't see anything at all, then, but the swinging flash of the blade as it bit into his brain. He stayed on his knees, his lips drawn back from his teeth, his body covered with icy sweat.

Presently he crawled over and got his shoulder against the sleek enamel front of the refrigerator and pushed himself upward along it.

The telephone stopped ringing.

The sharp stillness shocked against him. Clive shivered. He moved forward, struck the corner of the breakfast table and knocked it over, and went on without noticing it. He caught the door jamb and clung to it, staring into the living room. It was full of shadows, heavy around the sick light from the windows.

He said, 'Laurel.' There was no answer. He let go of the jamb and crossed the room. His step was steadier. He found the switch.

The hard yellow glare showed Laurel. She lay on the floor, her cheek cradled on her forearm, her chin tucked under the curve of her bare white shoulder. She seemed relaxed and very comfortable. Clive knelt beside her.

There was blood at her nostrils. There was blood, not much of it, clotted in her hair above the nape of her neck. There was blood, just a little, on the knotted grip of Mick Hammond's blackthorn stick, lying beyond her outflung hand.

He laid his fingers on her throat. The pulse was dead under them. The warmth was already going out of her flesh.

Laurel Dane was off her spot, for good.

CHAPTER FIVE

IT WAS quiet in the apartment. The swarm of men with cameras and measuring tapes and sketching pads and powders and camel's-hair brushes had finished and gone away.

Laurel had gone away, too. There was only a chalked outline on the rug to remind anyone that she had ever been there. It was curiously impersonal. It was like the things children draw in the sand and mark 'This is you.'

Edmond Clive paced up and down in front of the windows. Hot afternoon sun lay squared on the floor. He watched his black shoes move across it and thought, The rain's over.

Detective-Lieutenant Jordan Gaines of the Central Homicide Bureau stood by the door, talking in low tones to a grinning little man named Korsky. A uniformed cop sat in a corner, balancing a shorthand pad on his knee and studying the other occupants of the room with an amused and nasty speculation.

Jonathan Ladd Jones sat stiffly on a straight chair. He had not shaved and there was a dazed look about him. Mick Hammond was on the couch where Laurel had slept her last real sleep.

His hands hung loose between his thighs. He stared ahead of him, at nothing.

No one spoke except Gaines and Korsky, and their mumbling was only a sort of detached underlining of the silence. No one seemed to want to meet anyone else's eye.

Gaines had tried hard to crack them. Hours, in an empty apartment across the hall, Clive in one room, Mick Hammond in another. Now he was trying something new. Clive lighted his last cigarette and threw the pack away. His stubbled face twitched spasmodically, like the face of a man addicted to narcotics. The cop in the corner began a monotonous kicking of his heel against the chair rung. Korsky laughed a hard little laugh and Gaines said, 'Fine!' Korsky went on talking.

Suddenly Gaines said aloud, 'Okay, Korsky. That's all I need right now. Go on down and take care of Mrs. Hammond.'

Hammond brought his attention slowly to Gaines. His eyes held a terrible hate. Korsky went out. A uniformed man closed the door again from outside. The one with the shorthand pad straightened up in pleased anticipation. Johnny glanced quickly at Clive, and away.

Gaines came toward them. He was a big man, fleshy but not soft. He wore a well-cut blue suit, the set of which was spoiled by the thick pad of muscle across his back, relic of pick-and-shovel days before he started pounding a beat. His face was sun-reddened, healthy, appearing rather stupid until one noticed his pale, shrewd eyes.

He said, 'Well, boys?'

Clive stopped pacing. 'Look, Gaines. Either book us or let us go. I'm getting goddam sick of this stalling.'

'We've told you,' said Hammond. 'Over and over we've told you. What more do you want?'

Gaines settled down in an armchair. His toes almost touched the chalked outline. He studied it.

'There are four possible answers,' he said. 'One, you may be telling the truth. Two, you may have framed it between you. Three, Hammond may have slugged Clive and gone on from there. Four, Clive may have doped Hammond and ditto.' He looked up. 'You're a smart guy, Ed. How do you figure it?'

35

Jonathan Ladd Jones stood up. 'You goddam thick-headed son of a bitch! Ed's telling the truth, and if he says the other guy is, he is. What about the window in the back door? What about the phone call Ed got? What about the slug in the back?'

Gaines nodded. He was not angry. He seemed to have a great deal of time and not to care particularly what he did with it.

'The window in the back door. Uh-huh. A neat piece of work. The wooden frame removed carefully, without scarring. The glass held securely with masking tape. The nails in the frame clipped short from the underside, except four which were oiled to slide easily. The frame replaced. And we have a quick, noiseless way to reach in any time we want to and unlock the door.'

He pulled out a sack of tobacco and began making a cigarette. His thick scarred fingers made his neat clothing look incongruous.

'Of course,' he said, 'you all had fairly free entry into this apartment. You'd have had as much opportunity as anyone else.'

Clive started pacing again.

Hammond said, 'You found the marriage license and the picture. You know Laurel was afraid of her husband.' He hesitated over 'Laurel' as though the word had edges on it.

'I know you say she said she was.' Gaines struck a match with his thumbnail. 'Korsky checked with the switchboard girl at your place, Clive. The guy who phoned you was whispering. Anybody can whisper. Even Johnny Jones, maybe.'

Johnny swore.

'Listen, Gaines,' said Clive, with ugly patience. 'Laurel was killed sometime after one o'clock. I hung up on George about twelve-fifty-four. I suppose Korsky checked that, too. I walked across into the kitchen and somebody slugged me. Even your sawbones admits that this bump on my head must have put me to sleep for at least an hour. I didn't wake up until Johnny phoned around two, and I was too groggy to get there. Then I called you.'

'You're making it tough for me, Clive. I could take you down and let the boys sweat you.'

'You do, and I'll burn the breeches off you in court.'

Gaines sighed. 'That shyster lawyer of yours is another one I'm gonna get some day.' He leaned back, looking bored and plaintive. 'This is the god-damnedest case I been handed yet. People get slugged, and murdered, and other people walk in and out like a regular parade – at least the bolt's off the front door – nobody sees or hears anything and Hammond here sleeps through the whole thing like a baby. A hell of a case. You know what I think? I think somebody's lying to me.'

Clive said, 'That's tough.'

'You're right, it's tough. But I'm tough, too. I'm a regular rump steak, I am.' He heaved onto his feet and began to walk around aimlessly. 'Korsky's been doing the preliminary check. Clive, you and Hammond and the girl put on a swell floor show at the Skyway Club last night.'

Clive was standing by the open bedroom door. The smell of lavender came through it faintly. He closed his eyes and then moved away, like a man who doesn't see very well.

'Then you all went to the dressing room,' Gaines continued, 'and only you two know what happened there, except that somehow Clive got shot, but when you all came out again you seemed to have brotherly love just squirting out of your ears. Now I ask you, fellas! I've heard all about what happened earlier in Clive's office. I know all about your hating each other's guts for twenty years or more. And then all of a sudden you're practically in bed together, and with the same dame. Does that make sense?'

Clive's lean face was expressionless, except for the nervous tic. 'Sure it does. I kicked Mick out of my office, yes. Then he turned up at the Skyway Club because Laurel had promised to help him. She had a soft spot for sick cats. I didn't have anything to get sore at her about. If she'd been in love with him, what the hell? She didn't owe me anything. It just made me sick to look at him, so I tried to walk out and Laurel blew her top. So I figured it was better for her if I stayed. I was afraid she might crack up, she was so jittery. Nothing happened in the dressing room, except Hammond moaned about how everybody hated him, and some guy in the alley nearly finished me.'

Gaines said sleepily, 'You wouldn't be working for Hammond, would you? Covering a client, like?'

'I kidded the bastard along because I didn't want Laurel howling at me. Whatever else he told you, forget it.'

37

'Okay, okay. It's just funny you back up his sleeping beauty yarn.'

Mick Hammond was staring at Clive. His expression was that of a sick man who realizes suddenly that the doctors have been lying to him and he isn't going to get well. Clive seemed to have forgotten that he was in the room.

Gaines yawned. 'The hell with these midnight murders. . . . You wanted Johnny Jones awful bad last night, Clive. Why?'

'He's the only one can tuck me in bed the way Mama used to.'

'Do any drinking at the Skyway Club?'

'Some.'

'More when you got here, maybe?'

'Maybe.' The bottle and glasses were plain evidence.

'Hammond went right into the bedroom, didn't he? Then Laurel told you all about her life history and went to sleep on the couch. And you wanted Johnny Jones something awful.' Clive turned away irritably. 'You wanted Johnny Jones,' said Gaines, 'because you were so tight you couldn't be sure you'd see Laurel's husband if he did come.'

'All right,' Clive snarled. 'So I was drunk.'

'The bedroom door was closed, was it?'

'Christ, yes! How many more times do you want it?'

'How did you know Hammond was asleep?'

'I saw him when I went in for the blankets.'

'But you were tight.'

'All right!'

'H'm,' said Gaines softly. 'Hammond, your wife has a lot of money, hasn't she?' Hammond didn't seem to hear him. 'Your brother- and sister-in-law came along with her. They make swell witnesses. Seems everybody knew about Laurel Dane. A scandal wouldn't exactly set you in solid with your boss, would it?'

Hammond shivered slightly. He paid no attention to Gaines.

'We haven't talked much about the murder weapon being your stick, Hammond.'

Clive said impatiently, 'Anybody could have used it. You'll find my prints on it, from when I put it on the table. Or was it wiped clean?'

'It was wiped clean. So was the front doorknob, both sides. Not the back though, even though both doors were unlocked.

Funny, huh?' Gaines chuckled suddenly. 'So you were lushed last night. Shouldn't withhold information, you know. Well, that's all. You can go now.'

'What's the joke?'

Gaines said sullenly, 'I may be a chump, but not that big a one. The way things stand that shyster of yours would have you out so fast it isn't worth wasting the ink to book you with. All I'm saying is, just be around when I want you again.'

'You know my address,' Clive said. 'I've got a lease.'

Jonathan Ladd Jones licked his lips, which were dry and pale. 'You're holding Hammond for the kill?'

'Suspicion. Too many loose ends to tie up in one morning, but – ' Gaines shrugged – 'guys with lousy reputations and rich wives have beaten little girls' brains out before this.'

He opened the door and spoke to the man outside. Mick Hammond moved on the couch.

'Eddie . . .'

Clive went out.

There were a lot of reporters in the hall. Usually Clive was friendly with the press; it paid. Now he was aware of them only as something blocking his way. He pushed one man in the face with impersonal viciousness. The others got out of reach. Clive heard Johnny's voice behind him but not the words he said.

There was a cop in the alley behind the building. He let them by. A crowd stood around the front entrance, gawking hungrily. Somewhere a kid was yelling headlines.

Clive hailed a cab and got in, with Johnny at his heels. He put his face in his hands and sat without speaking. The sun burned hot through the window. The cords in Clive's neck stood out like ropes.

He said suddenly, 'I did everything there was to do. Nobody could have known about that goddam door.'

Johnny looked out at the hills pressing rough and close against the rain-washed town. 'It was just one of those things,' he said. 'Nobody could have helped it.'

'She was glad I was there. She was scared, and she was glad I was there.'

'Nobody could have done any more, Ed.'

A little later Clive found himself in his apartment without remembering how he got there. Johnny was shutting the door.

Clive said, 'Get out.'

'Like hell I will.'

Clive showed his teeth. He drew his hand back, but he didn't do anything with it. He seemed to have forgotten Johnny before the blow was even started. He went over to the liquor cabinet and got a bottle of Scotch and a glass, and then sat down in the big armchair by the table.

He spilled quite a lot of the whisky but managed to get some into him. He got up again and started to pull his coat off. Abruptly, with his arms still in the sleeves, he pitched over and hit his face on the floor, and lay still.

Jonathan Ladd Jones dragged him into the bedroom, covered him carefully with a blanket, and went out again. There was plenty of Scotch left in the bottle.

CHAPTER SIX

IT WAS nearly two the next afternoon when Ed Clive settled back from the table with a cigarette and his third cup of black coffee. He looked pale, gaunt, and about ten years older, but otherwise he was himself. Jonathan Ladd Jones was stretched out on the couch with a full belly and his eyes closed, enjoying it.

Clive said, 'Johnny, I am on a spot.'

'Uh-huh.'

'What do you think about Mick Hammond?'

'If I didn't know you, Ed, I'd say you were the most low-down dirty son of a bitch in southern California.'

'I had to sell him out! Gaines had the two of us figured for the job. I could see that idea sneaking around in back of every question he put to us. He figured we found out Laurel was two-timing both of us and decided, because we were kids together, to bury our hatchets in her.'

'He didn't say so.'

40

'Why would he tip his hand? But it's what he meant. Why did Mick and I suddenly get so friendly? Why did I back up his sleeping beauty yarn if I hated him as much as I said I did? Yeah. And there was just sense enough to it to make it dangerous. I couldn't do either of us any good sitting in the can with Gaines's boys pushing my teeth in. Christ, I'm just three jumps away from the gas chamber right now, and I don't like it!'

'What about Hammond?'

'I'll get him out of it.'

'If somebody doesn't get you first. You know Gaines is playing smart with you.'

'He's got to. He can't find the way out of the tangle by himself, so he's using me – Edmond Clive, the Seeing-Eye dog, tame and guaranteed housebroken. He's got Mick to keep the papers happy, and Korsky digging for clues, and all he has to do is park his backside on a cushion and wait till I'm dumb enough to lead him somewhere.' He ground out his cigarette angrily.

Johnny said, 'You weren't lushed, of course.'

Clive grinned. 'I hope Gaines hasn't a sharp ear. Anyway, I gave him an out and he took it.'

'Yeah. He took it so quick it scares me. You know, Ed, you don't look so much like a Seeing-Eye dog to me. You look more like the goat they stake out to make the tiger hungry.'

'You're a hell of a big comfort to me!' Clive swore. 'It ought to be such a simple case! It adds up beautifully most of the way, and then – blooey. The only reason Gaines let me go at all was because he couldn't decide how much I was lying.'

'You can't blame him.'

'No. He knew damn well if I was going to sell him a bill of goods I'd make it a better one than that.'

Johnny rolled over and looked at him. 'Ed – you're sure Hammond didn't do it.'

'I tucked him in myself. When I went back to wake him up after Laurel was killed he hadn't even moved his hand from where I put it.'

'He could have been smart enough . . . All right, all right! We'll drop it right there!'

Clive sprawled out in the armchair and started another cigarette. 'About the only other thing I'd bet on is that the guy who

41

slugged me is the same guy that woke me up to tell me Laurel was dead. If so, he's the one who phoned me, and I'll lay odds he did the shooting, too.'

'Uh-huh. Laurel's husband?'

'Or a hired hand. We'll know better when Gaines gets the dope from New Orleans.'

Johnny yawned. 'Well, everything looks straight enough to me. Eliminate Hammond, and that just leaves Beauvais.'

'Sure. But somebody had a key to Laurel's door. He was using it, just before I passed out. I shot the bolt on that front door myself, and checked it later. But when I came back after the murder it was off. Did the guy with the key get in – which means did Laurel let him in – or did the man in the kitchen open the door himself?'

'You're asking. Sure Farrar wasn't in on this somewhere?'

'I don't see where ... and Laurel would never have given him a key.'

'He could have stolen it out of her dressing room. Or made an impression in soap, or something.'

'Sure. So could anybody else in the city of Los Angeles. Then there's the question of the front doorknob being wiped for prints, and the back one not. Also, the question of Mick's cane.'

'That looks clear enough to me,' Johnny said. 'The killer simply picked up the handiest thing and hit her with it.'

Clive gave him a cold stare. 'Somebody was interested enough in Laurel to search her room, probably to make sure she was the right girl – she'd dyed her hair, remember. Incidentally, I'd say that would indicate Laurel's husband hired the job done – he'd have known her, black hair or not. This same guy took a lot of time and effort to fix up that back door. He checked up on me to see if I was going to be a nuisance. And then he walks in depending on finding the "handiest thing" to hit her with?'

'Well, hell, maybe he had a better idea. Maybe he wanted to hang the kill on somebody else.'

'That,' said Clive softly, 'is a thought.'

'Hey, that reminds me.' Johnny got up on his elbow. 'I finagled an interview with the apartment manager. He said Laurel's place was burgled a little over two weeks ago, along with five or six others. The management paid off and hushed it up, so as not to scare away the customers.'

'You see what I mean,' Clive said sourly. 'Monkey wrenches.'

He rose and dialed the number of Central Homicide. In a minute he had Gaines's sleepy voice on the other end. Clive greeted him genially.

'Hello, you sweet bastard. How are your trained seals?'

'They get around. Want anything special, Clive? I'm busy.'

'Tough life for an honest cop. What did you get on Beauvais?'

'Just a minute.' Clive heard papers shuffling. There was a typewriter going somewhere in the background. Gaines breathed heavily into the mouthpiece.

'Just came through a half-hour ago. Dion Beauvais is his right name. Born in New Orleans. Thirty-nine, height five feet ten inches, weight one-seventy-six, build medium, hair black, eyes brown, complexion swarthy. Marks, knife scar left breast, two-inch ditto under jaw. Several arrests. Only one conviction. Manslaughter, and it was a setup. Should have been anyway second-degree.'

'That all?'

'No. Seems Beauvais is quite a guy around the French Quarter. Has trouble fighting off the dames. It was one of his lady friends shived him. Seems she didn't like his getting married.'

'To Laurel?'

'Yeah. Only, like she said, her name was Sue Tanner then. Beauvais was pretty stuck on her. Cut up rough when she ran away.'

'Yeah,' said Clive. 'Know where he is now?'

'I know where he was on the morning of the day after the girl was killed.'

'Go on.'

'He was walking out the front gate of the Louisiana State Pen.' Gaines's voice had a laugh under it.

Clive smiled without humor. 'Nothing like prison for a good, clean, airtight alibi. But even convicts have friends, you know.'

'Don't fret, pal. We got an order out to pick him up for questioning, if we can find him.'

'Did he have any special gang, or a steady side-kick?'

'No, he seems to travel mostly alone. But we're checking it.'

'What kind of a jolt did he get?'

'One to ten, and served three. He was paroled.'

'And that's all the news?'

'That's all,' said Gaines pointedly, 'that I'm telling.'

'You scare me,' said Clive, and hung up. The hell of it is, he thought, you do. He looked down at the newspapers strewn on the floor. Murder of Night Club Singer. Prominent Detective Involved. His lips drew back from his teeth. He kicked the newspapers.

Johnny jumped up and said, 'Huh?'

'My picture,' said Clive. 'It stinks.'

He picked up his hat. Johnny yawned, stretched, and came after him.

'There's a stake-out on you, Ed.'

'Fine,' said Clive. 'We'll get 'em out in the fresh air and sunshine.'

'Ed . . .'

'Yeah?'

'If I hadn't been out jazzing that blonde when you wanted me . . .'

'You,' said Clive quietly, 'are a hell of a one to talk.' He gave Johnny's small hard shoulder a shake and a push. 'Move, will you? We got work to do.'

They plowed through reporters in the hall. Clive picked out the undistinguished little guy in the background who was not a reporter and waved to him. He discovered that movement made the wounded surfaces under his arm rub together unpleasantly. He put his hand in his pocket and went downstairs.

The switchboard girl had half a dozen calls for him. Johnny had seen to it that none came through. Two were from Thomas Benson, attorney at law. Four were from Jane Hammond.

Someone said, 'Hello.'

Clive turned. 'Well I'll be damned! Hello, Sugar.'

The girl at the switchboard was a nice girl. She didn't like the way Sugar March was dressed, but she couldn't help looking at it. Clive had to admit it was something even Methuselah would have noticed on his nine hundredth birthday. She wore her usual platinum hair and blood-red war paint. Her sweater was red, too, about four inches long, and not very concealing. There was quite a stretch of softly firm belly between it and her slacks, which were white, shiny, and snug. Her sandals had five-inch heels.

Clive shook his head admiringly. 'This California climate! Only two days ago it was cold and rainy, and now look. You sure you won't overheat, Sugar?'

She smiled. 'I want to talk to you.'

'Well, I'm pretty busy . . .'

'About Laurel.'

Clive studied her a moment. Then he steered her into a small anteroom and closed the heavy portieres.

'Okay,' he said. 'Talk.'

Sugar walked leisurely over to the window. She put her huge cloth bag down on a side table and fished a cigarette out of it.

'I've got plenty of time.'

Clive jerked her around roughly. 'Did you have something to say, Sugar?'

Her eyes were furious. 'You lost her, didn't you? You weren't really so damned smart. And now the little bi – '

Clive slapped her across the mouth. She drew a deep harsh breath. Her eyelids closed. She swayed into him.

'But she is dead,' said Sugar thickly. 'And now . . .'

He pushed her away. 'Talk, or get out!'

'All right, God damn you! Someone came to the Skyway Club the evening before she was killed. Someone that hated Laurel. It was early, and Laurel wasn't there yet, and I'm the only one that saw them.'

'Who was it?'

Sugar smiled. 'This is my night off, Ed. You know where I live.'

'Christ, you've told me times enough!'

'Someone that hated Laurel, Ed. Enough to want to kill her, and say so right out in public.' She licked her smeared lips. 'Maybe, if you're nice to me . . .'

'You haven't told the police?'

'No.'

Clive said speculatively, 'I don't think I want to wait till tonight.' He raised his hand.

45

She laughed, but her eyes followed it. 'With all those reporters out there? And the hotel staff? I'll scream my head off.' She picked up her bag. 'I'll be looking for you around eight.'

Clive shrugged. 'Okay, Sugar. There's just one thing you haven't thought of.'

'What's that?'

'Maybe I killed Laurel myself.'

She stared at him, at his hard, sensuous face. Then she said again, 'Eight o'clock, Ed,' and left.

Jonathan Ladd Jones was waiting at the curb with Clive's car. There was a black sedan across the street. The little man from the hallway was just getting into it. There was a second man at the wheel.

Clive whistled through his teeth, and waved. The men looked pained. He called amiably, 'We'll take it slow,' and added an address. Then he climbed into his own car.

'For Chrissake,' said Johnny, 'was that Sugar March?'

'It was.' Clive slid down in the seat and tilted his hat over his eyes. 'Gah! The things a decent dick has to do. Remind me to write a book advising youths to avoid the profession. Take up something respectable, like crimping. I want to see Sammy.'

The black sedan made an illegal U-turn to follow them. They passed Sugar walking down toward the Boulevard. Johnny glanced at Clive and grinned.

'You look,' he said, 'like you'd bit on a bad oyster.'

'Bitten,' said Clive smugly. 'Got your gun?'

'No.'

Clive reached under the dash and pulled the flat Smith & Wesson .38 from its clip. He dropped it in Johnny's side pocket and then looked out the back window. They were close above Hollywood Boulevard now, hitting the press of afternoon traffic. A woman driver pulled out from the curb behind them, temporarily blocking the street, and the red light came on at the corner ahead.

'Pull over for a right turn,' said Clive. 'Okay. They can't see you for a minute. Pick up Sugar and stay with her till I come back. That'll be about eight at her place.'

Johnny opened the door. He leered. 'Think I'll be safe with her?'

Clive slid over under the wheel. 'It's Sugar I'm worried about. If she does know something I'd like to be sure she lives long enough to spill it. Just take it easy, son. If she attacks you, lay that rod alongside her head.'

'I can think,' said Johnny, 'of better lays than that.' He vanished.

Samuels lived in modest opulence in the north-of-Wilshire section of Beverly Hills. Clive parked in front of the bastard-Spanish house, got out, and stood waiting. The black sedan hesitated and then swerved in behind him. Clive leaned on the door and smiled.

'I'll try not to keep you boys too long. There's a service station just down there, and a drugstore that probably sells cokes, so if you should want anything don't hesitate to run along. I'll wait for you. And, oh, yes – I'm sorry my pal had to leave so suddenly. Urgent business. You know how it is.'

They knew. They told him about it. He listened, failed to learn any new words, and went on up to the house.

Samuels was not happy to see him.

'Every goddam cop in southern California riding the pants off me, and now you gotta turn up.' There were shadows under his eyes as blue as his jowls. He wore a yellow silk shirt and wrinkled green slacks and woven sandals that creaked. 'Well, come on in.'

He led the way into a long whitewashed room with heavy beams and a gaudy tile fireplace. He shooed three fat swarthy kids out of a litter of comic books and motioned Clive to a chair. The kids stared and rushed away, yelling. Somewhere out in back a woman's voice chimed in. It was all rather unsettling to Clive. He had never pictured Samuels away from his tuxedo and his Skyway Club.

He was suddenly tired, and he hated Sammy's face.

'I suppose you've told all this to the police . . .'

'Damn right I have!'

'Well, once more won't kill you. I want to know anything you can remember that might have any bearing on what happened. Anyone asking for Laurel, anyone hanging around the club at odd hours, anything Laurel may have said or done that was out of the ordinary.'

47

Samuels said angrily, 'I've told the whole goddam bunch of you I don't know anything about it, except what went on the night she was killed. And that still makes you and the Hammond guy the best bets!'

'You're stringing along with the majority. Did Hammond's brother-in-law ever come into the club?'

'Jesus, how should I know!'

'I'm asking you, Sammy.'

Samuels glared at him. Finally he said, 'Well, a couple or three weeks ago some guy and a dame came in while Hammond was at your table with Laurel. The dame was plenty classy, a looker. The guy might have been her brother. Anyway, she was all right. Pretty friendly with Laurel, no trouble. Course, you can't always tell with dames. But this guy, he's had a couple and he's feeling feisty. I called the boys, just in case, and then Laurel got up to sing, and pretty soon the gimp started acting like his pants were on fire, he was so anxious to get out of there. So they left. And that's all. I don't know who they were.'

'They ever come back?'

'Only the gimp.'

'Did Farrar come back from the bar in time to see the row we had?'

'I didn't see him again that night.'

'Who was tending bar?'

Samuels thought a minute. 'Vince. Vince Klingman.' Clive wrote Klingman's address on an envelope and stood up. 'One more thing. Farrar was making a play for Laurel while I was out of town. Ever see him hanging around her dressing room? When she wasn't there, I mean.'

'I saw him in the back hall a couple times, but I don't know whether she was there or not.' He got up with heavy ill-nature. 'My God, I got a business to run! And the best singer I ever had goes and gets her brains knocked out.' He creaked down the hall and flung the door open. 'Listen, the next dame I get, you stay away from her, see? You and that gimpy pal of yours, if they don't choke you both in the gas chamber. I got enough grief all by myself!'

Clive looked up at the palm trees rattling in the afternoon breeze. 'Yeah. Yeah, I guess we all have, Sammy.'

He went to his car and drove off, taking the black sedan with him like a toy on a string.

Vince Klingman lived in a neat, old-fashioned cottage near Western Avenue. The lawn was green and the white fence had all the pickets in it. Klingman himself was down on his knees, setting out little square chunks of earth like chocolate cake with green sprouts on top. He was thick and middle-aged, with a contented face.

Clive leaned on the gate. 'Hi, Vince. You look busy.'

Klingman looked up. 'Mr. Clive.' He rose to his feet, smiling. 'Well. Won't you come in?'

'Thanks.' Clive pushed the gate open. Klingman wiped his hands on his earth-stained pants. 'Stock,' he said. 'It's a little late for it, but I love the smell. Wish I had more time for the garden.'

'It looks swell. Vince – I just want to ask a couple of questions.'

'Sure. Uh – about Laurel . . .' Klingman went on awkwardly. 'We all liked her around the club. And – well, I know how you . . . Well, you get me.'

'Yeah. Thanks, Vince.' Clive sat down on the porch steps. He was abruptly envious of Klingman and his garden and his serene face.

'You know Kenneth Farrar, don't you?' He described him. Klingman nodded.

'He was in the bar the night Laurel was killed. I built him a pousse-café.' Klingman's expression showed what he thought of men Farrar's size who went in for things like that.

Clive said, 'Laurel and I had a little trouble. Maybe you knew about it.'

'Well, those things get around.'

'Did people go out of the bar to watch us? Farrar, for instance?'

'You know how folks are. Somebody says, "There's a fight!" and right away everybody's got to go watch it. Farrar went, too. I didn't see him come back.'

'You ever see him hanging around Laurel's room when she wasn't there?'

Klingman frowned. 'I don't think . . . wait a minute. Sure. She was singing, then, out front. I went back to the toilet in the back

49

hall, and I ran into Farrar just outside her door. He was a little tight, and I knew he was trying to make Laurel – those things sort of circulate, you know – so I didn't think anything of it.'

Clive nodded. 'Uh-huh. One more thing, Vince. Ever know of anyone asking for Laurel? Anyone, maybe, with blood in his eye?'

'So many people drift in and out, Mr. Clive. It's only the regulars you get to know. Guys were always asking about Laurel. You know how it was.' Klingman scowled uncomfortably at his boots. 'Sometimes people got pretty sore about it. Sometimes the fellas, sometimes their dames. I don't know of anything lately, though. But, hell, Laurel was a good kid. She had her faults, like any of us, but she was a good kid.'

A yellow cab came down the street, fast. Jonathan Ladd Jones jumped out before the tires had stopped screaming and ran up the path.

Clive stayed where he was, on the steps. He said flatly, 'Sugar.'

Johnny stopped. He had the dazed, incredulous look of a man who has just been kicked fairly hard in the stomach.

'Yeah,' he said. 'She's dead.'

'Murdered?'

'No. No, she wasn't murdered. She's just – dead.'

CHAPTER SEVEN

CLIVE STOOD up. Klingman stared from him to Johnny.

'You mean Sugar March?'

'Yeah,' Clive said. 'The Skyway Club seems to be losing personnel fast. Poor Sammy. Thanks, Vince. Take care of yourself.'

He went out to the car. Johnny paid off the cab and climbed in beside him. He looked sick.

'For Chrissake, Ed, don't give me that dead-pan stuff. There wasn't anything I could do. I waited in a doorway to let her get ahead of me, and she got into this crowd waiting on the corner for the light to change. Maybe twenty people, mostly dames and service men. Just an ordinary bunch. You know those crazy shoes Sugar had on. Well, I guess she just got too near the edge and lost her balance. There was a guy turning the corner, trying to beat the yellow . . .'

Clive got a flask out of the glove compartment and gave it to Johnny. 'Killed instantly?'

Johnny gulped from the flask and shivered. 'Right under his wheels. It sure made a mess of her.'

'And you were watching her all the time? Nobody could have pushed her?'

'Like I said, there was a crowd and you know how those dames mill around. But it looked like a clean accident to me, and that's what everybody else thought. They were all screaming, "She fell off! She fell off!"'

'Nobody you knew in the crowd.'

'Nobody I saw, anyway. Hell, a Boulevard corner right in the shopping hours! And after it happened you couldn't see anything. God, what a madhouse! I hung around just long enough to be sure she was dead. Then I got a drink in the nearest bar and came after you. Sammy told me you were here.'

Clive shoved his hat back and sighed. 'Well, that's one possible lead shot to hell. Nice, pat accident. You're sure nobody was following her?'

'Nobody was near her until she got into that bunch. Nobody was paying any attention to her, and there wasn't anybody but just women with packages and baby carriages and stuff, and four or five soldiers. Cripes, just the way they move around could have pushed her off, with those silly shoes. I've seen it happen lots of times. Been pushed off myself.'

'I wonder if she kept a diary.'

'We could go see.'

Clive scratched his lip reflectively. 'I hope the cops will accept the accident theory. Because it's going to smell awfully fishy – Sugar just having seen me, and then you ducking out and being on the corner when she was killed.' He kicked the starter, looking as though he tasted something sour. 'This slays me,' he said, 'but I'll have to do it.'

He stopped at the first drugstore and called Gaines, telling him the whole story of Sugar's visit.

'I'm going to her place now. Maybe she left a lead of some kind. I'll wait for you. Bring her key and come unofficially, and you won't have to worry about a search warrant.'

Gaines said he'd be there. Clive went back to Johnny.

'Got another job for you, kid. Sugar wasn't exactly thick with any of the other employees, but there's a chance she may have talked to somebody before she realized what a trump card she held. Question them all. Find out if anything else happened that might mean something now, and check up all you can on Farrar. Hop to it, and I don't care if Gaines's little stooge goes in the same cab with you.'

'Okay.' Johnny handed him the gun. 'I guess I won't be needing this. Where'll I get in touch with you?'

'Go on to my place when you're through. I probably won't get back to the office for a year, the way things are breaking.'

Johnny left for a cab rank across the street. One of the men got out of the tail car and followed him. Clive drove away.

Sugar's address proved to be south of Sunset, an apartment over four garages at the back of some dingy flats. Gaines came almost as soon as he got there. They walked down the driveway. A hard-faced woman in blue pajamas put her head out the window and watched them.

Clive grunted. 'You're scaring the lady with those big flat feet.'

They climbed rickety wooden steps. Gaines used the key he had taken from Sugar's bag at the morgue. The woman decided they were all right and took her head back inside.

The apartment was about what Clive expected. There were a lot of things in it, but not one of them was a hint about who had come into the Skyway Club to threaten Laurel's life.

Out on the street again, Gaines said, 'The driver backs up Jones's story. Says the dame suddenly tipped over in front of him.'

'Oh, well. Maybe she was just having fun with me.'

'We'll check on it, anyway.' He studied Clive shrewdly. 'You played this one smart. Keep on doing it.'

Clive smiled innocently. 'Why, sure. Anything at all to keep you happy.'

He returned to Beverly Hills, stopping at a small, swanky office building on Brighton Way. The door marked *Kenneth Farrar – Private Investigator* was closed and locked. Knocking brought no response.

Clive had Mick Hammond's address from the newspapers. It turned out to be a big Georgian place set well back from Sunset Boulevard, on the winding, wooded stretch west of Beverly Hills. The grounds were beautifully landscaped. Beyond a high evergreen hedge Clive caught the glint of water in a turquoise swimming pool.

A tall, correct, cold-faced butler took Clive's card. 'Come in, please. I'll speak to Mrs. Hammond.'

Clive thanked him and went in. The hallway was a decorator's masterpiece, but it didn't feel like home. The butler indicated a chair and vanished.

The chair looked uncomfortable, and Clive was too edgy to feel like sitting down anyway. He wandered past the curving white staircase toward French doors that opened on a wide bricked terrace. It faced west, holding a golden heat from the late sun. Scarlet ramblers burned on the walls and there were beds of spicy stock. It was an expensive garden, but Clive wouldn't have traded it for Vince Klingman's. It was only a stage set, like the hall. He leaned on the edge of a tile-topped table, to wait.

Richard Alcott came around a wing of the tall hedge, climbing the steps to the terrace. He stopped when he saw Clive. The color drained out of his face and then surged back again, so strongly that his skin was almost black.

'You bastard,' he whispered. 'You dirty rotten bastard.'

'I didn't poke you so hard, Alcott. You caught me at a bad moment, or I wouldn't have poked you at all.'

'Just how do you mean that?'

'I mean you were drunk – like you are now. It isn't considered sporting to wallop a man when he's drunk.'

'I'm not so drunk I don't know what's going on. I know why you're here. You're trying to save that bastard's neck. The two of you did it together, didn't you, and you're trying to get your hooks into Jane and the lawyer. Well, it won't do you any good! You understand that?'

It came to Clive that there was more in Richard Alcott than whisky and rage. There was fear.

'Dick!' It was Jane Hammond, looking lovely in dark blue slacks and a flowered silk shirt. Her face was startling. It was like Mick's, tempered and fined and a little unearthly, only there was steel in it that would never be in Mick's.

She said, 'Dick, please go and lie down for a while.'

His lips made an ugly pretense of smiling. 'Of course, Jane. I realize I'm unsuitable to the present company.'

Jane stiffened. Somewhere off behind them a car drove in and stopped.

'Yes, most unsuitable,' Alcott said. 'I've had a drink or two. That's shocking, isn't it? Shocking, to a man who makes his living from murderers and thieves, and a woman who doesn't care if her husband kills the slut he bedded with.'

Jane turned absolutely white. Clive said quietly, 'Get out.'

Alcott swung toward him. He was on his home ground, but more than that his fear was driving him to boldness. He saw Clive's expression and hesitated. Something moving out on the lawn caught his eye. He grabbed at the excuse.

'Well,' he said viciously. 'So little Vivien finally remembered she had a home. It's a pity there isn't a good expressive word like "bitch" for a she-cat.'

He swung on his heel and went into the house. Clive watched him.

Jane said abruptly, 'I wish you'd hit him.'

Clive's mouth twitched. 'There's plenty of time.' He went to the low wall. He was shaking slightly.

Vivien Alcott was walking across the green hollow toward the swimming pool. She wore her crimson coat and she moved with a vague slowness as though she might be asleep and dreaming something nice. She disappeared into a small white Georgian bathhouse.

'They let me see Mick this morning, Mr. Clive. He hardly speaks of the murder. All he talks about is you.'

Jane Hammond stood beside him, her brown strong hands touching the roses. 'He's told me about you, over and over, in this last year. He's made me feel something of what he feels. That's why I'm trying so hard to think that there must have been a good reason for what you did to Mick.'

'And if there wasn't?'

'I think I'd want to kill you.'

'You believe in Mick, don't you?'

'In this last year, with all my heart. Before that, too, only I was afraid sometimes he'd never find himself.' She faced Clive. 'You haven't told me why you turned on him like that.'

Clive's dark eyes were impenetrable. Down by the pool, Vivien Alcott came out in a bright red bathing suit and cap. Her legs and arms were very brown. She was short and rather thick, without softness. She slid into the water, slowly, arching her head with a queer sensual pleasure, like a cat being stroked. She began to swim, easily and without splashing, making clean, purling turns at the end of each lap.

Clive turned away with nervous ill-temper. He lighted a cigarette, snapped the match into a bed of stock, and came back.

'It doesn't matter why I did what I did. All that matters is saving Mick from the gas chamber – and incidentally, saving myself, too. The least they can get me for is aiding and abetting, and Gaines will do his best to hand me the big rap. He doesn't like private dicks who get in his hair, and he's only letting me run until he can make up his mind who's lying. Unless I get a break, and damned quick, I wouldn't give a nickel for either one of us.'

'I think,' said Jane, 'that you must have changed a lot, Mr. Clive, since Mick knew you.'

'That doesn't matter, either. Will you help me, or not?'

The day was almost gone. The thin, foggy chill of evening crawled up from the beaches to the west, bringing a taint of distance and the sea.

Vivien Alcott climbed dripping out of the pool. She pulled off her cap and shook her hair back and stretched, lifting her brown arms high toward the rusty sun.

Jane Hammond said, 'What do you want me to do?'

'I have no authority. You could call a cop now and have me thrown out for bothering you. So I want you to give me a free hand here – with you, your family, the house.'

55

She was surprised. 'But why?'

'Somebody hung this frame on Mick. Maybe by accident, maybe not. But Mick told me about the letters. There may be a connection.'

'I don't see . . .'

'Oh, for Christ's sake! Somebody's been trying for six months to persecute you and Mick into splitting up. Your brother has been trailing Mick for weeks, peddling nasty stories about him and Laurel and even taking you to the Skyway Club to prove them. God knows what little sister has been doing, but I'll bet it's plenty. And both of them knocked themselves out talking, to make sure Gaines would arrest Mick.'

He dropped his cigarette and stepped on it, watching her stonily.

'You came to me, and I turned you down. Maybe it was just an act and you're writing the letters yourself, to get rid of Mick. Or maybe you got fed up suddenly. Maybe you followed us to Laurel's apartment and hit her with Mick's cane and went away happy.'

Anger burned up in her, giving her a sort of frosty glow. When she spoke it was with great care.

'I had no motive to kill Laurel Dane. I suppose I can't expect you to believe this, but I understood what was between her and Mick. I even understood his going home with her, and I was glad if he could find a few hours of peace.'

'Yeah,' Clive said. 'But you haven't answered me yet.'

She stared at him without speaking. The sun dropped out of sight. Shadows crept into the hollows and along the hedges, reaching up for the darkness that was coming out of the sky.

'I suppose,' Jane said, 'I shall have to let you do as you please.'

Vivien Alcott came out of the bathhouse. She had her scarlet coat on again.

'I suppose you read the afternoon papers, Mrs. Hammond,' Clive said. 'The District Attorney's office has received "secret information" in this case. I'm willing to bet that the writer of those letters has passed them on where they'll do the most good.'

'That'll make it worse for Mick.' Her face was hidden now in the dusk, but her voice held enough. 'What Richard told you

56

'. . . well, either he or Vivien could be the one. But that wouldn't necessarily mean . . .'

'That the sender of the letters killed Laurel or had anything to do with it? No. That's the beauty of this case. Nothing necessarily means anything. It would only be a possible motive to land Mick in the death house. Where do you keep the letters? I want to see them.'

'In my safe deposit box. But there are people besides Richard and Vivien . . .'

'Sure, sure. There are one hundred and thirty million people in the United States. All we have to do is pick the right one.'

She said sharply, 'I should think the first thing to do would be to find the man who was in the kitchen. He's certainly the most logical suspect.'

'You're forgetting there was also someone at the door. Someone with a key.'

'But the phone call! And this Dion Beauvais . . .'

'Has a copper-bottomed alibi. And there isn't one shred of evidence to connect him with the case anywhere. Hell, it could have been anybody! Anybody can whisper over a phone. Anybody that's been to the movies can fake a tough accent. Anybody can clip me from behind with a blackjack when I'm not looking.'

'Why, hello, Mr. Clive!' Vivien Alcott's high heels clicked over the terrace floor. She seemed wide awake now, and vivacious. She gave him her hand. It was square and strong, and still cold from the water.

Clive shuddered and let go of it.

'My goodness!' she said. 'Am I that bad?'

'Your hand. It startled me a little, being so cold.'

Vivien sucked her breath in. Her face was only a sort of coppery blur in the afterglow, but he could see the line of her little teeth and the brightness of her eyes.

'That's right,' she said huskily. 'She was cold, wasn't she – when you found her?'

CHAPTER EIGHT

NO ONE spoke for a minute. Tree frogs chirped. Dim lights began to show from houses on the neighboring slopes, given halos by the mist, and there was a burst of illumination from the hall.

Jane Hammond was the first to move. Her voice was flat. 'Let's go in.'

Vivien Alcott walked beside Clive, so near that his hand brushed her coat.

She said, 'You were really as close to it as that, and you didn't see anything?'

'No.'

'Did it hurt much, getting hit like that?'

Clive laughed. 'I hardly notice those things any more. You get hardened to it.'

She studied his face intently. 'I guess a detective has to be tough. Are you tough, Mr. Clive?'

'How do I look?'

'Tough. Awfully tough.'

Jane said, 'Vivien, for heaven's sake!'

Vivien went in through the door and turned around, her hands deep in her coat pockets. She smiled at Clive, corner-wise.

'If he doesn't like it, he can say so. He would, too. I think he'd hit a woman if she spoke out of turn.'

She put her hands on his arm with sudden childlike seriousness. 'Mr. Clive, you said Mick is innocent. Did you mean that? I mean really, because you know it, and not just because you used to be his friend?'

Everybody stopped dead.

'Well I'll be damned,' said Clive. 'The last I heard you were talking sixteen to the dozen to make sure Mick got it.'

'And if he killed her, I hope he does! But – ' she hitched away from him – 'but hell! You don't like seeing even Mick executed for something he didn't do.'

Jane Hammond opened her mouth, and closed it again. Vivien spun slowly on her high heels and came back to Clive.

'After I read what you said in the paper, I thought maybe Mick was telling the truth, because I didn't think he'd have the guts to kill even a girl, let alone knock out a man like you, unless you let him.'

'Maybe I did. Maybe I was lying. The police think I was.'

Vivien's lips made a moist red O. 'You are tough. Really tough!' She came in against him, not too close. 'I don't think you were lying, Mr. Clive. I think you'd lie better than that. I think you'd be an awfully good liar if you wanted to.'

'Of course he was lying!' Richard Alcott stumbled part way down the stairs and leaned against the white virginal curve of the banister, staring over. He was very drunk. 'He knows he was lying. He and that bastard did it between them and they're both guilty as hell. Why are they letting you run around, Clive? And what are you doing in this house?'

Vivien laughed at him. 'He's making an investigation. Maybe he'll give us all the third degree.' She turned shining pale eyes on Clive. 'I'll bet you'd know how, too. I'll bet you've even had it done to you. You have, haven't you?'

'Once or twice.' He had an idea she'd like it if he took off his clothes and showed her.

Alcott was dangerously flushed. His veins protruded. 'You won't investigate me. You have no authority.'

Jane said quietly, 'I've given him the authority.'

Alcott looked at her, a long time. 'You would, wouldn't you?' he whispered. 'Anything to save him. Anything at all to keep that bastard from getting what he deserves. Do you know what you are, Jane? You're a cheap, common . . .'

'Shut up.' It might as well have been the flat of Clive's hand across Alcott's mouth.

Alcott took hold of the banister and yelled, 'You haven't any right here! She can't give you the right. You can't question me. You can't lay a hand on me. I can have you arrested if you try.'

'That scares me.' Clive laughed. 'With a murder rap hanging over me, that scares me a lot.' He stepped forward, holding his body erect and easy. 'You're scared, sonny,' he said genially. 'Only a guy with something to hide starts squawking before he's hurt. What have you got that you're afraid to tell?'

'Nothing. Nothing! God damn you, you can't bully me in my own house . . .'

'Here, or somewhere else. It doesn't matter.'

Alcott's color began to be frightening. 'Jane. Jane, you can't let him. This is your house. You own it. I'm your brother, Jane. You can't . . .'

Jane let her cold blue eyes travel slowly from his blond head to his shoes. 'But I can,' she said. 'Once, a long time ago, I might have cared. But not any more. Mr. Clive has a free hand in my house as far as I can give it. What he does and what penalty he may have to pay are at his own discretion.'

She turned away as though the sight of them all made her want to be ill. Alcott went gray under the purple.

Vivien giggled. 'Blood pressure. We're always hoping he'll have a stroke, but he never does.'

The doorbell chimed.

The butler came from somewhere beyond the staircase. He came so quickly that he had obviously been listening, but his face showed nothing. His heels made a loud noise on the polished floor. Clive realized how quiet it was in the hall. Alcott seemed to have stopped breathing.

'Good evening, Mr. Benson,' said the butler.

A small neat man came in, carrying a large brief case. He nodded to the butler, swept his small sharp eyes around the tableau at the foot of the stairs, sniffed, and pinched his small bloodless mouth even tighter.

'Well,' he said. 'Well?'

Richard Alcott doubled up suddenly. 'I'm sick,' he said. 'Oh, Christ, I'm sick.'

The butler paused. His correct front dissolved enough to show a resigned and patient loathing. Clive thought probably that Richard Alcott's being sick almost anywhere in the house was nothing new around here.

'I'll help you,' he said, and went up the steps. 'Where's the bathroom?'

'Get away from me, you bastard.'

60

'I wish you'd learn a new word. That bastard routine gets tiresome.' He got a hand under Alcott's arm. 'Come on.'

Alcott pulled away. He gagged, let down at the knees, and changed his mind.

'Top of the stairs,' he whispered.

They started up. Alcott was taller than Clive, and heavier. He clung to him, his legs dangling.

'You,' said Benson. 'You're Edmond Clive.'

'Oh, God, yes.' Clive was beginning to sweat. The top of the stairs was a long way off. Alcott retched loudly.

'I want to see you, Mr. Clive.'

'The bathroom will probably hold three. Come right along, but make it fast, brother. Fast.' Vivien giggled.

Alcott made a convulsive surge up the last four steps and pawed at a door. 'Open it. Oh, God. Oh, God.'

Clive doubted whether God was worried much. He got the door open. It was an opulent bathroom, done in apricot and chocolate brown. Alcott made it, but just. Clive leaned his back against the door. He lit a cigarette, hooked his thumbs in his belt, and waited. After a while Alcott sat back on his heels. Clive examined him with open contempt.

'You're a hell of a fine specimen,' he said.

Some of the nastiness came back into Alcott's face and, with it, the fear. He had less strength to hide it now. It looked out starkly from his eyes.

'You leave me alone. If you touch me – '

'I know. You'll call a policeman.' Clive's lip curled. He bent over. 'Go ahead, sonny. Scream your lousy head off, and see if it makes the bruises stop hurting.'

'You wouldn't dare! I'm a sick man. You wouldn't dare ...'

'You're drunk, Alcott. Drunk and scared. Talk up.'

'I don't know anything. I tell you I don't know anything! What makes you think I do?'

'I'm an old dog,' Clive said. 'I've been in the game a long time. I can read signs that aren't half as big and bright as the one you're wearing.' He sat down on the edge of the glistening tub. His manner, all at once, was quite companionable. 'You began to show it out there on the terrace. Then you poured more in on top of the load you were already carrying, hoping

I'd dissolve in the alcohol. But I didn't, so you started yelling about your rights. That was a dead giveaway, son. Remember that. If you're guilty, never object to questioning.'

'I'm not guilty! I haven't done . . .'

'Smoke?'

Alcott swallowed and said, 'No!'

'Where were you,' asked Clive, 'when Laurel Dane was killed?'

Alcott's body grew rigid. He watched Clive from under lowered lids, oddly as though his physical self were a stronghold and he a creature at bay inside it.

'I was at home,' he said. 'In bed.'

'Can you prove that?'

'No. Nobody in this house ever knows where anybody else is, except perhaps at mealtimes. We all have our own cars. There are three ways you can go out without anyone seeing you. We don't keep a chauffeur and all the servants are inside the house.'

Clive nodded. 'That seems an excellent arrangement. You could commit every crime in the calendar and never get caught. You follow Mick to the Skyway Club that night?'

'I – I started to. But I knew it wasn't any use. Jane had told me to mind my own business. She didn't care about Laurel, the bitch. So I just drove around to a few bars and came home. It was raining, and I – I didn't feel so good.'

'You certainly hate Mick's guts.'

'Don't you?'

Clive shrugged. 'What do you think?'

'I don't know,' Alcott said slowly. 'I don't know.' His mouth twisted with venom. 'The bastard! I hope they convict him. I hope they . . .'

'You're sure he's guilty.'

'I don't care. He deserves it anyway. He's a dirty rotten – '

'I know. Bastard.'

'Do you know what he did?' Alcott's voice was shrill now, like a woman's. 'He took my girl away from me. He had Jane and he had her money, but he couldn't keep his hands off Anne. He took her down to the beach and made love to her and she broke off our engagement the next day. She said she wouldn't live in the same family with a man like

62

Mick, and besides . . .' He shut up suddenly, withdrawing again into himself.

Clive laughed. 'And besides,' he finished, 'after Mick had worked out on her you looked like a pretty cold potato. Not a bad motive, at that.'

Alcott glanced up. There was only fear in him now – cold and naked and ugly. He said, with no voice at all, 'Motive?'

'Sure.' Clive smiled at him. 'For sending those letters.'

Alcott's colorless lips made three distinct tries before they could get any words out.

'Letters? Those letters Jane got about Mick?'

'Yeah. Those letters.'

'Alcott's head fell back. His eyes closed. He drew a shaky breath, and then he laughed. He laughed a long time. It got fairly close to hysteria, but it didn't slip over.

'I didn't send the letters,' Alcott said.

Clive's voice didn't give away any more than his face did. 'Mind if I search your room?'

'Hell, no. Move in and live there if you want to. Only for Christ's sake let me alone. I want to sleep.'

He crawled on his hands and knees to the door and pulled himself erect and turned the knob. Clive watched him wobble across the hall and disappear into a bedroom. After a minute he went slowly down the stairs again.

The butler was waiting in the hall. He stared fixedly at a point above and beyond the top of Clive's head, which annoyed Clive. He didn't like to be reminded that he was no skyscraper.

The butler inquired whether Mr. Alcott would be needing anything.

'A lot of things,' Clive told him, 'including a swift kick in the teeth. But right now I think he wants to be alone. Got a telephone?'

'In there, sir. When you're through, Mrs. Hammond asks if you will join them in the library.'

'Thanks.' Clive started as though to move past him, and then stopped, close. 'Just between us boys,' he said, 'what do you think of all this?'

For a moment there was no response. Then the mask cracked open. 'I think,' said the butler in a low, clear voice, 'it stinks.

63

It would please me to learn that the entire family was headed for prison, for life. Excepting Mrs. Hammond, who is a white woman.'

'How about Mr. Hammond?'

'I don't know. He's changed since his accident, but before that . . .' He shrugged. 'Swine,' he said bitterly. 'Pigs, sows, and swine!'

'Uh-huh. Know anything about the letters Mrs. Hammond has been getting?'

'Only that whoever sent them deserves a stretch in hell.' There was actually an angry flush in his flat cheeks. 'I wouldn't have put up with them if it hadn't been for Miss Jane. Not after old Mr. Alcott died. This house! This rotten, filthy madhouse! And Miss Jane, to have married a man like Hammond!'

Clive looked at the floor. 'Yeah,' he said. 'Know where any of the family were between one and two A.M. yesterday?'

Yesterday. Yesterday, hell. It was a hundred years ago. He could feel the marks of all of them on his face.

'No, sir.' The butler went on to explain what Richard Alcott had already told Clive. Clive thanked him and went into the small paneled alcove that housed the telephone. He called his apartment. Johnny Jones wasn't back yet. Clive left the number for him and hung up. He sat scowling, worrying his lower lip with his thumbnail. Then he called Gaines.

The big man growled surlily in his ear. 'For Chrissake, I was just going to dinner. What do you want?'

'If I gave you a detailed answer to that one, you'd have a beard too thick to strain your soup through. Listen, sweetheart. You might take Laurel's key and check around to see if anybody can remember making a duplicate lately.'

Gaines sighed. 'We're only a bunch of dumb flatfeet, but we try. I've had the boys working on that one since yesterday afternoon.'

'Any results?'

'Do you know how many guys make keys in Los Angeles and vicinity? Vicinity! That's about all this lousy town is – vicinity!'

'Yeah. I'll cry about that when I have time. In other words, you haven't anything new.'

'Not yet. Unless . . .'

'Unless what, dammit?'

'Oh, probably nothing. Only they brought a guy into the morgue this morning, early. Accident case. He tried to go downstairs on his neck. I wouldn't have heard about it, only somebody remembered that we were checking on keysmiths . . .'

'I get it,' Clive said sourly. 'Another fluke like Sugar March. It had to be an accident, did it? Nobody could have tripped him? Nobody could have broken his neck and then shoved him downstairs?'

'Medical report says accidental death. I wouldn't know. He lived alone in one of those dumps east of Skid Row, and there were no witnesses. He was pretty old and shaky on his pins and people do break their necks legitimately.'

'It had to be a keysmith, though, and not a street cleaner or a barkeep or even a hustler.' Clive swore. 'A couple more coincidences and you can lock me up in a paddy with the paper dolls. How about the March girl?'

'Accidental death. My belly's biting holes in me. Will you sign off and let me eat?'

Sure, sure,' said Clive pleasantly. 'Go ahead and eat, and I hope you strangle.'

He slammed the receiver down and went out. He was sweating. He walked across to the library door and stopped. He closed his eyes and shivered. For a moment he looked physically ill.

CHAPTER NINE

THE LIBRARY was like the rest of the house. It was big and comfortable, done in dark blue and a soft dull rose. A woman's room, but not the kind that would stifle a man. The woodwork was white, the wall masses broken up with bookshelves and a few excellent pictures, the lamplight shaded and restful. And yet somehow it had an empty feel, as though it were not really lived in.

Jane Hammond looked up from the depths of an armchair as Clive came in. 'How is Richard?'

'Sleeping it off.' He gave her a reassuring smile.

Vivien Alcott bounced up off a couch, all flushed and excited. She had shed the red coat, and the brown dress she wore was pretty tight.

'You've been missing all the fun. I thought Jane was going to murder Benson before you got back. Did Richard tell you what you wanted to know? Did you hit him?'

He grinned. 'Where did you get so bloodthirsty?'

'Runs in the family. We all like our beef rare. Come over and sit down.'

She caught his left arm, hard enough to make him wince and bite his breath off short. She let go quickly and stood away.

'Gee, I'm sorry! I forgot. You got shot, didn't you?'

'A little. It's all right.'

'Mr. Clive.' Jane Hammond rose abruptly. 'Mr. Benson isn't going to defend Mick.'

The lawyer said testily, 'I didn't say that at all. I simply pointed out . . .' He glanced at Clive and pressed his lips together.

Clive said, 'Just what did you point out?'

'I simply said that a straight plea of innocence was a ridiculous waste of time.'

Vivien giggled. 'Not guilty, and not guilty by reason of insanity.'

'Insanity,' whispered Jane Hammond. 'Insanity! And the stain of murder on Mick for the rest of his life.' Her eyes blazed. 'I won't have it! It's cruel and unfair. Mick is innocent, and it's got to be proved!'

The lawyer reached a thin, angry hand into his brief case and threw a newspaper open on the table.

'Look at it! *Love Nest Killing.* Remember what I have to work with and stop asking for miracles!' Benson fixed Jane Hammond with a hard, uncompromising stare. 'This is a shocking thing. There's public feeling about it. I've spoken to the the District Attorney, and I assure you that there'll be no mercy from him. I'll do my best, Jane. But please remember that I wouldn't have touched this case if it hadn't been that you're Tom Alcott's daughter.'

'I know that. I also know that you believe all these things of Mick. You think I was a fool to marry him, and we both deserve what we're getting.'

Vivien broke in sharply, 'Well, you do! Mick married you for your money, he's kicked you around like a cur pup, and you don't care about any of it as long as you can have him to sleep with.' She stepped forward, trembling, her fists clenched. 'Richard was right. Any woman that will take what you've taken from Mick is no better than a – '

'Vivien!' The lawyer was using his courtroom voice. 'Stop that at once! You should be ashamed of yourself.'

'Why? It's the truth!' Her words began to stumble. 'She doesn't care about anybody but him. She doesn't care about her own family. She doesn't care if he killed that woman, if she can have him back!'

Clive put his hand on her shoulder. 'Take it easy, kid.'

She shivered violently. Her head went back. She struggled for a moment to breathe. Then she turned out from under his hand and walked to the couch and buried her face in a corner of it.

Jane said, to no one in particular, 'I'm sorry.'

The lawyer shrugged. He picked up his brief case.

Clive said, 'You're a hell of a fine lawyer.' He pointed to the newspaper. 'That's no courtroom. You haven't any right to try Mick Hammond in that.'

'I must do as I think best, Mr. Clive.'

'Mick's told you he's innocent.'

'Yes.'

'And you don't believe him.'

'No.'

'And you don't believe me, either.'

'Did you expect me to?'

'Hell, why should you be unique?' He was suddenly furious. 'God damn it! Doesn't anybody think I have a brain? Would I try to get away with a corny yarn like that if it wasn't true?'

'I'm sure I couldn't answer that,' said Benson.

'No. No, I don't suppose you could. All right. So you're convinced that either Mick or I did the job, and that one of us is stooging for the other?'

67

Benson nodded. 'Either that, or you were simply too drunk to know what was going on, and tried to cover it on the spur of the moment with that fantastic tale.'

Clive took a quick, nervous walk to the window and back again. He stopped in front of Jane Hammond.

'My lawyer said practically the same thing when I talked to him on the phone this morning, only he wasn't as polite about it. A plea of temporary insanity is the safest thing for Mick.'

He might as well have struck her.

'I'm telling you the truth,' he went on angrily. 'No one believes my story, and, unless I can turn up something to prove it, no one ever will believe it. Gaines and the D.A. are going to be satisfied with what they have. In view of his accident and his nervous condition, Mick might have a chance – and maybe you'd better grab at the best straw there is.'

She said, 'You know Mick didn't kill her.'

Clive looked away from her. 'When I went to wake him, he hadn't even moved his hand, with the quilt folded under it. I had a fight to stir him, even then.'

'He's like that, when he hasn't slept for a long time.' She closed her eyes. 'Mr. Benson – if you won't change your mind, we'll get another lawyer.'

Benson stabbed his cold, small gaze from one to the other. Then he raised his shoulders. 'Very well,' he said. 'I'll do what I can.'

He went out, without saying good night. Vivien was gone, too. It was suddenly very quiet.

Clive said awkwardly, 'Well . . .'

Jane Hammond came to stand in front of him, searching his eyes.

'You're a strange man,' she said. 'I think a person could hate you bitterly or love you very deeply, but nothing in between. I think I hate you for the way you treated Mick. And yet I believe you'll do your best to save him.'

He said brutally, 'It's my neck, too.'

'But you could have saved it by not telling the story you did. By saying that Mick struck you down from behind.'

'I can still do that.'

'Are you going to?'

Clive said, 'No.'

She let her head drop forward. 'I trust you. I don't know why. Perhaps it's that I have to, or . . . I've been thinking. If turning on Mick the way you did was a trick to throw the police off, to give you a chance to find out what really happened, then of course you couldn't tell me. You'd be afraid I'd tell Mick, or give it away somehow, and then the police would be sure that you were guilty, too.' Something was tightening inside her throat, blocking her voice. 'I hope that's the way it was. I hope you aren't lying to me now. Because if you are . . .'

'You're forgetting something,' he said. 'I have another reason.'

'Yes – I was forgetting. You loved her, didn't you?'

Muscles tightened sharply in Clive's face. 'Yeah.'

She moved away from him, pushing the hair back from her forehead. 'Why do things have to be this way? Why can't there ever be any happiness or peace, no matter what we do or how hard we try? What does God think we are? How long does He think we can stand it?' She began to cry, in hard, racking sobs.

Clive put his arms around her. He brought her head onto his shoulder and held her there, gently.

'I don't know,' he said. 'Only they shove the cards in your hands on the day you're born, and you can play 'em any way you want to.'

After a while she whispered, 'Thanks,' and straightened up, fishing for a handkerchief. Clive grunted and gave her his.

'Dames who give out like that should carry sponges,' he said. He smiled. 'Better get some sleep now. It won't help anybody if you slip your cable.'

'I know. I'm sorry. It's just that . . .'

'Go on to bed. I'll tell Jeeves to take you up a tray.'

'His name is Mulligan.' She caught her breath between a laugh and a sob. 'I never believed it either.'

At the door she took his hand and pressed it, and went away up the curving stairs.

Mulligan glided up to Clive's elbow.

'She'll want a tray,' Clive said. 'Something that'll help her to sleep.'

'Yes. Right away.' Mulligan added, 'I hope, for her sake, things aren't as bad as they look.'

'Yeah,' said Clive. 'But I wouldn't take any bets on it.'

He was halfway out the door when he heard the phone ring. Mulligan went back and answered it.

'For you, Mr. Clive.'

It was Jonathan Ladd Jones, and he was feeling sorry for himself.

'Gawdamighty, my tongue's hanging clear to my knees! I never knew so many people worked for Sammy. And Sugar never dropped a hint to any of them. Nobody else heard anybody threaten Laurel. Farrar's been hanging around her dressing room, but I knew that myself. Nobody noticed anyone else doing it, but that doesn't mean anything. There was hardly ever anyone in the hall, and you can get into it from both the club and the alley.'

'I knew that,' said Clive.

'Okay! So you know everything I know. Any luck with you?'

Clive said slowly, 'I don't know yet.'

'Coming home now?'

'That depends.'

'Had any dinner?'

'No, mama.'

'Well, you ought to get some dinner.'

'I'm not hungry.'

'Look, Ed, it's not good to . . .'

'For Chrissake, can't I even feed myself? Get down to head-quarters and get all the dope you can on the stiff with the broken neck they brought in this morning. Go on over to the guy's flophouse and see can you earn what I pay you. I'll catch up with you as soon as I can.'

Johnny cursed him, bitterly and at some length. Clive grinned and hung up. He said good night to Mulligan and went out, pausing on the dark driveway to locate Richard Alcott's windows. A light came on while he was watching, and the blinds were pulled down. Clive went on to his car.

He opened the door. Something rustled inside, and Clive dropped sideways like a cat.

'It's only me,' a small voice said.

Clive straightened up, sweating. 'What,' he said, 'the merry aitch are you doing here?'

The answer was slow in coming, and it wasn't really an answer. 'I blew off in there, didn't I?'

'I never saw it done better.'

'You think I'm pretty much of a heel, don't you?'

'Well, a thing like that doesn't exactly advertise a girl's charm.'

'No.' This time there was a very long gap. Clive shot an impatient glance at the house. Alcott's light was still on.

Vivien said, 'I'm sorry.' She sounded about five years old.

Clive laughed. 'You don't owe me an apology. I'm sort of a heel myself. Besides, I'm Mick's friend, and that makes me one of the family.'

'You don't think much of us, do you?'

He said quietly, 'I think a lot of Jane.'

'Yes.' Vivien sighed, a peculiar sigh that might have meant anything. 'I thought you would. Please get in. I want to talk a minute.'

Clive slid under the wheel. He could feel her round, strong thigh against his.

She said, 'This probably won't make any difference to you, but I'm going to tell you anyhow. I used to be in love with Mick.'

'The woman scorned, huh?'

'You could call it that, I guess. But there's more to it. You see – I'm not pretty. Jane is. Jane is everything I'm not. Jane always got everything when Father was alive, and he left her all his money. All Richard and I got were trust funds. You can see what he thought of us.'

The bitterness of her laugh startled him. 'Maybe he was right. Richard's a nasty drunken little swine, and I – ' She broke off short, and then went on again half jokingly. 'Richard and I got our unstable nerves from our mother. Richard and Jane both look like Father, but Mother was tall and fair too. Nobody knows whom I look like. Everybody always said maybe I was a changeling.'

She gave him a tip-tilted smile. 'Personally,' she said, 'I've always thought I was a bastard.'

'Well,' said Clive. 'Well!'

'And if you think that helps any, you're crazy!'

'No. No, I don't imagine it would.' He shifted, but the wheel pinned him. He couldn't get away from that warm, vibrant thigh.

'So now you know,' said Vivien wearily. 'I hate Mick, and I hate Jane, and I hate Richard, and I hate myself.'

'Doesn't that get a little tiresome?'

'Oh, God,' she whispered, 'you don't know.'

After a pause Clive said easily, 'That explains the letters, then.'

'Letters? You mean the ones about Mick?'

'Yeah. Richard told me all about your sending them.'

'He would.' Her voice didn't show anything but her peculiar brand of family affection. 'He would try to blame them on me! Well, I didn't send them. I'm sorry I didn't, but I didn't. If I'd thought of it and had known how to find out all those things about Mick, I probably would have done it. But I didn't.'

'Well,' Clive said, 'that's that, then.'

'I never met a detective before.' She sounded eager as a child. 'What will you do now?'

'Detectives never tell.'

'I'm sorry I pulled your arm. Does it still hurt?'

'No.' He laughed. 'I'm tough. Remember?'

'Yes. I remember.' She hesitated. 'The man that hit you – you know, in the kitchen. I should think, being so close to him and everything . . . haven't you any idea who it was?'

'Guys who make a business of things like that are pretty careful, and a blackjack doesn't have much personality. It could have been anybody.'

'But you're going to find him, aren't you?'

'I'm going to try.'

'You scare me when you sound like that.' Her hand came up to his where it lay on the wheel. 'The papers said that you and Laurel – '

'The papers said! All right, God damn it, yes! I loved her.'

She let her fingers slide away across the taut cords of his wrist. 'I'm sorry.'

He shook his head irritably. 'Skip it. I just haven't slept much lately.'

She pushed herself away, out of the car. 'I never met anyone like you before,' she said. 'Perhaps if I had . . .'

She was gone, leaving a queer little whimper on the foggy air. Clive didn't look after her. He got out the flask and took a stiff one, and one more to wash it down. Then he started

72

the car, tramping on the throttle to make it backfire, and drove onto Sunset Boulevard. He didn't go far. There was a tree some hundred feet west of the Hammond gate. Clive parked in its shadow. His chaperon was still waiting patiently.

Because the house was set higher than the surrounding ground, Clive could see the light in Alcott's room. Almost immediately it went out.

Clive waited.

About five minutes later a long dark convertible rushed out of the Hammond driveway and headed east.

CHAPTER TEN

EDMOND CLIVE was good at following cars. The three of them – the convertible, Clive's coupé, and the police tail car – went down Sunset to Beverly Hills, slackening pace when they hit the more traveled streets. At Camden the convertible crossed over to Wilshire and headed toward Los Angeles.

They went as fast as the law allowed, and no faster, stopping carefully for red lights. They passed the dimmed-out Miracle Mile, Western Avenue, and then the copper-sheathed tower of Bullock's store. Presently they were on the wide causeway splitting Westlake Park. The still water of the lake was like a shield of polished iron under the sky. The convertible turned right on Alvarado, and then onto Seventh Street. Theater parking had jammed the curbs. It turned again, onto the dark side of the park, and slid in beside a fire plug.

Clive hung back. The tail car was on his rear bumper now. The street was deserted.

Richard Alcott got out of the convertible and walked quickly into the dense shadows of the trees. Clive left his car in the street and followed. Alcott was moving fast toward the lake, and not making much noise about it. There was a wide graveled path beside the water. Alcott avoided this, keeping on the grass where he was covered by the shrubbery. He seemed to be aiming for a spot where the shore line made a jog inward and the trees came close to it, overhanging a stand of pampas grass.

Clive bent over and ran without sound, making a circle. He came down to the lake ahead of Alcott and crouched beside a clump of the saw-edged grass.

Alcott's feet crunched softly on the gravel walk. He had his hand in his pocket. He paused in the shelter of the pampas, listening, standing black against the paler darkness of the water. Then he took his hand out of his pocket and raised it, high, like a woman starting to throw a ball.

Clive stood up, fast. He caught Alcott's upraised wrist just as it began its forward sweep. Alcott let go a strangled yell. Clive kicked him back of the knee and pulled his arm over his shoulder. Something dropped heavily. Alcott twisted around. Clive's shoulder hunched slightly. His fist traveled about six inches and hit square. Alcott fell on his back, jerked briefly, and lay still.

Clive got out a small flashlight. Almost at once he found what had fallen. It was a Colt .45, with a silencer. Clive stared at it. 'Well,' he said aloud. 'Well I'll be damned!'

Somebody was tramping around in the bushes behind him. A man said gruffly, 'Hey, what goes on?'

Clive turned. The beam of his flashlight speared Alcott's face. There was a sudden sharp feminine scream.

'Migawd, he's killed him! Joey . . .'

'Relax, sister,' said Clive. He was holding his left shoulder now, his face twitching with pain. 'I only hit him a little.'

Somewhere a man was making angry noises among the trees, coming closer. The flashlight beam showed a little red worm crawling out of Alcott's wide-open mouth.

The woman said hoarsely, 'You brute!'

Clive didn't answer that.

The woman said, 'You get a cop, Joey. You go right away and get a cop.'

Clive laughed. 'Never mind, Joey.' He raised his voice. 'Hey, Junior! Over this way!'

The plain-clothes man panted up. He had his gun out, and he looked hungry and resentful.

The woman shrieked again.

'Bandits! Joey, you get me out of here! Don't you dare touch us, you two. Joey, you take me right away . . .'

'Yeah,' said the plain-clothes man. 'You do that, Joey. Quick, before I forget I'm a gentleman. Go on! Scram!'

They went. Her voice carried clearly. In the future Joey would probably pick a less private spot in which to do his necking.

'Dames,' said the plain-clothes man. 'Yah!' He frowned at the revolver lying beside Clive's foot. 'Okay, Clive. What gives?'

'Plenty.' Clive handed him the flashlight and stepped carefully around the gun. 'Don't touch that.' He kneeled and sopped his handkerchief in the cold lake water and slapped Alcott in the face with it. Alcott pushed himself up on his elbow, retched, and fell back again, but he was conscious.

Clive said pleasantly, 'In a few minutes you are going down to headquarters and be booked for attempted murder. Down there you will sing your head off. But I'm in a hurry and I'd like to hear about it now.'

Alcott shut his teeth together. 'I won't talk without my lawyer.'

'The cops can hold you a long time before you can have a lawyer, son. How are your kidneys?'

'My kidneys?'

'Not too hot, are they, with all that stuff you swill down? They can keep you from going to the john for a long, long time. It doesn't leave any marks on you, but it isn't funny.'

Alcott's gaze was fixed on Clive. He said nothing.

'They can keep you awake, too. Fifty, sixty, seventy hours. No water. No cigarettes. No fresh air. Lights burning your eyes blind. Sometimes they do tricks with a telephone book. That's fun, Alcott. You'd be surprised how much beating a guy's head can take from a telephone book and not show anything.'

He paused. He was smiling, rather kindly.

'Vivien said something about high blood pressure. Be too bad if you were to have a stroke because you wouldn't talk. But you couldn't blame the cops if a guy had a stroke, now could you?'

Hoarsely, between his clenched teeth, Alcott began to curse.

Clive's hand shot out and took him hard across the mouth. Moving very quickly, he caught Alcott's shirt and dragged the dead weight of him to the edge of the lake, so that his head hung over into the water.

Clive said very softly, 'You shot me in the back from a dark alley. You hit Laurel from behind. Did you knock that old man downstairs the same way, or was he feeble enough so you dared to face him?'

Alcott writhed under Clive's grip. His hair moved sluggishly in the cold water.

'I didn't. I didn't kill anybody.' His eyes rolled toward the plain-clothes man. They showed white around the irises. 'You! You're a policeman. Make him stop!'

The plain-clothes man shrugged. 'I just came along for the ride.'

Clive said, 'You plugged me, Alcott. Were you that sore about that whack in the belly?'

Fingers tore at his coat sleeve. 'You can't prove . . .'

'You were trying to get rid of the gun. Your fingerprints are on it. There's a bullet in the wall of Laurel's dressing room that'll match the barrel. Did you pay somebody to make that phone call or did you do it yourself?'

'Phone . . . phone call?'

Clive shoved his face under and dragged him up again instantly, coughing and blowing.

'The phone call, Alcott. The one you made threatening Laurel's life.'

'Oh, Christ, I didn't! I didn't even know . . .'

'Did you go through the alley or the club when you stole the key from Laurel's dressing room?'

'I didn't! Why would I want to? She wasn't anything to me.' Alcott strained his head up, away from the water. 'How did you follow me here? How did you know?'

Clive said, 'What do you think I am – a baby? You were scared stiff. Not about the letters, but about something. Why do you think I let you go? I knew you'd make a break for it.'

'Oh, God,' moaned Alcott. 'Let me up.'

'As soon as you talk.'

'I didn't have anything to do with it, I swear I didn't . . .'

'I wonder,' said Clive conversationally, 'how long you could hold your breath under water?'

Nobody said anything for a minute. The dark water rose and fell, and somewhere a duck quacked sleepily.

Alcott whispered, 'All right.'

Clive pulled him back from the edge. Alcott was completely relaxed now, his eyes closed.

'Can I have a cigarette?'

Clive lit one for him. Alcott began to talk in a toneless voice.

'I didn't mean to shoot you. I meant to shoot Mick, and you stepped in front of me. I bought the gun and the silencer after Anne left me. I couldn't make up my mind to use them. I was afraid of murder. And then, when I knew Mick wasn't ever going to get what was coming to him from Jane, I . . .'

He rolled his head, coughing over the smoke. Clive said, 'Take your time.'

'I sat in my car that night, alone, outside the Skyway Club. I was thinking about Anne, and about Mick there, playing with another woman. I was thinking about the money, too. He married Jane for her money – money that should have been mine. I'm the son! What right did Jane have to my money, the bitch? My money, going to a bastard like Mick, who was cheating on her in public with a night-club slut and she wouldn't believe it!

'I got my gun and went around into the alley. It was raining and there was nobody around. I knew Mick went back to her dressing room a lot. I looked through the window and I saw him sitting on the couch, right in front of me. I wanted to blow his head off, so he couldn't take the money that belonged to me, or the woman that belonged to me, any more.'

He stopped. He was beginning to shudder in regular spasms.

Clive said, 'So you fired at Mick, and I stepped in front of you.'

'Yes. And then I was scared. I could have killed Mick then, but I was scared. I thought you were dead, and I never knew before what it would feel like to kill a man. I'd been drinking in the car and I got sick. I knew somebody would be coming out. I ran down the alley and got in my car and drove away. I stopped once on the way home. I was sick. I was home all the rest of the night, in bed.'

Clive studied him for a long time without speaking.

'Alcott,' he said at last, 'I think perhaps you've forgotten something. I think you haven't told me what you did between the time you drove away from the Skyway Club and the time you went to bed.'

Alcott's body grew slowly rigid. 'I told you . . .'

'I think after you ran away you took a few more drinks to settle your nerves, and you got to thinking. Maybe the second time wouldn't be so bad. And you began to see how you could take care of Mick so that you yourself wouldn't be suspected. You decided you were really a pretty big guy. I'd socked you one, and you'd paid me out, and as far as you could see you were safe. Be nice to do the same thing for Mick . . .

'I'm not sure about the key. Maybe you'd had the idea in the back of your head for a long time. Maybe you got it from Laurel's dressing room, or maybe you stole it from Mick. Anyway, you had a key to her apartment. You went up there . . .'

'No. Clive, I swear to God – no!'

'Did you hire it done, then? Was that your strong-arm boy that clipped me?'

Alcott drew a long breath. 'Clive,' he said very slowly, 'I didn't kill her. I didn't kill anyone, then or later.' His eyes met Clive's, held them fairly. He whispered, 'I wish I had, though. I wish to Christ I had!'

Clive stood up. The plain-clothes man said, 'He's passed out.' Clive seemed not to hear him. He looked down at Alcott, somberly abstracted. The plain-clothes man lighted a cigarette, watching him curiously.

Presently Clive gave his shoulders a hitch and turned around, bending over the gun. He found a pencil, and hooked it carefully through the trigger guard.

The plain-clothes man nodded at Alcott. 'Funny thing. Guys like that, you don't really have to do anything. Just talking scares the bejesus out of 'em.'

Clive grunted. 'You should see him tackle a woman. Hell on wheels. Throw some water on him.'

The plain-clothes man picked up Clive's wet handkerchief and went to work. Alcott came to, and Clive spoke to him.

'Listen, and get this through your head. I have this gun. I will get the bullet. Junior here is a witness to your confession, so don't think you're getting away with anything.'

The plain-clothes man had a funny look on his face. Alcott began to struggle onto his knees.

78

'You're no good to this case,' Clive said, 'and you'll be a lot of harm to Jane if the papers get hold of you. I'm the only one that got hurt and I'm willing to forget it – on condition.'

'Condition?'

'Yeah. Try and behave like a human being around Jane, and as soon as you can after this is over take yourself and your dirty tongue away somewhere and stay a while. A long while. Get it?'

'Yes,' Alcott whispered. 'Yes. I got it.' His face was only a pale gleam in the darkness, unreadable. He balanced on his knees and then tried standing. Clive watched impassively.

'Don't talk to Jane. Don't talk to anybody. And remember the jail is yawning for you if your foot slips.'

Alcott didn't say anything. He lurched away across the gravel path.

The plain-clothes man said, 'Well . . .'

Clive's brows went up. 'What's the matter, Junior? Conscience got an ache?'

'Well, he's gotta connection with this case . . .'

'Sure. He can make it a little tougher on Mick's wife, but that's all. I'm the injured party, and I'm not doing anything about it. So where does your conscience get off?'

'Well . . .'

Clive pulled out his wallet. He handed the man a couple of bills. 'That's no bribe, Junior. That's a poultice for the ache.'

Junior whistled. 'I could poultice a lot of aches with that. But if Gaines starts asking questions . . .'

'Why should he? As far as he knows Alcott never left the house. Why confuse the poor lug by telling him?'

The plain-clothes man shrugged. 'Okay. I'm just a hired hand, anyhow. Let's go.'

They went. When Clive drove onto Wilshire, Alcott's car had already started creeping back toward home.

Clive went up to Homicide to see Gaines. Korsky was with him in his dingy cubicle, sitting back-to-front on a marred chair and smoking a cheap cigar.

Gaines glanced up from behind a littered desk. 'Decided to give yourself up?'

'My God,' said Clive. 'What a comedian.' He sat down uninvited and began to add more smoke to what was already rolling under the ceiling. Gaines went on making a cigarette. It was hot. Korsky examined Clive with bright, hard eyes.

Clive told about the letters. There was not much point in keeping them quiet any more, and the police laboratory had a better chance of finding out things about them than he did.

When he was finished Gaines said, 'We been checking on Kenneth Farrar. Want to hear about it?'

'Yeah.'

'Shoot, Korsky.' Gaines became absorbed in the actions of a fly walking across the ceiling.

Korsky talked without taking the cigar out of his mouth.

'He tells a straight story. He was crazy about the girl, but she couldn't see him. After the fight you picked with him he had a drink and moved on. I checked him through four or five places. He got home about a quarter to one, according to the night clerk, and he didn't go out again. The back door is locked after ten o'clock and only the clerk and the manager have keys. Besides, the clerk can see down the hall to the back stairs and the door itself makes a noise. Nobody went near it.'

'Fire escape?'

'That comes down right over the back door. He'd have heard it.'

Clive nodded. He showed neither surprise nor disappointment. The silence lay heavy in the airless room.

After a while Gaines said, 'There were no prints but yours and Hammond's and the girl's. That doesn't help you any.'

'No.'

'Farrar doesn't, either.'

'No.'

'There isn't a lot of hope on the Beauvais angle – even if you weren't lying.'

Clive shrugged.

'Probably those letters won't help any more than the rest.'

'It's possible.'

Gaines tilted forward in his chair and crushed out his butt. 'Why,' he asked softly, 'should I bother with any silly damn letters? Why shouldn't I book you right now and throw the whole thing to the D.A.?'

Clive's face twitched slightly. 'Because Mick didn't do it. Because I didn't do it. Because we didn't do it.'

'Think of a better reason.'

Korsky let his breath go with a harsh little rasp. 'I can think of a better one. Eddie didn't realize how silly he was going to look, saying he was dumped on his pratt in the kitchen. So now he's got to find a fall guy to save that ugly mug of his.'

Clive said, with no particular emphasis, 'I can top that.'

A curious tautness came over Gaines. 'Yeah?'

Clive nodded.

'Well, go ahead.'

'With that in the room?' Clive indicated Korsky with his thumb.

'Why not?'

'I'm sentimental, that's all. I don't want to blast the boy's bright faith in the sanctity of the Police Department.' He sighed. 'But we all have to grow up, don't we?' He leaned his elbows on his knees, flipping his cigarette in the general direction of the cuspidor. 'You remember Joe Rappatoni?'

Slow crimson flowed up to the roots of Gaines's hair, leaving a white line around his lips. He sat perfectly still, staring into Clive's eyes. Korsky straightened up on his chair.

Gaines said, 'Get out, Korsky.'

Korsky started to say something, changed his mind, and went out. Gaines got to his feet, leaning over the desk. Clive stopped the words in his mouth with a quick gesture. He went noiselessly to the door and pulled it open.

Korsky caught himself on the door jamb.

Clive smiled. He kicked Korsky accurately and with force in the upper belly, pushing out straight with his heel. Korsky ran backward across the hall, fetched up hard against the opposite side, and slid down to a sitting position on the floor. He looked as though he would be there for some time.

Clive said, 'I've been wanting to do that, pal.' He closed the door and leaned his shoulders against it.

Gaines said harshly, 'What are you trying to pull?'

'Blackmail.'

81

'What do you think you know about Rappatoni?'

'He was a louse. If I'd been your sister I'd have shot him, too.'

Gaines waited a long while. Then he said carefully, 'You can't prove my sister had anything to do with that mess.'

'I can make a damn good try.'

The fly buzzed industriously on the ceiling.

Gaines came around the desk. 'I knew you were a bastard, Clive, but I never thought you'd pull a thing like this.' He cursed him obscenely. 'You haven't got a thing that will stand up in court. They hanged a man for that killing.'

'Sure. And Little Cuppy killed a lot of guys in his time, too. But Joe Rappatoni wasn't one of them.'

Clive took his shoulders away from the door. He kept his voice low, but it was guttural with anger.

'You'd be surprised what I've got that will stand up in court – against you and half the big shots in this state. I make a collection of things like that, so when some influential son of a bitch backs me into a corner I'll have a chance of getting out again. You asked for it, Gaines. Now I'm telling you. Lay off me! You think I'm bluffing, go ahead and call me. Maybe it's worth it to you to pin a bum rap on a private dick you don't like. I don't think it'll be worth it to your sister.'

After a long interval Gaines turned away. He walked over to his desk and put his palms on it, flat, and said over his shoulder, 'Get out.'

Clive grinned, without humor. He opened the door and went out. Behind him, Gaines began to curse in a choked whisper.

Korsky still sat on the floor. His mouth was wide open. Whistling, wheezing noises came out of it.

'Try a cubeb,' said Clive kindly. 'Good for asthma.'

The outside air felt ice cold when it hit him. His chest muscles were twitching, and he broke four matches before he could get his cigarette going.

He laughed and started walking, toward the nearest bar.

CHAPTER ELEVEN

JONATHAN LADD Jones had left a note stuck in the door of the keysmith's room, 'Waiting in #4B.' Clive scowled and went down the stairs again. He prowled in the dirty yellow smear of light that came from two feeble bulbs set back and front. The frayed carpeting tried to trip him, and when he touched woodwork it was greasy with the memories of ancient cooking. The place smelled of many people, many things, none of them clean.

He found the number finally and knocked. The voice of Jonathan Ladd Jones came from beyond.

'C'min, c'min, whoever you are.'

He sounded very happy. Clive opened the door. The stench of the hallway was beaten back immediately by a more powerful one that had been cooped up inside. The inside odor was mostly gin. There were other things – perfume, stale smoke, musty fabric, sweat. But predominantly it was gin. Clive staggered slightly. He shut the door and propped himself against it. He shoved his hat back and stared.

'Well,' he said. 'Well, blow me down.'

A small room with blotched plaster and stained paper on the walls. The usual articles of furniture, very old, very tired, very sad. Unshaded bulbs glared overhead. There was a lopsided armchair opposite the door, and there seemed to be several people sitting in it.

On closer inspection it turned out to be only Jonathan Ladd Jones and a blonde. She was a big, healthy blonde. She was sitting on Johnny's lap, and she covered everything but the top of his head and his shoes. Johnny wormed his face through a froth of pink chiffon ruffles and said, 'Hiya, Ed.' His spaniel eyes were bright and unfocused. He waved, causing liquid to slosh in the glass he held.

Clive said, 'Hi,' and waved back.

The blonde gave him a huge damp grin. 'C'mon in. Y'pal's been keepin' ya seat warm.'

'Nuh-uh,' said Johnny. 'Your seat, baby.' He giggled. 'God, my knees! You sure don't starve yourself.'

The blonde smiled. 'I like to give 'em their money's worth.' She jerked her head up suddenly and let out a screech that made Clive jump. 'Kethrin! Kethrin, here's ya boy!'

Kethrin came from an adjoining room. She wore something loose, Nile green, and pretty slinky, only she didn't have much to slink with. Her hair was a deep maroon and her face slid away from under popped brown eyes as though it were too tired to stay put.

She held up a fresh bottle of cheap gin and said heavily, 'Oh boy, now we can have a party.'

Clive took a deep breath. 'Now wait a minute, sister. I've got work to do.' He smiled patiently. 'Johnny. Johnny, dear. I sent you down here to investigate something. Remember?'

'S'what'm doin'. 'Vestigatin'.' He nudged his face forward, causing interesting reactions under the pink ruffles. 'Big case,' he said. 'Very big case.'

'Yeah. I can see that. But there was a corpse, remember? A male corpse, with a broken neck.'

The blonde shuddered. Johnny groaned. 'F'Chrissake sit still. 'M bein' ground to a powder.' He looked at Clive reproachfully. 'I got what you wanted, Ed. Just ask the girls.'

The blonde said, 'You tell'm, Kethrin. I can't bear it.' She hid her head on Johnny's shoulder.

Kethrin said, 'Well . . .' She was standing close to Clive now. She was runty enough to make him look like a good-sized man. She held out the gin bottle.

Clive said, 'No, thanks. What was it you had to tell me?'

'We could be more comfortable over there.'

'I don't think so.'

'I talk better when I'm comfortable.'

Clive got out a five-dollar bill. 'That help any?'

'Well . . .'

He held the bill out of reach and waited. He was wondering what the oxygen content of the air was and how long he could continue breathing. He felt green.

'I saw a man,' said Kethrin.

The blonde whinnied as though Kethrin had said something very funny indeed. Johnny's feet kicked. 'Stop it,' he said. 'You tickle.'

Clive looked innocent. 'A man. Any special kind?'

'Just a man.'

'How, when, and what was he doing?'

'Coming upstairs. I didn't hear him until he stumbled in the hall outside. When I got the door open he was halfway to the next floor.'

'Slowpoke,' said the blonde viciously. 'Gettin' old.'

'I could be your daughter.' Kethrin shrugged and added, 'Hell, I could be, at that.'

'About the man,' said Clive.

'Oh, him. Well, he was sorta tall and he had on a black coat and a black hat jammed over his eyes. I couldn't see his face.'

'Old or young?'

'He was taking the steps like he had plenty of pep, all right.'

'Then what?'

'Then I went back to bed. Pretty soon I hear a hell of a racket. I look out the door and there's this old guy that makes keys lying on his belly at the foot of the stairs, with his head folded under.' Other people start coming out, too, but I'm nearest so I get there first. I see he's dead, all right.'

She shivered, and for a moment her face was pitiful.

'I guess maybe I scream or something. Then I look up the stair well. I don't know why. Maybe I just want to look away from – him. Anyway, it's dark up there but I think I see something, a black coat maybe, moving up. Then people start coming out into the halls above, and I ain't sure I hear what I think I hear – the sound of the door onto the roof, opening and shutting.'

She drank from the bottle. 'Okay,' she said, when she had her breath again. 'How's about that dough?'

Clive gave it to her. 'Did the keysmith usually go out as early as that?'

'Nuh-uh. But he wasn't going out. He didn't have nothing on but a shirt and underpants. Way I figure he must of headed for the can and tripped just at the head of the stairs. He was an old guy, and the carpet's full of holes.'

Clive nodded. 'Thanks. Okay, Johnny. We go home now.'

The blonde raised her head and blinked at him. 'Home?' she repeated. 'Go home?'

'Uh-huh. You know – home. Everybody has one. Sort of a place to go to, all your own.'

The blonde looked down at Johnny. 'You gotta home?'

Johnny buried his face in pink ruffles and let his head ride up and down on the heaving of them. 'Home,' he said, 'but no mother.' He wept.

'You wanna go to it?'

'Why would I wanna go home all by myself? 'M lousy company.'

She crushed him tenderly to her bosom and glared at Clive. 'You heard him. He dowanna go home.'

Kethrin giggled. 'Plenty of gin, big boy. Stick around and have some fun.'

Clive smiled. 'I'd love to, baby. But I'm working a case. It's tough, but we have to be brave about those things.'

The blonde took a deep breath. Johnny's head rose and fell. His eyes were closed. The blonde said distinctly, 'He is staying.'

Clive went a little closer. 'Johnny!'

Johnny smiled drowsily. 'Can't come, Ed. Somep'n holdin' me down. Awful sorry.'

The blonde said, 'If you wanna scram, go ahead. We c'n get along without you. Can't we get along, Kethrin?'

Kethrin said they could. She said, 'One from four makes more gin.'

The blonde said, 'See?' very hard, through her teeth. Clive got out his wallet again.

'Will this get you up, babe, or do I use my boot?'

The blonde measured Clive carefully and then laughed. 'Get him!'

Kethrin sucked noisily on the bottle, considering. 'He ain't so awful big,' she decided, 'but he's tough. Maybe you better take the dough.'

The blonde picked up Johnny's head by the hair and laid it against the chair back. She rose, fishing around by her feet for an empty bottle.

She said, 'I'm sorta tough myself,' and raised the weapon, shaking her arm loose from the pink ruffles. It was about the size of Clive's thigh. She moved forward.

Kethrin giggled and took herself and her gin out of the way. 'Oh boy,' she said. 'Oh boy.'

The blonde let fly. Clive ducked. The bottle hit the door behind him. Johnny started and sat up.

Clive said evenly, 'You come one step closer, honey, and I'll land you one square in the wind.'

'You,' said the blonde, 'are no gentleman.'

She started one from below the knee. Clive had plenty of time to get out of the way. The only thing he hadn't figured on was the bottle he stepped on. There were a lot of bottles. The girls seemed to keep them around as mementos of happy times. There was one under his heel when he stepped back, and it nearly sat him down flat. The blonde's fist caught him on the side of the head. Clive turned over three times and hit a table, causing a crash and an explosion of splinters.

Kethrin set her bottle on the floor, clapped her hands together, and said solemnly, 'Whee.' Clive rolled over, shaking his head and kicking pieces of table out of his way. The blonde advanced, breathing heavily.

'Now,' she roared, 'he busts my furnicha!'

Clive lay on his back and stared, fascinated. A foot in a large pink mule rose into the air and rushed down at him with the aim and authority of a pile driver.

He caught it close to his stomach and threw it away, hard. The blonde sat down. Plaster ripped and fell somewhere below.

Johnny said suddenly, 'He's my pal, y'unnerstan'? You can't do that to him.'

Clive didn't see much sense in that remark. He succeeded in untying himself from the wreckage of the table and retrieved his hat. The blonde remained seated, blowing like a winded horse.

Johnny said, 'Y'unnerstan'? You can't do that to my pal.'

'Oh,' said the blonde. 'Oh, can't I!' She got up. Clive wouldn't have believed that she could do it that fast. She was squarely between him and the door.

He jammed his hat on and made sure his feet were free of bottles.

The blonde looked at him. She took a good long look. Then she turned suddenly on Jonathan Ladd Jones.

'All right,' she said. 'If that's the way you feel about it.'

She picked him up by the collar and the seat of the pants and yelled, 'Open that door, you horse-faced little bastard!'

Clive decided she must mean him. He opened it. Johnny shot out into the hallway, lit on all fours, rolled over, and fetched up on his back with his feet propped against the wall.

Kethrin waved.

Clive raised his hat politely and went out, fast. Behind him the door began to give out sounds like a drum being beaten rapidly and with force.

Clive whistled. 'If she does that well with gin bottles, what couldn't she do pitching for the Yankees!'

Quite a few people were hanging over the banisters and out of doors, grinning. He nodded at them.

'Nice kids,' he said. 'Trouble is, they're a little too refined.'

He got hold of Johnny's collar and dragged him bodily down the stairs. The cold air outside revived him somewhat. He waited until Clive had started repeating himself and then smiled cherubically.

'That clue was worth the five bucks, huh?'

'Oh, sure! That heavy-duty tank damn near breaks my neck, but it's worth it!' Clive wrenched the car door open. 'Go on. Get in.'

Johnny was unabashed. When Clive had the car going, headed west again, he said, 'At least you know somebody was around that didn't belong there when the old guy was killed.'

'Yeah. Somebody. A man with no face. Just a black coat and hat going upstairs. Maybe. And maybe that lass with the maroon hair was so lushed that she might have seen Winston Churchill riding by on a pink barrage balloon.' He grated the gears savagely. 'That's the hell of this case. Nobody has a face. Nobody even has a voice. Just shadows and whispers and keys turning, and death in somebody's heart, and no way to get any of it out into the daylight.'

Johnny shot a glance at him. 'You had any dinner, Ed?'

Clive laughed. 'Okay, mama! Just don't try and hold the spoon for me, will you?'

He had his dinner, trying not to think that he should be having it at the Skyway Club, trying not to think that he wouldn't ever be having it there again. He listened while Johnny told him what he knew about the keysmith. The man's stand had been near Fifth and Broadway, and there was no more chance of identifying one of his customers than of picking out a particular sea gull in a flock of thousands.

He brought Johnny up to date on the Hammond family and the situation with regard to Gaines. Johnny was immensely pleased with the latter. He called Gaines a number of things, none of them complimentary, and then sighed.

'Anyway, that lets both Farrar and the guy with the whisper out as shooting suspects.'

Clive laid his fork down. 'Farrar. I think, Johnny, we will go and have a talk with Mr. Farrar.'

But they didn't. Clive took the precaution of calling, first. It was a long way to Beverly Hills, and he had to think of gas and tires. Farrar was not at his office, nor his apartment. He had come in shortly after six, changed his clothes, and gone out again. No, he hadn't said where.

Clive introduced himself and asked some questions about Farrar's alibi. The clerk was anxious to talk. He hoped to get his name in the papers. Clive didn't learn anything Korsky hadn't told him.

Going back to Hollywood, Clive said, 'I'd give a lot to know what Farrar does with his spare time.'

'I could tell you.'

'Don't. I've heard enough smut for one day.'

'Anyway, what difference does it make? He's got an alibi.'

'Sure, sure. Everybody's got an alibi, except the two people that didn't do it. Farrar's clean, Beauvais is clean ... Was it you that sneaked into the kitchen and slugged me, Jonathan Ladd Jones?'

'Yeah. With my Aunt Fanny's antimacassar. What do we do now?'

'Get some sleep. After that ...' Clive scowled. 'Farrar may not be deliberately keeping out of my way, but he isn't making it easy for me to see him.'

'Would he?'

'Perhaps not. But he's no pattycake, and if he's got an alibi, why is he worried?'

'Maybe it's just coincidence.'

Clive said evenly, 'If one more person says "maybe" or "coincidence" in my hearing once more I will boot his teeth out through the back of his neck. Anyway, I'm going to do a little research on Kenneth Farrar, unless something hotter turns up. I'll stake out on his apartment early in the morning. You take his office. We can keep in touch through the switchboard girl.'

Johnny yawned. 'Waste of time, Ed. I don't like Farrar any better than you do, but there's no reason to think he had anything to do with Laur – with what happened.'

'Up to now there's been no reason to think anybody had anything to do with it. Only Laurel's dead. Besides, what do you care if I waste your time? I pay for it.'

'Sure, sure.' The car stopped in front of Johnny's bungalow court. He climbed out and then stuck his head back through the window. 'For cripe's sake get some rest, will you? You've got a disposition like forty yards of barbed wire.'

Clive grinned and went home. He let Chuck put the car to bed. Gaines had either not supplied him with another tail or he simply had not paid enough attention to notice. The hall was empty. He unlocked his door and stepped inside, thinking lovingly of sleep.

Somebody jammed a gun in the pit of his stomach and kicked the door shut all in one movement.

'Hold still,' said a voice out of the darkness. A soft, slow voice with a lilt under it that comes only from having Irish blood. 'Just hold right still. This rod's got a hair trigger.'

Clive did as he was told. A hand ran over him with expert speed, found nothing, and went away. The gun muzzle took itself out of his stomach. There was a feeling of someone moving back.

'Turn the lights on, Mr. Clive. Then just stand still.'

'I'm a high school pony,' said Clive. 'I stand the first time you tell me.' He reached unhurriedly for the switch. 'Anyway, I've been wanting to see you, Mr. Beauvais.'

The lights went on.

90

CHAPTER TWELVE

THEY STOOD easily, looking at each other. Beauvais held his Police Special .38 as though he had forgotten he had it.

He was not the man in Laurel Dane's picture, except that he still had his big pantherish body and his swarthy good looks. But he had aged and hardened, and there was no laughter in him. His skin was pale with the bleaching of three years in the cell blocks, but it only made the brown of his eyes browner and the black of his brows and hair blacker. The lines around his mouth were like scars, cut deep.

Laurel's husband. The first man she loved, the only man she married, the man who had taken steel because of her. It didn't register. Clive thought, That wasn't Laurel. That was a redheaded kid named Sue Tanner, a girl I never met. And he never met Laurel. But they were both dead, lying in a dark drawer, not feeling the darkness or the cold. Red hair, black hair, it didn't matter. There was only silence now, and the long, long night.

Clive said, 'I didn't kill her.'

Beauvais moved his chin. 'Sit down. I want to listen . . . and I don't want to hear anything but truth.'

Clive walked over and sat down, not hurrying. He leaned forward with his hands lax between his knees and started to talk.

'I knew her for two years. There was nothing between us but feeling. Monday evening she told me she was afraid. Somebody had searched her apartment. She thought it was you, or someone sent by you. She asked me to help her and then – withdrew the request. I stayed with her anyway. Mick Hammond, who was her friend and nothing more, went to sleep in the bedroom. She went to sleep on the couch. Somebody tried to get in the front door with a key and when I started for it somebody slugged me from behind. When I came to she was dead. Hammond was asleep.

He didn't kill her. He had no reason to kill her. I've talked to Mrs. Hammond, and I know.'

'Go on.'

'All the rest of it's in the papers.'

'Go on.'

'Someone had taken the glass panel out of the back door. It had been fixed for a long time. There were no fingerprints that didn't belong there. The front doorknob and the stick were wiped clean. The front door was opened, but nobody knows whether the person with the key got in or not. The man in the kitchen could have done that to divert suspicion from himself. Or he could have torn his gloves, or even taken them off while he was talking to her.'

'Go on.'

Clive looked up. Beauvais leaned forward, tense, his lips drawn back showing his teeth. His eyes were not quite sane.

Clive said, 'What more do you want?'

'What you've been saving for the last.'

'Who was he, Beauvais?'

The gun made a small, blind movement. 'Tell me how he sounded, what he said, what he did. Go on.'

'He called me on the phone. He didn't have a voice. He whispered. He told me to stay out of his way, that Laurel's number was up. Later, when I was lying in the kitchen, he slapped my face to bring me to. He said, "I just wanted you to know, pal. Laurel's off her spot – for good." He was still whispering. Then he laughed and hit me on the jaw and went away.'

'He whispered,' said Beauvais softly, and smiled. His teeth were very white, very strong, very beautiful. 'He slugged you?'

'I think so.'

'He killed her?'

'Don't you know?'

Beauvais ran the red tip of his tongue across his pale, tight lips. He didn't seem to be in the room any more. He was looking somewhere far beyond it, and his words were no louder than his breathing.

'Yeah. Yeah – I know.'

He turned abruptly, going noiselessly to the door.

Clive said, 'Beauvais!'

The dark man whipped around. His gun came up. Clive rose. 'Wait,' he said. 'This isn't just your fight.'

The muzzle twitched and steadied. Clive looked past it into Beauvais's eyes. 'It's my debt, too,' he said. 'You can't pay it alone.'

Silence answered him. Beauvais's right forefinger ridged, drawing in. There was sweat around his hairline.

Clive didn't move. The gun held steady. Beauvais shivered suddenly. His head went back a little, and then sideways. He let his breath out, hard. The gun hit the floor. Beauvais turned and walked toward the nearest chair, not seeing it clearly, and went heavily to his knees in front of it. He let his head and shoulders fall forward into the seat and stay there.

Clive poured a stiff jolt of whisky. He set the glass on the floor and took Beauvais by the shoulders and rolled him around. He growled at Clive and tried to push him off, but he was like a man fighting in a dream. Clive held the glass to his lips.

'It's okay,' he said. 'I know. Prison does things to you.'

Beauvais drank, rattling his teeth against the rim. He coughed and shuddered violently, letting his head drop into his hands. He had lost his hat. His hair was like thick curled silk.

'Three years,' he said hoarsely. 'Three years looking at dim walls and dim faces, lying on a hard cot and listening to the silence. No sun. No talk, no music, no wine. No sky, except a little piece way at the top that got caught in the bars. Caged up, me, like a roach in a matchbox, with nothing to think about but – her.'

The cords stood out on his black-haired wrists. His face was twisted like that of a child crying.

'I'd think about her – about the first year when she was mine and I didn't mind a knifing because of her. About the body and the white skin and the red hair of her, and the way her eyes could laugh. I'd think of feeding her pralines and walking with her down the Rue Royale, smelling the smell of the fever bottoms and the chicory, and then lighting candles to the Blessed Virgin in St. Louis, praying for a child. And then ... I hunted her for two years, and then I went to prison. I'd look up at the little piece of sky and wonder who she was sleeping with and beat the walls because I couldn't kill them both. And the screws would come and throw me in the hole.

'It was worse down there. No light, no sound. She used to come to me. She'd stand there shining in the darkness and sing, and I could hear her but never touch her. And I'd beat the walls some more.'

He held his hands out and stared at them. Clive saw the scars and two knuckles that had been broken. He poured himself a drink, got cigarettes, and came back. On the way he picked up Beauvais's gun and dropped it in his pocket.

He gave Beauvais a smoke and then said quietly, 'Who was he?'

'My cell mate for eighteen months. I suppose he had a name. I never heard it. Everybody just called him the Big Fella.' He got up suddenly and stood with his back to Clive. 'I had to talk.'

'Sure.'

'I been holding that a long time. I'm French-Irish. I haven't got frozen guts like some people. I had to talk.'

Clive nodded. 'Forget it.'

'Night sweats,' Beauvais muttered, 'and the jerks. I'm no easy-doer. Seven months after Big Fella got out I walked up and down that lousy cell, knowing he was looking for Sue, wondering if he'd find her, wondering if my parole would come through . . . When I walked out the gates the first thing I saw was Sue's picture in the *Times-Picayune*. It was a picture of her dead.'

Nobody spoke for a minute. Then Clive said, 'Tell me about this cell mate.'

'Can I have another drink?'

'Help yourself.'

Beauvais went over and got it. He was looking human again. 'He's a big guy,' he said. 'Shrinks me to a fly-weight when I stand beside him. He was in the rackets, strong-arm stuff, and the cops worked him over a few times. You could tell he'd been beaten around the head, and he couldn't talk above a whisper because some bull used a night stick on his Adam's apple and didn't know when to quit. He hated people, any people, but especially cops. He used to watch the screw like he wanted to take him apart bare-handed. He scared hell out of three other guys they tried him out on. They were too crowded to give him a cage to himself, so they dumped him on me.'

Beauvais started pacing restively. 'Funny thing. Big Fella kind of took to me. Maybe he figured I had troubles, too. He never talked much, but he'd sit there mooning at me like a dog and listen when I'd start screaming about Sue. At night when I'd have the sweats and the bad dreams he'd gentle me down, so as to keep the guards off my back. He . . .' Beauvais broke off, cursing, and ground out his cigarette.

'Did you send him to kill her?'

'No,' said Beauvais shortly. 'He wanted to find her for me. I was happy about that. I'd been paying guys to look for her, until they sent me up. After that it took all my dough to get me out again.'

'What were you going to do when you found her, Beauvais?'

Beauvais sucked his breath in harshly between his teeth. 'I don't know. I don't know. Something. Beat her, make her suffer, make her know I'm the man she married. Take her back to the Vieux Carré to stop the mouths that were laughing at me, and then fix her so there won't be any more men. I don't know. Something, maybe. Maybe nothing. I don't know.'

He raised his head. 'But she was mine! Nobody else had a right to touch her! Jesus Christ – to wait and wait and then find she's dead . . .!'

'This Big Fella – he was pretty fond of you?'

'I told you. He used to mop the sweat off me when I had a bad night, like I was his kid or something. He got the hole for three weeks once because a guy picked a fight with me in the yard and Big Fella took him on. He liked me. Yeah.' He looked as though the words tasted bitter in his mouth.

Clive said, 'Maybe he thought he'd be doing you a favor to put Laurel – her – where you wouldn't have to worry about her.'

'Yeah. Maybe.'

'You know where to find him?'

'He told me he had a cousin in Santa Monica, a dame. It was the only place he had to go for money to get started again.'

'You know her address?'

'Yeah.'

Clive picked up his hat. 'Wait till I see if the hall's clear.'

Beauvais said, 'Wait a minute.' He came up to Clive and took him by the shoulder and turned him around.

Clive said, 'Take your goddam paws off.'

Beauvais relaxed his grip, slowly. 'You were in love with each other.'

Clive said nothing.

Beauvais sounded almost lazy. 'Did you sleep with her, little man?'

Clive hit him.

Beauvais went over onto his shoulder blades. He got half-way up, fumbling at the cuff of his left sleeve, and Clive hit him again. He moved fast, and he hit with his whole body. Beauvais fell down again. Clive stood over him, but it was a long time before Beauvais stirred.

'God,' he said. He put his hand up to his mouth and stared at the blood on his fingers. 'God, what a wallop!' He threw his head back suddenly and roared, deep, healthy Irish laughter. 'And me thinking all the time I could break you in my two hands!'

Clive turned away.

Beauvais got up, mopping his face carefully with a thin linen handkerchief. 'I shouldn't have asked that.'

Clive's mouth twitched. 'The answer's no. I knew us both too well. I didn't want to make the mistake you did.'

There was silence. Beauvais put his stained handkerchief in his pocket and got his hat.

'Okay, Tarzan,' he said. 'Let's go.'

Clive switched off the lights. He didn't offer to give Beauvais back his gun.

There was no one in the hall, or on the back stairs. Clive got the car out and backed it down the drive, with Beauvais slumped low in the front seat. Nobody saw them. Three or four cars followed them down to the Boulevard. Clive went along Highland to Santa Monica Boulevard, and turned west.

After a while he said, 'I think we have a chaperon.'

Beauvais chuckled. 'You're kinda hot, too, huh?'

'No,' said Clive acidly. 'Gaines just loves me too much. He worries about the people I play with.'

'Shake him.'

Clive did some fancy maneuvering. Either he lost the trailing car or the driver was a very smart man. Clive couldn't be sure, because shortly afterward they hit the military dimout zone and a pea-soup fog on the edge of Santa Monica, and it was impossible to tell whether any of the half-dozen cars crawling after them under parking lights were following them.

'You did a neat job of cop-dodging, Beauvais. They've had an order out for you since Tuesday. How'd you get here, and so quick?'

Beauvais shrugged. 'I already had a ticket on the plane to L.A., under another name. I knew Big Fella was out here. I had a hunch he might have picked up her trail some way, and I wanted to see him. I got through the airport just before the flatties were set to catch me. Then I had to hang around out of sight until I could get you alone. I had to be sure . . .'

The way he said that made Clive's stomach quiver slightly. 'How'd you get into my apartment?'

'The bunkie I had before Big Fella was an expert on locks. He taught me to open anything with hinges on it.'

'Education,' said Clive, 'is a wonderful thing.'

They found the house finally, with no help from the fog or the dimout. They walked up a streak of broken cement between spreads of lawn that were about half wire grass and half native hardpan. Overgrown poinsettias rattled stiffly against the front wall, which was frame painted some indeterminate color, and not recently. The cold salt sweat lay on everything, eating, rotting, corroding.

Beauvais knocked.

Clive looked back down the street. He could see nothing that looked like a tail, but, considering visibility, that didn't mean a thing. He settled his shoulders uneasily.

A peephole in the door opened, shooting a little spear of light across Beauvais's jaw. A man's heavy voice said, 'Yeah?'

'You John Kelleher?'

'Who's askin'?'

'I am. I want to talk to your wife.'

'Oh, you do?' It was a voice that belonged with a thick neck and big red fists with scars on the knuckles. 'I'm particular who talks to my wife.'

Clive said quietly, 'Just a moment, Mr. Kelleher.' He dug something out of his pocket and pushed past Beauvais, holding his hand close to the light.

Kelleher grunted. 'I shoulda known.'

'Police business,' said Clive, putting the badge away. It was a perfectly good, perfectly legal police badge. The plain-clothes man who lost it never could understand how it happened. 'We just want to ask a few questions. Open up.'

The peephole closed. Clive muttered to Beauvais, 'For Chrissake, take it easy!'

Kelleher matched his voice. He wore khaki pants and an undershirt that smelled of hard work. There were freckles and a fuzz of red hair across his beefy shoulders.

'Come in,' he said.

The living room was small, furnished out of a time-payment store and the five-and-ten. But it was swept and polished and dusted, and the only untidiness was Kelleher's dirty shirt hanging over a chair arm and a drift of papers on the floor beside it.

Clive removed his hat. 'Mrs. Kelleher?'

She was over by the phony fireplace, standing very straight with her bony hands locked at her waist. Her faded house-dress still had cheerful flowers in it, and it was fresh. Her graying hair was cut short and the wave was homemade, but it glistened with brushing. Her eyes were blue, very wide, very frightened.

Beauvais said roughly, 'Where is he? Where's your cousin?'

Kelleher shoved by the two men. He put his arm around his wife and said, 'My wife ain't done nothin'. She ain't responsible for nothin'. And if you start bullyin' her, cop or no cop, I'll fix your wagon, so help me God.'

Clive smiled, a pleasant and friendly smile. 'There'll be no bullying.' He said that as much to Beauvais as to Kelleher. 'There are some questions we'd like to ask your cousin, Mrs. Kelleher, and we hoped you could tell us where to find him.'

Her eyelids flickered down. 'John,' she whispered, 'please put your shirt on.' Kelleher went slowly to get it, not taking his eyes off the two men. The woman said, 'I don't know where he is. Has he done something?'

'That's what we want to find out. He doesn't live here?'

'No. I don't know where he lives. He wouldn't tell me.'

Beauvais said, 'But he comes here. You give him money.'

She parted her fingers and knotted them again in a different sequence. Kelleher came back to her, buttoning his shirt. He left the tails outside.

'I'm frightened of him,' she said. 'I haven't the money to give him, but he . . .' She made a vague gesture and went on rapidly, 'He wasn't always like that, you see. I knew him when he was a little boy. He's been hurt. He doesn't look at things like he used to. I . . .'

'I understand.' Clive's voice was gentle. 'Can't you give us any clue to where we might find him?'

She shook her head. 'He was here this afternoon. He wanted fifty dollars. I told him I couldn't give it to him. He said he had to have it, that he was going away and wouldn't bother me any more. When I said there wasn't any way I could get fifty dollars he was angry. I thought he was going to make trouble, but he went away.'

Kelleher snarled, 'I've wanted to make trouble for that son of a bitch myself, but the old woman wouldn't let me.'

'I was afraid, John. He – isn't right.' She moved toward Clive. 'Please, don't let him know I've told you anything. Don't let him hurt us.'

'He isn't going to hurt anybody, Mrs. Kelleher. Not any more. But we've got to find him. Surely he must have dropped some hint. Please try to think!'

Mrs. Kelleher walked jerkily, halfway across the room and back.

'He coughed a lot. His throat was hurt, you know. He said once that this beach air was killing him.'

'There's a lot of beach, Mrs. Kelleher.'

'But he didn't tell me anything more!'

Clive grabbed Beauvais's arm and stopped him from doing whatever he'd been going to do. 'Please, think hard.'

'I am . . . Once when he came in I was writing down the grocery list. I asked him for some paper, and he gave me an old garage bill. I thought that was funny because he doesn't have a car. When I mentioned it he said it was just something he picked up, and then he snatched it away from me and stuffed it back in his pocket. But I'd already seen the name and address on it.' She paused, frowning. 'That's what I couldn't understand. Why he should mind, I mean. The bill was months old, and it wasn't his name.'

Clive said carefully, 'Do you remember the address?'

'I didn't pay much attention. It was a Jewish name, I know.'

'Take your time, Mrs. Kelleher. It probably doesn't matter, but I'd like to check on it.'

She paced up and down, her face screwed up in an agony of concentration. No one else moved or spoke.

'Venice,' she said suddenly. 'That was it. Venice. Avenue . . .' She stopped. Clive held his breath. She shut her eyes and made writing motions on the air. 'Thirty-seven. Avenue Thirty-seven. I don't know the house.'

Clive relaxed. 'Thank you, Mrs. Kelleher – Mr. Kelleher. Sorry to have had to bother you. And don't worry about trouble. We'll take care of that. Come on, Beauvais.'

Beauvais said, 'It wasn't his bill. What difference . . .'

'Come on!'

Beauvais hesitated, and then went. Kelleher closed the door behind them with unnecessary emphasis. The street was just as it had been, dark and cold and full of fog. Clive coaxed the motor back to life.

'You damn fool!' he said. 'Why do you suppose he'd care if she saw somebody else's garage bill unless it meant something to him? He said he picked it up. Okay. He found it in a closet or somewhere in the house where he's living. The tenant may be different, but the address is the same.'

Beauvais gave a surly grunt. 'Know where the street is?'

Clive laughed. 'I think so. I lived most of my childhood one block over, on Thirty-eight.'

'He may have left town already.'

'Maybe. But he's broke. I think he'll wait a while before he tries rolling anybody. If he caught a rumble on it he'd be in hot water. That trick voice of his has its drawbacks.'

'Okay. Get going.'

They didn't talk, driving south along the coast. They left Windward and the Venice Pier behind them, taking the new asphalt road where the car tracks used to be. Clive remembered the little red trolley bucketing back and forth down the long line of telephone poles to Del Rey, making a noise like the New York El. He'd always ridden up front where you got the full effect of the bouncing, and could watch the dogs scatter off the tracks ahead.

Past the hill on Thirty-five where he'd chipped the cartilage in his knee skating, and then the place where he had seen his first corpse – a drowned woman brought out of the sea. He slowed down, risking his spotlight in brief flashes. The curb was solid along the beach side to the right. At the left narrow asphalt roads dropped down the hill to the flats. Thirty-six, Thirty-seven. One more block and you're home. Hot gingerbread and milk after school. Only home isn't there any more. They pulled it down to make way for a derrick, and there hasn't been anyone to bake gingerbread for a long time now.

Clive turned left off the highway, let the car drift its own length down the hill, and then set the hand brake, leaving the gear in reverse. He chuckled suddenly.

'I used to coast my bike down this hill. There's a right-angle turn at the bottom. I used to be able to take it with my hands in my pockets.'

'No kidding!' said Beauvais. 'That's swell.'

'Yeah. It was.'

They got out. The sea was very close, lashing the beach with big thundering waves and then backing off with a slow hiss. It didn't sound any different. It smelled the same, too, except that now there was a heavy pungence of oil and sump-water under the clean salt. Once there hadn't been anything but sand and the sunburned houses and the wind off the water. Now there were derricks, thick as flies on a dead dog. The vacant spaces that used to be covered with tough little wild flowers in the spring had scars like malignant ringworms where the sumps had stained them, littered with bones from old rigs and chunks of broken concrete.

Clive rubbed his hand over his face. It felt slippery with the fog-damp on it. Somewhere to his right a well rig choked and sighed like an old man going upstairs.

'All the houses are across the highway, toward the beach,' he said. 'You stay out of sight. There might be another big guy living here, and I wouldn't want you blowing the wrong head off.'

Beauvais said, 'I'll take my gun back.'

Clive reached in and got his own .38 from under the dash, and then handed Beauvais his gun. Beauvais was standing very close to him, a paler shadow against the night.

'I'm cutting you in on this because I guess you got a right.'

'I bought it, pal. With a crack on the head.'

'Yeah. Only don't get in front of my gun.'

Clive's mouth was ugly. 'Don't take on too much to worry about.' He went away, scrunching sand under his feet.

They crossed the highway, stumbling over the curb, and split up. A dog began to bark furiously. Clive climbed ghostly steps and knocked on the first door. A thin young man in dirty denim pants and a faded T-shirt stuck his head out. There was a radio playing loudly.

Clive said, 'I'm looking for a man who lives on this street. A very big man who talks in a whisper. Know him?'

'Sure. He lives down by the canal. Tried to get my kids to come inside his shack the other day. I ain't lettin' 'em play down there no more.' He studied Clive. 'Law?'

Clive moved his head closer. The blaring radio covered his voice. 'Got a phone?'

'Nuh-uh. But there's one across the street.'

'Okay. Give me a couple of minutes and then go over and call the cops. Tell 'em where to go, and tell 'em to make it fast. Got it?'

The young man nearly lost his grip on the cigarette in his mouth. 'Jeez! Sure. Yeah, I got it.'

Clive started away.

'Hey. The house –'

'I know the house. Thanks.' Clive vanished into the fog. Beauvais drifted up, guided by the grating footsteps.

'Well?'

'He's down by the canal. There's one shack all alone in a flock of oil wells, nice and private. I'd almost forgotten it was there.'

'Canal?'

Clive felt for the curb with his foot. A car crept by, pushing a dim globe of light ahead of it.

'Yes,' he said. 'Part of the old "Venice of the Pacific" build-up, when the development was going to be something special. There's a whole system of them. They get water from an ocean inlet down at Del Rey. We kids used to spend most of our time down there, fishing and swimming.'

You wouldn't want to swim there now. The banks are black with seeping oil, and the water's black, too, and it stinks. There aren't any fish in it now.

They went back down the hill, past the heave and groan of the well, groping their way in the blind dark. A zone of silence and a feeling of space, and then Clive heard the rhythmic creak of a walking beam and a motor that sounded different from the first. He found Beauvais's arm and pressed it.

There was light seeping through the fog, a dirty yellow stain on gray-black wool.

Beauvais laughed without mirth and started forward. Clive held him. He was standing with his head raised, listening. Beauvais jerked away.

'Getting chicken?'

Clive didn't answer that. He stood a moment longer, but all he could hear was the rig and the sound of water slipping in from the sea, going with a furtive rush under the lock a hundred feet away. He shrugged irritably.

'I've got an itch between my shoulders that says we didn't shake our tail. Don't ask me why. It's just a feeling I get.'

He followed Beauvais, taking the gun out of his pocket, and walked beside him up three rotting wooden steps. Beauvais hit the door with his doubled fist.

Clive waited, not conscious of any excitement, not conscious of anything but the slow footsteps moving toward them over a warped and sagging floor. The old woman with the cats used to live here, he thought. Seventeen cats, and she nailed herself in at night. Mick and I used to play with the kittens.

Beauvais stood close to the door. The gun in his hand caught a dull glint from the light. His voice was tender, the kind of an Irish voice that sings about Molly and the Rose of Tralee.

'Big Fella. It's me, Di. Dion Beauvais.'

Silence. Long and heavy, choked with fog and the smell of the black sea water. Clive shifted his weight forward.

Beauvais said, 'It's okay, Big Fella. You did me a favor. I just want to say "Thanks."'

A rusty bolt pulled through its ring. A yellow glow fanned out, pushing past the man that filled nearly all the space in the door frame. Beauvais was smiling. He might have been greeting his bride.

Moving very fast, Clive brought his gun barrel down across Beauvais's wrist.

CHAPTER THIRTEEN

THE BULLET hit the rotten step and kept going. The gun fell out of Beauvais's hand almost onto the hole. The mist snared the noise of the shot, wrapped it up, and threw it away far out in the empty night. Clive kicked the gun off toward the canal and dropped back down the stairs.

'Hold it,' he said. 'Just take it easy.'

Beauvais held his wrist in his left hand and cursed in a flat, venomous whisper. His fingers were out of sight under his cuff. The man in the doorway had not moved or spoken.

'Ease that shiv out, Frenchy, and let it drop. Try anything and I'll blow your hand off.'

Beauvais stood absolutely still. His eyes burned. The big man faded backward, just the shadow of a movement.

Clive said, 'All I want from either of you is talk. I can shoot you both in the belly and still have all the time I need.'

They stood, the two of them – not stirring, not breathing, staring down at Clive. He waited. Beauvais let the knife slide out from under his sleeve.

'Kick it,' said Clive. 'Hard.' Beauvais kicked it. 'Now, both of you. Raise your hands slowly and clasp them behind your heads. Yeah. That's right. Now sit down. Keep your hands where they are.'

Beauvais said, 'There isn't room.'

'Make room.'

Beauvais sat, bending at the knees like a panther bellying down under the whip. Big Fella got down beside him. He wore loose slippers and dark pants and a heavy sweater. His hair was cropped close to the scalp, curling tightly. His face was heavy, sullen, and without expression, the flesh scarred and lumpy. He was big. He made Beauvais look like a growing boy.

Clive said, 'We'll have some law here any minute now. So just relax.'

'You dirty double-crossing bastard,' whispered Beauvais. 'You goddam . . .'

'Di.' Big Fella turned his head. 'Di, listen.'

Clive knew that voice. His guts knotted inside him.

Beauvais snarled, 'Shut up.'

'You tried to shoot me, Di. You hadn't ought to done that, not without lettin' me tell you.'

'Shut up!' Beauvais's head jerked back and forth and his feet kicked.

'But I didn't kill her, Di. Hear me? I didn't kill her.'

A peculiar stillness settled on the three of them.

Beauvais looked around, moving nothing but his head. 'You're lying.'

'No. No, I ain't.'

'God damn you, you're lying!'

'Listen, Di.' The big man's manner was as gentle and patient as a woman's with a sick child. 'Back there in the cell I used to watch you sweat, thinkin' about this dame. You used to talk about her when you was asleep, and cry and yell till I'd stuff the blanket in your mouth to keep the screw from hearin'. It got so I didn't like seein' you sweat over this no-good bitch. I says to myself, he'll never stop thinkin' about her while she's alive. He'll kill himself, thinkin' about her. So I says to myself, I'll find her and put her down for good, so he can forget her and maybe sleep nights again.'

'She was mine,' Beauvais said. 'Nobody else had a right to touch her.'

'Sure. But they'd of shagged you, Di. You couldn't never have made it. The johns would of sent you up to the gas-box without even askin' you if you was guilty. But me – hell, they don't know I'm alive.'

Beauvais sat still, his dark eyes wide and queer. There was no hint of a siren. Clive heard muffled thunder, and realized that it was the beat of his own blood in his ears.

Beauvais said, 'Go on.'

'I bummed around a long time after I got out, but I couldn't get no line on the dame. Finally I had to come out here to get dough from my cousin, and right away I walk down a street and see a picture of this black-haired broad in front of a joint where she sings. It looks like the picture you carry, Di, but she's different with her hair black. I got to be sure. So I hang around and find out where she lives, and then I pull a job in the apartment house. I take five or six places, so she won't worry about it, and I find your picture, Di, and the marriage license.'

Big Fella's painful whisper was coming faster now. 'I fix up the door so I can get in any time. I know I got to hurry because pretty soon you'll be out and you won't maybe have a good alibi. I go up there several times, but there's always some hitch. People hangin' around, a party across the back porch. Then this guy –' he jerked his head toward Clive – 'gets back in town, and it's walkin' out time for you, and I know I got to do this job that night if she's got the whole Marine Corps in her room. So I go up there.'

Clive was tensed forward. Sweat mixed with the fog-rime on his face. He wasn't listening for the siren any more. He was hearing Laurel's drowsy voice saying, *I'm glad you're here. Ed. I'm so glad you're here.*

'It looks like a cinch. The gimp goes to sleep. She goes to sleep. And then this guy –' Big Fella laughed, a strange little sound with no mirth to it – 'he goes to sleep, too. Easy, like knockin' down a butterfly. I start out of the kitchen. Somebody's tryin' a key in the front door, but it's bolted and the girl don't wake up, and pretty soon they go away. And then this Hammond guy comes out of the bedroom. . . .'

Clive took one step toward him. He said, 'You're lying.'

Big Fella laughed. 'Sure, pal. Prove it. Let the johns prove it.'

Dion Beauvais said, 'Go on.'

'Hammond looks around. He thinks it's funny his pal ain't there. He calls a couple times and even looks into the kitchen, but he don't see nothin' but darkness. He decides maybe his pal went out for a beer. Anyway, he's happy 'cause now he don't have to slug him like he was goin' to. He picks up his stick off the table and shakes the girl awake. She looks at him and all of a sudden she gets scared and tries to run. And he hits her in the back of the head with the stick. He makes sure she's dead. Then he wipes off the stick with his handkerchief and lays it down and goes over and opens the front door. Nobody's around. He wipes off both knobs and the bolt and closes it again, leavin' the bolt off. Then he goes back to bed again, all fixed up.' He gave a brutal chuckle. 'We're all fixed up. Him and the girl and me and my pal here. I wake him up to tell him the good news and put him to sleep again. Easy. He's a tough guy. He don't scare. But he handles easy.'

He kicked off his slippers, one after the other like machine-gun bullets, into Clive's face. Clive fired twice by sheer instinctive reflex at the sound of their bodies tumbling off the steps. Beauvais yelled. There was a sort of animal grunt from the big man, and then there was no sound at all, no movement, no sight of anything in the smear of light by the doorway.

Clive faded sideways into the dark. He hadn't forgotten Beauvais's armament lying somewhere on the sand. You could find things again, and Beauvais hadn't sounded like a man ready for the cooling board when he yelled.

He crouched, listening, shaken with anger so cold and over-powering that it caused a physical nausea. There was still no siren. He crawled forward, slowly.

Sand came flying out of the night. It hit him squarely in the eyes, and he was as blind as Samson. Somebody's feet scruffed, running fast. He snapped a shot at the noise, shaking his head and blinking. The fine grains scoured his eyeballs and set the tears flowing.

Somebody came up behind him. Clive turned to fire, and somebody dived in low and knocked him backward. He twisted and clawed, trying to find something to shove his gun against and pull the trigger. A hand caught his wrist and pushed it up, and Beauvais yelled, 'Hit him! Hit him!'

Clive swung a left-handed haymaker at the sound of Beauvais's voice. It connected. Something broke under his knuckles.

The weight shifted on his legs and Beauvais cried out harshly. He didn't let go of Clive's wrist. Clive doubled his knees up into his chest and let go.

He got both heels under Beauvais's jaw. Beauvais rose up and fell backward. The force of the kick turned Clive clear over. His wrist tore loose from Beauvais's grip, and he was still hanging onto his gun. He was halfway to his feet when the edge of Big Fella's hand took him across the back of the neck like a poleax.

Clive fell on his face. Big Fella stooped over and took his gun and then kicked him in the side, not specially hard.

'Easy,' he said. 'Tough, but he handles easy.'

He stood still a moment, listening. Beauvais was on his knees, slobbering blood through his fingers.

Big Fella said suddenly, 'I hurt. God damn you, you burned me.'

He leaned over and hit Clive twice under the ears, like a child in a tantrum. Clive's body jerked. He moaned slightly. Big Fella hooked his hand in Clive's collar and dragged him over to the steps, throwing him down on them like a sack of wheat. He went back to Beauvais.

'Di. Did he hurt you, Di?'

Clive got his eyes open. There was sand in them, and more of it in his mouth. He got his hands under him with great effort and pushed up, and then twisted his hips so that he was sitting on the stairs instead of lying on them. Presently he could see, not very clearly – a couple of dim shapes in the dirty yellow fan of light.

Big Fella had one hand pressed to his side. The other one held Clive's revolver. Beauvais got up off his knees, unsteadily, holding his jaw together with his hands.

He said thickly, 'I'm okay. You get him?'

'Yeah.'

'What took you so long?'

'He burned me. He had me down for a minute.'

Beauvais took his hands away slowly from his face. His lips were mashed. He had bled over his chin and down his shirt.

He said hoarsely, 'Were you lying about not killing her?'

'I didn't, Di. I swear to God I didn't.'

108

'Give me that gun.'

Big Fella held it out. Beauvais took it. He stepped in close and shoved the muzzle into the big man's stomach.

Big Fella's hands stayed limp at his sides. 'I'm tellin' you, Di,' he said simply. 'I didn't kill her. I was there, but I didn't kill her.'

Beauvais stared up into his eyes. Clive tried twice to get up and bruised himself falling back again. He thought, Mom always told me it was too lonesome to play down here. She always said I'd get hurt.

Beauvais shuddered and let the gun drop. 'And I almost killed you. You got a long record in this state. You might have got the book for the apartment job alone, but you did it anyhow.'

'Sure.' Big Fella coughed, rubbing his throat. 'Sure, Di.'

Beauvais made a sound that was almost a sob. He whirled toward Clive.

'We'll go, Big Fella. We'll take his car. But I got something to do first.' He raised the gun.

Big Fella knocked it aside. 'There ain't no rush, Di. He was kiddin' about cops. The bull house ain't more'n a mile away. They'd of been here a long time ago if they was comin' at all.'

He moved forward, stumbled, and looked stupidly at his feet. There was nothing under them. He shook his head and went on. His eyes were little curved gashes in his face, glittering and colorless as window glass seen through slits in a curtain.

'Plenty time,' he whispered. His face screwed up. 'I hurt, Di. He burned me, and I hurt.'

Beauvais raised the gun again. 'We'll hurry and get a doctor.'

'No. I done all the time I'm goin' to. Ain't easy findin' a croaker that won't spill his guts. I'll heal up without one. I done it before. Only I'm takin' this guy first.'

Beauvais ran his tongue over the crusted blood on his lips and laughed. He took his finger off the trigger and laid it along the barrel.

Clive's face tightened. He pushed his shoulders forward, clawing at the bottom tread. His skin was greasy with sweat.

Big Fella walked slowly, ahead of Beauvais. Clive got up off the steps. Big Fella put his hands out, in a clumsy sort of way. He was smiling. Clive tried to go past him to get at Beauvais.

Big Fella's fists moved so fast they blurred. Clive went back and cracked his head on the doorsill.

The pain jarred some of the numbness out of the nerve centers along his spine, and it made him mad. He rolled over, making his feet come in under him. Big Fella laughed.

'Get him, Di. He's tough. He don't stay down.'

Clive turned and threw himself into the big man's knees.

Big Fella's hands slid along his back, just too late. The two of them overbalanced and fell. Clive let go. Big Fella's knee hit him in the chest. Clive coughed his breath out and twisted sideways, aiming in a low kick.

It never landed. Beauvais came in and laid the flat of the gun along Clive's temple. Clive dropped heavily. Beauvais kicked him. He held his broken jaw in his left hand and tried to boot Clive's face in. Clive covered up, but it hurt. He tried to stand, and Big Fella hit him across the buttocks, knocking him flat.

Clive rolled over on his hip and swung his legs in a circle. They took Beauvais below the knee and staggered him, and before Big Fella could do anything about it Clive had grabbed Beauvais's ankle and brought him down. Beauvais screamed, protecting his jaw. Clive kneed him in the stomach. They rolled. Clive tried to get Beauvais's face, but all he hit was a couple of muscular forearms. He got hold of Beauvais's right hand and tried to pry the gun out of it.

Big Fella caught Clive around the neck from behind. Clive let go of Beauvais. He reared backward and pushed himself up, trying to get his heel in the big man's crotch. Big Fella turned his hip. He hit Clive in the kidneys, tightened his elbow lock not quite hard enough to snap Clive's neck, and then loosed him, stepping back.

Clive staggered and turned around and took both of Big Fella's fists under the jaw. He fell down. After a while he tried to get up again.

Big Fella said pleasantly, 'You hadn't ought to work so hard, pal. You'll wear yourself out.'

Clive snarled. He could see nothing but lights where there were no lights. Big Fella waited until he was on his hands and knees and then kicked him in the stomach. He watched patiently while Clive threw up his dinner and then kicked him three or four times more, not hurrying, choosing his spots.

Clive retched and sobbed and pushed himself away from the sand, two or three inches.

'Hard boy,' said Big Fella. 'Very tough. But you handle, brother.'

Beauvais said, 'Turn him over.'

Big Fella lifted Clive like a cat lifting a kitten and rolled him on his back. Clive hit him twice in the face. Big Fella laughed. 'Get the pansy,' he said. 'Pattin' my cheek.' He laid Clive across his knee, holding his head back by the hair, and took both wrists in his right hand.

Beauvais said, 'Clive.'

Clive looked up, not as though he saw anything clearly. His lips pulled back from his teeth.

Beauvais called him three names in a voice as soft as a lover's touch and hit him left and right across the mouth with the barrel of the .38.

'That's for the two you gave me.'

Blood ran down Clive's throat. He started to strangle. Big Fella let him drop in the sand.

'Let's go,' he said. 'I hurt. I wanta go somewheres and lay down.'

'Sure,' said Beauvais. 'Sure. We'll just haul him over to the canal and throw him in. He'll like that. He used to swim there when he was a kid.'

Big Fella chuckled. He nudged Clive's jaw with his boot. 'Hear that, pally? We're goin' for a swim.'

Clive let his breath out harshly and jerked as though he might still be trying to get up. Big Fella laughed, grabbing a handful of his coat collar. He dragged him away toward the black water sliding in under the fog.

A horn began to scream frantically, up on the highway. Big Fella stopped. His mouth twisted. He let go of Clive and put both hands to his side. 'For Chrissake, what's that?'

Clive's face touched something hard, lying on the sand.

Beauvais stood listening. The horn blew and blew. Clive heard it dimly. It didn't mean anything. The hard object under his cheek was cold. There was something familiar about it.

'The goddam fools!' said Beauvais. 'They'll have somebody down here. Kick him in and let's go.'

Big Fella lifted him by the collar again, and Clive saw the shape of the hard thing, black against the paler sand.

A gun.

His hands trailed past it as Big Fella walked. He picked it up, with infantile clumsiness. He could smell the water, cold, heavy with salt and oil. He was afraid of the water.

The horn stopped blowing.

Big Fella stumbled, and Beauvais said, 'Hurry up.'

Using both hands, Clive raised the gun and fired it into the gray thickness of Beauvais's body. Beauvais did nothing for a moment, except to tip sideways a little with the force of the bullet. Then he folded up at the joints and pitched down.

Big Fella stopped. He let Clive fall and stood staring at Beauvais.

'Di. Di, what happened?'

Beauvais moaned. Big Fella bent over him. Clive tried to pull his gun hand out from under him. He wanted to shoot Big Fella. He wanted it so badly that he cried.

Big Fella said, 'Oh, Christ,' very softly. He staggered, pressing his side. Beauvais coughed, a slow deep spasm. Blood poured out of his mouth. Big Fella put an arm around his shoulders.

'We'll find a croaker. Take it easy, Di. Just take it easy. . . .'

It took him a long time to get Beauvais up into his arms. Clive watched him lurch off into the fog and cried because he couldn't pull the gun free.

After a while he stopped crying. The canal rustled close to his head and the night was cold and he hurt. He wanted to sleep. There was some reason he shouldn't – something to do with Mick. The incoming tide swirled around the lock. Maybe that was it. Maybe Mick had slipped on the stringer and fallen in and been pulled under the gate. There were barnacles down there, on the sharp red rocks.

Clive moaned, and the blood ran sandy in his throat.

Somewhere, far off on another planet, someone screamed.

The dark shut down.

CHAPTER FOURTEEN

EDMOND CLIVE'S conscious mind broke the surface suddenly like a flying fish, with the same effect of spray inside his skull. He opened his eyes, and then everything was white.

He stirred. Very slightly, but too much.

A piece of the whiteness detached itself with a rustling noise and leaned over him. He squinted, trying to focus.

After a while he whispered, 'Your face is on upside down. Take it away.' He retched, and the sweat rolled down his cheeks.

The nurse wiped him with a cold towel and said, 'Just lie still, Mr. Clive.'

'My God,' he said. 'Mick.' He started to get up. The pain hit him then. Really hit. He lay under it dazed and quiescent, and it was a long time before he heard the nurse again.

'That's better. Everything's all right. Lie still.' He began to curse her. He was almost crying.

And then a masculine voice said heartily, 'Now, now, we can't have any of that. You've taken quite a beating and you'll just have to be good for a while whether you like it or not.'

A tubby little man in white clothes stooped over the bed. He had a round red face with glints on it where the glasses were.

Clive said carefully, 'There's something I have to do.' His lips felt as though someone had put them through a meat grinder.

'It can wait. Now behave yourself, or I won't let you see your visitor.'

'Visitor?'

'A Mrs. Hammond. She's been waiting several hours for you to wake up. Feel like seeing her?'

Clive shut his eyes. 'Not now or ever,' he said. 'But bring her in.'

The nurse peeled back his sleeve and swabbed a spot on his arm. There was the glitter of a hypodermic needle.

'What's that for?'

'Sleep,' said the doctor. 'It'll give you ten or fifteen minutes with Mrs. Hammond, and then back to dreamland.'

Clive decided not to fight it. 'How long have I been here?'

'Something over forty-eight hours.'

'Will I live?'

'Well, for a while we thought the easiest thing might be to throw you away entirely and start fresh.' The hypo needle jabbed and stayed there. 'But the X-rays didn't show anything but three cracked ribs and some minor internal injuries. God knows why.'

Clive said unemotionally, 'They wanted me to know what was going on all the way through, right up until I finished drowning. You don't kick a man too hard when you want him to last.'

The nurse looked a little sick. She pulled his sleeve down again and went away.

Clive asked, 'How long am I in for?'

'That depends. Aside from everything else, your nerves are in bad shape and you need the rest.'

'Rest,' said Clive. 'Yeah.'

The doctor left and Jane Hammond came in. She stood by the bed in a wash of golden sunlight from the windows. She wore a plain moss-green dress and a simple hat. She was cool and lovely and it hurt Clive to look at her.

He knew without asking, but he said, 'They lived to talk?'

'Only Beauvais. He died the next day.'

'That was long enough.' Clive turned his head away.

Jane Hammond sat down on a white chair beside the bed and took his hand. 'Ed – please don't look like that. You couldn't help it.' She touched his forehead gently. 'Your poor face. They must have hurt you terribly. To go through all that, and then . . .' Her head was suddenly down close to his shoulder. She wasn't crying. She was breathing too deeply, and the sound had an edge on it, like the breathing of a child exhausted beyond tears.

Clive put his hand on hers.

Presently she said quietly, 'I've been with Mick all they'd let me. He still says he didn't do it. I believe him.'

The light on Clive's face made it hollow like a skull under the hard bones. He said, 'If you were someone else I'd lie to you.' He felt her lift her head, but he kept his eyes away. 'The big man didn't murder Laurel. Beauvais was on the kill about it, and he convinced Beauvais. You know the truth when you hear it, Jane, whether you like it or not. We both heard it, that night.'

Her voice was little more than a whisper. 'Then you think . . .'

He turned to her now, a level, searching look. 'You're the only one, Jane, who could know whether Mick had a motive.'

She held his gaze a long time, without wavering. 'He had no motive.'

'All right. No, I don't think Mick's guilty. I think the big man was lying about him because it was the easiest story to tell. I think the murderer is the third person, with the key. But that doesn't help us. It doesn't help Mick. It doesn't swing any weight with a jury.'

'No.'

They were silent for a while. Then Clive sighed and rubbed his palm across his eyes and winced.

'Got a cigarette?'

She lighted one for him, with fingers as steady as marble. 'Mick's innocent. There must be some way to prove it.'

'It looks as though it'll take a bigger man than I am to do it.'

'Then you'll have to be a bigger man,' said Jane. 'You're the only man there is.'

He looked at her. 'My God,' he said, and smiled somberly. 'That's putting it square in my lap. Okay, Jane. We'll try.'

'Thanks, Ed . . .' After a minute she said, 'Vivien's been haunting the hospital. I finally made her go home and rest. I think you've made a conquest.'

'Yeah?' He laughed. 'God, I'm getting sleepy! Where's Johnny?'

'He's been in and out, acting like a hen with one chick. He'll be furious that he missed you.'

Clive's eyelids flickered down. The cigarette drooped in his mouth. 'There are questions I want to ask, but I guess they'll have to wait . . .' The smoke tasted good. The pain was getting dull and far away.

Jane said, 'There's one more thing. They – buried Laurel this morning. Beauvais made the arrangements before he died.'

Clive's face showed a brief shadowing. Jane said gently, 'I was there, for both of you. She looked very lovely.'

115

She went and stood by the window. Clive seemed to be asleep, with the smoke drifting up idly from the cigarette. Then, without opening his eyes or moving, he said in a slow half-whisper:

'Sleep dwell upon thine eyes, peace in thy breast . . .'

Jane turned around.

'. . . Would I were sleep and peace, so sweet to rest . . .'

'Ed!'

He raised his lids a crack. 'Huh?'

'You were quoting Shakespeare!'

'My God. Shows what dope will do . . .' He smiled foggily. 'Don't tell it around. The hard boys would keep undressing me to see the lace on my drawers.'

The last words came very slowly. When she reached the bed he was across the gulf and away. Jane leaned over and took the cigarette from his lips. She didn't make any noise going out.

Clive slept well into the next morning and woke up feeling pretty good, all things considered. Jonathan Ladd Jones came in, bringing Gaines with him.

'All right,' said Clive. 'Do your gloating quick and get out.'

Gaines examined him like a man studying a work of art. 'Nice job they did on you, Clive. A very nice job. What did he use on your kisser?'

'The barrel of my own gun. Go ahead and laugh.'

'I already have.' Gaines shrugged. 'You should worry. You plugged 'em both. Did you know you nearly got Beauvais the first time?'

'I heard him yell.'

'You creased his back. It was that close. And the big guy was filling up inside all the time he was playing with you. Jesus, the vitality that gorilla had!'

'I'll pat myself on the back when I'm not so sore. Where the hell were you flatfeet, anyhow?'

'That's right, you wouldn't know, would you?' Gaines sat down beside the bed. Johnny leaned on the windowsill, smoking.

'First off, I want to say that what you did to my tail car wasn't funny. I won't kick about you wanting to go alone with Beauvais – I guess you had to play it that way, then. But slashing tires just isn't patriotic!'

Clive stared at him. 'What are you talking about?'

'You sneaked up and cut the rear tires on the tail car that was waiting across the street from your apartment house.'

'You're crazy.'

Gaines sighed. 'Okay. I can't prove you did it, and I don't at this time give a damn. I'm through playing games with you. I don't have to any more. You gave me what I wanted on a silver platter. You're cleared – and the way it happened, by God it's worth it!'

Clive's mouth twitched. He said nothing.

'Well,' Gaines said, 'it seems that the guy you told to call the cops tripped over his own feet going across the way to phone. He cracked his skull. His wife found him and called a doctor, but he was out for a couple of hours. When he came to it was a while longer before he could make anybody understand, and by the time the boys at the Venice station finally did get word, it was all over but to call the ambulance and the morgue. You were out cold with your head in the canal, Beauvais was beside the road, also out cold, and the big fellow . . .'

Gaines chuckled. 'Funny about him. He'd of died anyhow in a couple of hours, but your car didn't seem to want to take any chances.'

'My car?'

'Yeah. You left it parked on the hill, remember? Must of been careless about the brake, because she broke loose and drifted down on top of him. He'd had to put Beauvais down and was crawling up toward the highway, and your car caught him square before it went off in the sand. Dead as a mackerel with the tire treads marked plain across his neck and back.'

Clive said, 'Just a minute.'

Johnny straightened up. Gaines's eyelids narrowed.

Clive said slowly, 'I distinctly remember setting the hand brake hard and then putting the gear in reverse. She couldn't have drifted.'

Gaines lifted his beefy shoulders and dropped them again. 'She did.'

'God damn it, I know what I did! And I know something else, too, if you'll shut up and let me think.' He closed his eyes and scowled.

'I had a feeling somebody was following us when we went down there. Didn't see anyone – it was just one of those notions you get. And then, some time before I passed out, I heard a horn up on the highway, screaming its head off. It bothered the boys a lot, and it saved my life, because that was when they stopped to listen and Big Fella threw me down on top of the gun.'

Gaines nodded. 'Quite a few people heard that horn. A couple of men even went out to see what was up. But the fog was thicker than a suit of woolen underwear and it was late and nobody wanted to stick his neck out too far, so I guess they didn't look very hard. Anyway, nobody saw the car and the horn quit blowing, and that was that. Probably some local wolf having a scrap with his girl friend.'

Clive said stubbornly, 'My car couldn't have drifted.'

'For Chrissake, what are you trying to hand me now? You cleared yourself, and it's not your fault your pal double-crossed you. We've got the right guy, the girl's paid for, and so why don't you relax?'

'I saw Mick Hammond after the killing, Gaines. He didn't do it.'

Gaines stood up. He rubbed one thick scarred hand through his hair and said slowly, 'I'll be a son of a bitch.'

'You were a long time ago. God damn it!' said Clive furiously. 'Mick didn't have the ghost of a motive!'

'So the big guy was lying.'

'About who killed her, yes.'

'You know how that sounds.'

'Sure. Like Beauvais kicked me harder in the head than he did. But somebody cut the tires on your tail car, and whether you like it or not, it wasn't me!'

Gaines blinked his pale eyes. 'I'm getting old, Clive. I can't take it any more. I got to get out of here before I fall down and start frothing.' He put his hat on and took hold of the knob. 'It must be the dope they gave you. I hope so. I guess I hate your guts as much as anyone I know, but I don't like seeing anybody crack up.'

Clive snarled and reached for the clock on the bedside table. The pain in his belly muscles doubled him up, and by the time he could breathe again Gaines was gone.

Jonathan Ladd Jones came over and put a cigarette in his mouth and held a match. Clive lay back, blowing smoke and holding himself together with his hands.

Johnny said, 'He's right.'

'He's wrong. Somebody followed us that night – somebody who didn't want the law butting in – somebody who fixed the tail car so it couldn't follow.' He looked at Johnny. 'You think I'm lying?'

Johnny studied the toes of his small shoes. 'Way I figure it, Ed, Hammond was your pal once. You're pretty soft on his wife, too. So . . .'

'You think Mick's a good enough actor to put over the show he's been giving?'

'I don't know.'

'Well I do. He's not. He didn't have any reason to kill Laurel . . .'

'Jane Hammond could be lying.'

'She could. It doesn't change things any. Mick didn't know it. He was ready to kill himself over the idea of losing her, but all he could say was how she'd stood by him.' Clive pitched the butt savagely across the room and doubled up again, gasping.

Finally he said between his teeth, 'Mick wasn't acting in Laurel's dressing room. He'd have told me then if Jane had ever said anything about leaving him.'

Johnny went over and stepped on the cigarette. 'All right. But why would the big fellow lie?'

'Beauvais had Big Fella figured for the job, and he was the most kill-crazy guy I ever looked at. All right. Big Fella didn't do it, but he knew he'd have a time convincing Beauvais. So he told the simplest story. Mick was already taking the fall. Why change it? Why drag in some third party that he probably never saw before, maybe couldn't even name? The newspapers had the crime all worked out and tagged for him. He just quoted, built it up a little, and put all his energy into getting over the one thing that mattered to him – clearing himself. And Beauvais believed it where he mightn't have believed any other yarn.'

'That's another of those "could be's," Ed. The jury isn't going to think much of it.'

'No, God damn it. Like the searching of Laurel's apartment two or three days before the murder, and the guy with the key who might or might not have got in. Like Sugar March. Like the keysmith, and my car drifting with the gear and the brake both set, and just happening to hit Big Fella, who was the only man who knew whether there *was* anyone else in Laurel's apartment that night. Like the horn that blew, and the guy that fell down on his way to call the cops, and the cut tires on the police car . . . Shadows, Johnny. Murder with no face. You feel it. You know it's there watching you, but you can't see it. You can't hear it. You can't even talk about it, because when you do what you say sounds farfetched and silly even to yourself. And Mick's going to die in the gas chamber because the murderer's smarter than I am.'

Clive stared at Johnny with bitter dark eyes.

'He's watched me from the beginning. He's let me front for him, let me grab at leads that didn't go anywhere, let me lock the door tighter on Mick with every step I took. Never showing himself, but always pushing things around so they broke just right for him and left me looking like a fool.' He laughed, a small hard sound in his throat. 'He must have enjoyed himself that night, watching me convict Mick Hammond when I thought I was going to clear him, and then eat boot leather and the barrel of my own gun. God damn him down to hell.'

Neither said anything for a while. Johnny came back and sat down, not looking at Clive.

'What do we do next?'

'Johnny . . . you don't have to stick.'

Johnny rose. 'Listen, Ed. It doesn't matter a goddam bit what I think. I'm only your stooge anyhow. Now tell me what you want me to do and I'll start earning my wages.'

Clive laughed. 'Sure, sure. Only don't get tough with me. I'm a sick man.'

Johnny rubbed his nose and turned away.

Clive said, 'The only definite thing we have to go on is the tire-slashing. It's just barely possible that someone may have seen . . .'

Lieutenant Jordan Gaines opened the door.

'Just like a cop,' said Clive. 'You ought to knock. I might have been in conference or something.'

'I called headquarters,' said Gaines. 'I wanted to check on that tire business.'

'Yeah?'

'Yeah. The Hollywood Division reports that several cars in that block were slashed that night, apparently the work of one of these kid vandal gangs that have been giving us such a headache since the tire ban. Several cars, Clive. So I guess that clears that up, doesn't it?'

Clive said, 'Yes. Yes, I guess it does.'

Gaines watched him. Presently he sighed. 'Jesus, that dead pan of yours! I'd like to borrow it the next time I play poker. The hell with you.'

He closed the door behind him. Clive lay perfectly still, without speaking.

After a long while Johnny said, 'Well . . .'

Clive stared at the ceiling. 'I'm getting old, Johnny. I'm eating dirt.'

'There's a long time yet before the trial, Ed. Maybe –'

'Are my clothes in that closet over there?'

'Hey . . .'

'Go get 'em.'

'Now look, Ed . . .'

Clive pushed the covers back. Johnny walked over to the bed. 'You weren't thinking of going anywhere?'

'You try and stop me, small size.'

'Sure,' said Johnny. 'Sure, Ed.' He slapped Clive fairly hard across the belly. Clive turned green and stopped breathing. Johnny pulled the blanket up, smoothed it, laid a pack of cigarettes on the bedside table, and put on his hat.

'So long, Ed. Be good.'

Clive's eyes burned. Johnny waved cheerfully and went out. Clive lay sweating quietly. Presently he grinned.

'The little bastard. I'll fix his wagon for that!'

Someone rapped on his door, a small rap. He said, 'Come in.'

Vivien Alcott slid herself in through the door and shut it as though it were made of porcelain. She wore a red wool dress under a short camel's-hair coat, high-heeled red pumps,

121

and no hat. She stood with her hands in her pockets, smiling hesitantly.

Clive said, 'Hello. Come on in.'

She showed her little white teeth. 'Are you sure you don't mind?'

'Sure.'

She walked across the room like someone tiptoeing on thin ice. Clive laughed, being careful not to jiggle his stomach.

'Relax! I won't break.'

She giggled. 'I brought you a present.' She pulled a flat pint of rye out of her coat pocket and held it up, shaking it slightly so that Clive could see the bead in the light.

'Well!' said Clive. 'Sit down, baby. Sit right down and make yourself at home!'

CHAPTER FIFTEEN

VIVIEN FOUND a couple of medicine glasses and brought them over.

Clive said, 'Take your coat off. You make me hot just looking at you.'

She smiled and laid it across the foot of the bed, and then bent over the table, pouring the drinks. Clive watched her, faintly comic with surprise.

She looked nice. She looked very nice indeed. The soft wool of her dress was gathered and bloused, so that her full sharp curves were hinted at rather than seen, and the way the whole thing was cut made her look taller and slimmer. The red color was deep and warm without being garish, and it reflected a most becoming glow across her brown cheeks. Clive noticed that she had one of those strong vibrant necks that would be pleasant to touch.

She knew he was admiring her. Her eyes had a depth and glow he had never seen before. She handed him his drink. Her nails were short, very clean, and covered with an unobtrusive polish. This time, when their fingers touched, hers were warm and electrically alive.

Vivien grinned suddenly, wrinkling her nose. 'You smell funny.'

'Chloroform liniment. Between that and the hot Epsom salts they've been soaking me in, I feel like a boiled potato.' He raised his glass. 'Here's to crime.'

She sipped her drink, studying him. 'You don't really mean that – about crime?'

'Sure I do. How else could I make a living?'

'Ed – Mr. Clive . . .'

'You were right the first time.'

'Ed, then. How did you happen to become a detective?'

'Well, it's kind of a silly story. Happened a long time ago, when Mick and I were kids. We had a couple of rafts knocked together out of railroad ties and packing boxes, and we used to paddle them around on the canal.'

'The same canal, where they almost drowned you?'

'Uh-huh. Only there wasn't any oil in it then. Anyhow, one day five or six big boys happened along and stole the rafts from us just for the hell of it. They couldn't have had any use for them. It nearly broke our hearts. I remember Mick squatting up on the lock stringer crying and calling them every name he knew. I got hold of one guy in the pool and tried to drown him, I was so mad, but he was about four times my size and it didn't bother him too much. He just held my head under and then went away. I think right then I made up my mind that when I grew up I was going to do something about big boys that went around swiping things from little boys.'

'You fought them,' said Vivien.

'I always did have a nasty temper.'

'Mick didn't fight, though. I'll bet he never fought. I'll bet he was just tagging around after you all the time.'

'You'll lose your money. I hero-worshiped Mick. He was everything I wanted to be.' He chuckled. 'Mick's mother was always a little condescending to my mother.'

'She just didn't know,' whispered Vivien.

He glanced up at her and grinned. She held his gaze briefly and then flushed, turning away.

'You're laughing at me. You think I'm a fool.' Her lips quivered. 'I'm not. I'm in love.'

'No,' said Clive kindly. 'I'm just a new kind of animal, and you've got me mixed up with Dick Tracy and a couple of other glamour guys. That's all.'

She turned. Her face was a little girl's face, desolate with the fear of misunderstanding.

'No. You're a man, Ed. You've got hard hands that can hurt, and a hard body. I've felt you tremble. I've felt your rough tweeds on my skin, and heard you breathe, and touched the hair on the back of your wrist. You're real, Ed. You're alive, and I . . .' She caught her breath harshly. 'If I were a nice girl I wouldn't say things like that. But I'm not a nice girl. And I've been thinking about you, all alone there in the fog and the darkness, being hurt . . .'

Her jaw locked and her head went back. Then quite suddenly she relaxed and finished her drink and said flatly, 'I'm a goddam fool.'

Clive stirred uncomfortably. 'I'm sorry, Vivien.'

'Oh, hell, no!' She made a motion almost as though she were going to throw the glass at him. 'Curse me, hate me, do anything at all, but don't be sorry for me!'

'I didn't mean it that way.'

She bit her lower lip and hiccuped slightly. 'I know. I guess –' her face crumpled between tears and sheepish laughter – 'I guess I have a mean disposition, too.'

Clive said solemnly, 'Just a pair of heels without a soul between us. Who shall we go and stamp on?'

'Whom.'

'You go around throwing grammar in my teeth and I'll throw something right back at yours.' He snapped his fingers suddenly. 'Baby, how would you like to be assistant to the great Edmond Clive? Limited engagement, and at no salary, but think of the prestige.'

Her eyes grew shiny with excitement. 'I don't understand.'

Clive laid a tender hand on his middle. 'Johnny's left me in the lurch. I want to get out of here, right now. Will you help me?'

'Oh, I don't know! Do you think you ought to?'

'Hell, yes! They've boiled most of the soreness out of me, and the rest will work off when I get moving. Anyway, God damn it, I've got too much to do!'

Some of the youth and animation left her face. 'Yes,' she said slowly. 'Jane told me how you felt. I don't think I really believed her. Ed –' she leaned toward him, serious, searching – 'Ed, are you sure you're not letting this get you, because of what Mick used to mean to you?'

'Mick's innocent, Vivien, and what I said before still goes.'

She dropped her head, so he couldn't see anything but her clean, shining hair. 'I believe you, Ed. I'll help you.'

'You don't hate Mick any more?'

'Hate him!' She rose and went around the chair and stood with her hands clenched on the back of it. Her eyes blazed palely. 'Yes, I hate him! And I hate Jane, too. I'll always hate them. I've suffered, Ed. Maybe you wouldn't understand, not being a woman. But it goes deep.'

'Then why are you going to help me?'

She clung to the chair, rocking on her red heels. Her mouth was sullen and cruel. After a long time she whispered, 'Because you make me.'

Clive watched her sombrely.

She whimpered and beat the chair legs up and down on the floor. 'You're cruel. You like to make people suffer. I hate you! . . . Nothing's the same any more. You've broken everything to pieces for me. It isn't fair for one person to come up to another person and speak and go away again, and change everything just by having done it. Anybody else wouldn't have mattered. But it had to be you. You – your voice, your face, the way you walk, and the look in your eyes – and something inside you. Something that frightens me. Something that could kill me. And yet I want it more than I've ever wanted anything in my life. Strength, Ed. A thing I never had.'

He said quietly, 'You can be strong, if you want to be.'

She looked away. 'Maybe. Maybe . . .'

'You could quit hating, too, if you wanted to.'

'Maybe.' She shuddered, drawing her chin in and twisting it up toward her shoulder. 'Maybe I'm finding something better than hate.'

'There's nothing better than hate,' he said, 'if you hate the right things. And nothing worse if you don't.'

Vivien relaxed her grip on the chair, drooping wearily. 'Jane's been good to me. It isn't her fault she's Jane. But it isn't my fault I'm me.' She put her hands over her face. 'Pour me a drink, Ed.'

The bottle was where he could reach it. He poured her one and she gulped it down, walking over to the window and back. Then she laughed.

'If you don't have a relapse,' she said, 'it won't be because I haven't tried.'

The hall door opened suddenly, right on the heels of a rap. The nurse poked her head in. The face on it reminded Clive of a lemon pudding – thin, pale, sour.

'The doctor won't like it, Mr. Clive, if you tire yourself.'

'The doctor,' Clive told her, 'would be surprised if he knew just how tired I plan to get.'

'I don't know that he would.' The nurse looked at Vivien. Vivien colored and looked at Clive.

Clive said gently, 'Miss Nightingale, in spite of my youthful appearance I am past the age of legal consent. My brow is not fevered, nor am I the least bit uncomfortable. So I don't really need you for a thing.' He gave her one of his sweetest smiles. 'There must be some unfortunate around here who has need of you. Suppose you go and look.'

She looked him fair in the eye. 'Very well, Mr. Clive. It will probably take me some time, so if you should want anything, don't bother to ring!'

She closed the door firmly. Clive shuddered. 'A hospital,' he said, 'is no place to be sick in. A man needs all his strength just for things like that.'

Vivien giggled. Except for a streaky appearance under the eyes she was normal again.

'Okay, chief,' she said hoarsely. 'Let's take a powder. What do I do first?'

'Oh, God – you go to the movies, too. Well, okay, babe.' He sounded very tough indeed. 'Grab de raggery out'n de closet and den scram. Stake out inna hall an' tip me quick if we catch a rumble from Dog-Eye.'

She stared at him. 'Huh?'

He leaned back on the pillows, laughing. 'The clothes, honey. Out of the closet. Then go outside and let me know if you see the nurse coming back.'

She said, 'Oh!' and went across the room. Clive sat up, very, very carefully, bending a little at a time.

'Whew!' he gasped. 'That guy sure had big feet.' Vivien put his clothes on the chair and hovered over him. He nodded. 'Untie the nightie and then beat it.'

She loosened the knots down his back. 'Hadn't I better stay and help? You can hardly move.'

'Outside, darling.'

She pushed the hospital gown petulantly over his shoulders and started for the door. 'All right, but you don't have to be coy. I'm not . . .'

'I don't care if you're the entire staff of a nudist colony. I still wish to put my pants on in private.'

'That's all right with me,' said Vivien stiffly. 'I'll bet your legs aren't pretty anyway.' She wrinkled her nose at him and went out.

Clive whistled softly, grinned, and shook his head. He began to dress himself, very gently indeed, as though he were made of thin Venetian glass.

Presently he called, 'Vivien. Oh, Viv!'

She came in quickly. 'No sign of Dog-Eye.'

'Swell.' Clive was sitting on the edge of the bed, holding the bottle of rye. He had on his shirt and pants and one sock. 'Finish with the feet, baby. They're too far away for me.'

She got down on her knees. 'H'mph! I thought you were tough.'

'Only during office hours. Other times I'm strictly the patty-cake type.' He tilted the bottle and winced. 'Oi! I'm stiff all over.' He drank.

'What's that for? Oil?'

'Nuh-uh. Heat's good for bruises. I'm trying it from the inside.' He felt better.

By the time Vivien got his coat on him he felt swell. He even felt good enough to grin at Dog-Eye when she opened the door after another of her double-time raps.

She took one glance and went out again.

'Rumble,' said Clive. 'Let's lam outa here.'

'Sure t'ing, chief. Here's ya hat.'

'Caster,' he corrected. 'Let us keep in character.'

He put his arm around her shoulders, as much because they were a nice shape as because he needed the support. He had hold of the knob when it was jerked away from him, hard. Clive let go a strangled howl.

'For Chrissake, what are you trying to do, kill me?'

The doctor planted himself in the doorway. 'I won't have to if you don't get back in that bed.' Dog-Eye was behind him, looking nasty.

'Sorry,' said Clive. 'I've got things to do.'

'Listen, Mr. Clive. You've taken a bad beating . . .'

'All right. It's my beating, isn't it? I can do what I want with it.'

The doctor studied his face, swallowed, and tried again.'Mr. Clive, please. I won't be responsible . . .'

Clive stepped closer. 'You got it, pal. You won't be anything but sorry if you don't get out of my way.'

The doctor was stubborn. He glared at Clive. Clive glared at him. He could feel Vivien trembling against him, red-faced with laughter bottled up in her. He took another step and placed his forefinger on the doctor's pudgy chest. He smiled genially, giving off strong alcoholic fumes. The doctor began to sweat.

'I'm a little drunk,' Clive murmured. 'Sometimes I get very nasty indeed.'

The doctor moved backward. Clive followed. They lock-stepped some way down the corridor.

Then Dog-Eye snorted. 'Let him go. The Department of Sanitation will take care of him if he dies in the gutter.'

'Very well.' The doctor side-stepped. 'On your own head be it. If you're still alive, for heaven's sake come back for a check-up at your earliest opportunity.'

'Sure. You know where to send the bill.' Clive tipped his hat to Dog-Eye. They went out. Clive had to support Vivien most of the way. She was helpless with laughter.

When she could see again she said, 'I have my car. Where do you want to go?'

All the humor was gone out of Clive now. 'I want to see Mick,' he said. 'But I can take a cab.'

'No. I'm in this, and I'm going to stay in.'

She drove well, too fast but with an instinctive sureness rare in a woman. Clive said something about it, and she smiled.

'I used to belong to a hundred-mile club. I got pinched for it twice. They didn't let me drive for eighteen months.' The unhappy look came back in her face. 'I suppose,' she said abruptly, 'you've been wondering why Jane puts up with Richard and me in her house.'

'I haven't asked, have I?'

'I'm going to tell you anyway. She has to. Father's will said she had always to provide a home for us. He thought she could make us into human beings, maybe. The damn fool!'

Clive said gently, 'Look, Viv. Why don't you stop kicking yourself around? Why don't you just relax and be a nice kid? You could, you know.'

She bit her lip. 'Not any more. I've done – too many things.'

'I think,' said Clive, 'you're kidding yourself.'

She sighed. It was almost a sob. Her face was very young and very tired. 'Maybe. I don't know. I don't know anything any more. I – just feel. And I'm weak, Ed. I told you that. I haven't any strength at all. Jane got that, too.'

They didn't speak again. She stopped the car presently and Clive got out by himself and went into the City Jail. The agony of motion lessened slightly as time went by, but the whisky was dying in him and mentally he felt like hell. He followed the jailer slowly down the corridor to Mick's cell.

Chapter sixteen

MICK HAMMOND was lying on his cot with his eyes closed, but he looked around when he heard the cell door open and then sat up, swinging his feet to the floor. Clive came in. The door rang shut behind him and the jailer's boots went away down the corridor.

Mick said, 'I knew you'd come.'

'Mick . . . about what I told Gaines that day . . .'

'Jane and I figured that out, Eddie. You had to, the way things were.'

Clive sighed. 'That's okay, then.'

'Sure. How do you feel?'

'A bit sore in the tripes – and a lot sorer in what is sometimes called the soul. I've done you a hell of a lot of good so far.'

'I'm not worried.' Hammond smiled faintly. His eyes were exhausted, but there was no hysteria in them.

Clive studied him. 'You've grown up, Mick.'

'Well, I figure it this way. If I get out of this I'll be grateful. I want to live as much as the next man, and I want to be happy, and I'd try awfully hard to build something worth while. But if I don't get out of it – well, if I'd behaved myself I wouldn't be here. I haven't anyone but myself to blame.' He laughed. 'Oh, I didn't feel that way at first. But I got to thinking, and that's the way it came out.' He added soberly, 'The worst of it is Jane.'

'Jane's holding up too well, Mick.'

'She's all right, Eddie. I know her better than you do. She's all right.' He grinned at Clive. 'You haven't done any breaking, either.'

Clive stared at him, blank-faced and faintly surprised. He said, 'I guess I haven't had any time.'

That pleased Hammond immensely. 'Sit down and have a cigarette.'

Clive found the one low stool and sat down, pushing his hat back. The smoke tasted good.

Hammond said matter-of-factly, 'Do you have any hopes of saving me?'

'I'm still trying. But I won't kid you, Mick.'

'You'll do it. You'll do it for Laurel.'

Clive said slowly, 'I don't know.'

'I'm not worried.'

'Hey, quit with that!' Clive laughed. 'I'm supposed to hold *your* hand, not the other way around.' He rose and wandered around the cell. 'What was the name of the woman who got you your job in the store, Mick?'

'Krebs. Mrs. Julia Krebs. Why?'

'Thought I'd like to talk to her. Know her address?'

'Cardiff Towers, over on Rossmore.' Hammond leaned back against the wall. 'Funny thing, Eddie. That job was what really held Jane to me. She said it proved I could work and be somebody if I wanted to.' He frowned down at his hands. 'People talk a lot about love, Eddie. Most of them don't know what the word means.'

Clive said, 'No.'

'I never did before. I didn't even realize that you were in love with Marian. God, what a fool I was.'

'Marian got over it. She married some kid from the East the year after you walked out on her.'

'But you didn't get over it.'

'I did all right. It was you going back on me like that that hurt the worst. It made me out such a chump. I guess you did me a favor at that, Mick. I quit hanging rainbows on things – and people.'

'Yeah,' said Hammond softly. 'I'm sorry.'

'Oh hell, let's forget it!' Clive's sudden grin took the edge off his words. 'Sit tight, kiddie, and eat your spinach, and Uncle Eddie will see if he can find a can opener for you.' He shook Hammond's shoulder, hard enough to make him wince. The jailer was already hovering in the background.

'Oh, Mick – I wanted to ask you. I noticed a long sort of gash on that blackthorn stick. Care to tell me how it happened?'

'I – well, why not? Vivien has a talent for needling people. My nerves were all shot after the accident. I hadn't slept much for over a week, and she just got to me one night, out on the terrace. I – tried to hit her. I didn't know what I was doing. Fortunately I hit some ornamental stonework instead.' Hammond made a wry face. 'That wouldn't sound so good to a jury, would it?'

'Not from your lawyer's point of view, no. By the way, is –'

'Benson is still defending me, with no hope at all.'

'That's great,' said Clive dourly. 'Did Gaines ask you about the stick?'

131

'I told him I shut it in the car door. I don't think he believes me. Vivien may have told him the truth anyhow. But it doesn't really matter.'

The jailer unlocked the door.

'Well, so long, Mick.' Clive started out, then stopped. 'One more thing. Does this Krebs dame do any kicking?'

Mick laughed. 'No! Why?'

'Because,' said Clive grimly, 'from now on I'm carrying a gun. And the next person that tries to feed me boot leather is going to get lead in him before he gets his toe off the ground!'

Vivien was waiting patiently outside. She reached over and opened the door for him. 'Okay, chief. Where do we go now?'

'Home.'

'Home! I thought we were going sleuthing.'

'Sure. But first I want a bath, so I don't stink of liniment. I want a clean shirt and a suit that doesn't have blood all over it. The first rule of a successful private eye is always to look like a gentleman. You may fool somebody when you least expect it.'

They went home. Chuck was very solicitous about helping Clive out of the car. Clive thanked him and then turned to Vivien.

'Come on up and have a drink. You've earned it.'

She bounced out happily, walking close to him and enjoying the stir they made going through the lobby. They had their drink upstairs, and then Clive said, 'Thanks for everything, Viv. And now . . .'

'And now I'm getting the brush-off.' She stood up sulkily. 'All right.'

Clive laughed. 'Don't be sore at me. It's just that I'm liable to have trouble enough carrying my own weight, that's all. And it wouldn't be any fun for you. Believe it or not, ninety-five per cent of the detective business is duller than hell.'

'What are you going to do?'

'Fish around and see what I get. I've got nothing to lose, anyway.'

'Just one thing.' She came to him, her eyes big and tender. 'Yourself, Ed.'

'You can't worry too much about that.'

132

'But I do! Ed, listen. If what you say is true and the murderer is still loose ... well, he's safe now, except for you. He isn't going to let you get close to him.'

He could see a mist of tears in her lashes and the quiver of her brown throat. He put his arms around her and kissed her. She lay close against him, not moving except for the lift of her round breasts.

'Kiss me again,' she whispered. 'Please.'

She put her head back. Her eyes were closed, her lips parted and hungry. Clive bent to her. Her body arched under his, her arms going around him, tight, inside his coat. Strong round arms and a strong round body, and a mouth that bruised his mouth with the cuts half healed across it.

Pain.

He pushed her roughly away and caught the back of a chair and stood bent over it. Vivien leaned against the door, where the force of his thrust had thrown her. He couldn't see her. He couldn't see anything at all for a moment. But the sound of her breathing came to him clearly. It was hoarse and guttural, like the breathing of an animal after a fight.

She wrenched the door open suddenly and ran out.

After a while he went and closed it. Then he poured himself a long drink and began to strip.

He treated himself to a lengthy soaking in a hot tub, finished with a cold shower, and shaved. He dressed carefully in a fresh shirt and striped tie, and a suit of brown Harris tweed. The easy hang of the coat concealed the bulk of the Colt automatic under his left armpit. His step was almost as springy as usual when he went downstairs.

Jonathan Ladd Jones had seen that his car was brought back after the police were through with it. He drove down to the Boulevard, not hurrying. No car followed him.

The light held him up at the corner where Sugar March had died. He scowled at it, whistling absently, until a snarl of horns behind him moved him on. No car tagged him on the way down to Vine Street. He parked and went up to his office, walking softly. He flung the door open quickly.

Jonathan Ladd Jones jumped three feet behind the desk. It was a neat trick, because his feet were crossed comfortably on the blotter. A bottle of Gilbey's Spey Royal teetered perilously beside them.

Clive shut the door. He hitched up his pants, hooked his thumbs in the waist band, and smiled.

'Well for Chrissake,' said Johnny angrily. 'That ain't fair. I left you flat on your back . . .'

'That you did. And if I didn't need all my strength I'd leave you flat on yours right now. Of all the double-crossing little rats!'

Johnny slid the bottle into the desk drawer and shut it with his foot. He said solicitously, 'How do you feel, Ed?'

'Like beating your head off. You don't know what you got me into.'

'The Alcott dame, I'll bet. I passed her on the way out. So she helped you crash out, huh?'

'Yeah.' Clive lighted a cigarette with quick, jerky hands. 'Get Gaines on the phone and ask him what they found out about those letters.'

Johnny stared at him and then picked up the phone. Clive stood by the window, smoking. Johnny asked questions, listened, and then hung up.

'The letters were pretty hot stuff, it seems. Up to and including a Mrs. Julia Krebs. Typed on dime-store paper with a Royal that cuts the capital Y's and E's in two. No prints. The D.A. was very grateful for the carbons.' Johnny settled back in the swivel chair. 'Look, Ed. Supposing you're right about Hammond being innocent, what have those letters got to do with it? It was Laurel Dane that got killed, and she didn't know Hammond much over two weeks. And how do you know the framing of Hammond was intentional? I think the killer just got a lucky break.'

'An assistant,' said Clive, 'is supposed to assist.'

'Sure, sure. But Laurel was the kind of a girl that – well, you know what I mean . . .'

'I know. Laurel bruised a lot of masculine egos in her day. Some of them might have stayed just as sore as Beauvais's. So we're right back where we started, and with a damn sight less to work on.'

'Less! I'd say nothing.'

'Yeah. Well, if that's the way the game's stacked, that's the way we'll play it.'

'What do you want me to do?'

'Nothing right now, except stay where I can get hold of you when I want you.'

'I'll be here all day. I'll stay home nights.'

'If you have company in, chum, keep one hand free for the phone and don't get too high to reach it.'

Johnny grinned. 'Sure. And take it easy, Ed. If you're right about Hammond, the real killer isn't going to –'

'That's already been pointed out to me.' Clive turned the knob. 'So long.'

Johnny said glumly, 'So long.'

'If you finish the bottle, call the liquor store and have 'em send up another. Have your meals sent up, too. You stick by that phone.'

'Well for cripe's sake,' said Johnny. 'It's a good thing I don't have to go down the hall to . . .'

Clive slammed the door and went downstairs. A man stepped quickly out of the janitor's closet and pressed the muzzle of an ancient horse pistol into his belly. The man was Richard Alcott, and he was cold, stony sober.

'In here, Clive.'

Clive obeyed. The janitor's closet was long and narrow with a small window at the end. Alcott locked the door.

Clive said, 'So you did kill her, after all.'

'That doesn't matter.'

Clive nodded at the pistol. 'That relic is apt to kill both of us if you fire it.'

'Are you afraid?'

'Of course I am.'

'So am I,' said Alcott slowly. 'But that doesn't matter, either.' He studied Clive for some time, as though searching for an answer, an explanation. He had not slept well, and his sobriety made of him a different and rather terrifying person. Clive realized presently what the unfamiliar quality was. It was dignity.

'What made you think I suspected you, Alcott?'

'I haven't thought about it. The murder isn't important now. There's something else.'

135

'Yes. Yes, I'm beginning to see. I manhandled you, twice. That's it, isn't it?'

'Partly.'

'And partly,' said Clive, 'the thing you've been running away from all your life finally caught up with you, and there was no place else to run.'

'Yes,' said Alcott, 'that's it. No place else to run. That's why I haven't had a drink since that night in the park. Drinking is no use any more.'

'And are you sure that killing me is going to prove your manhood?'

'That's what worries me. I don't know.'

'I can tell you. It won't.'

'Why?' He was asking the question seriously, as though he were a pupil and Clive the teacher. The big clumsy revolver remained centered on Clive's belt buckle.

'Because life doesn't work like that. It doesn't come in nice sharp climaxes that tie up your problem neatly and file it away in a drawer. The next day comes, and the day after that, and you think. And you're not sure. You're never sure.' He indicated the gun. 'You're calling in outside help, Alcott. That thing isn't any part of you. Anybody can pull a trigger.'

'That's true,' said Alcott. 'But you did abuse me, contemptuously, as though I were not a man like yourself. If I kill you –'

'You'll prove you can shoot an unarmed man. And that's all.'

Alcott said, 'You have a gun?'

'Yes.'

'Take it out.'

Clive stared at him. 'No,' he said slowly, 'I won't do that. You know, Alcott, sometimes dying is the easiest way out. Sometimes it takes the real guts to go on living.'

Alcott whispered, 'I should have killed you before you said that.' He let the gun slip out of his hand, leaning back against the door. 'I'm tired.'

Sweat stood out on Clive's forehead. In spite of himself he was trembling.

'What is it you and Vivien are afraid of?' he asked.

'Jane. We were born and bred in her shadow.'

'Why don't you get out of it?'

'Their attitude – Father's and Jane's – has always been that Vivien and I should stay near her. Good influence, a good home. She's afraid of what we'll do if we're turned loose.'

'Good God, you're over twenty-one!'

'Jane controls the money. You see?'

'Yeah. Then in plain English you've always been afraid to risk going hungry in order to make your own life.'

'That's it.' Alcott laughed, without humor. 'Things are funny, aren't they? Jane's so damned good, so perfect, so capable that Vivien and I practically in self-defense developed all our worst qualities. If Jane had had faults like anybody else . . .'

'Maybe you wouldn't have committed a murder.'

'Murder?' Alcott glanced up. 'Oh, the girl. I told you that night I didn't kill her.'

'I know you did.'

Alcott spread his hands. 'There's no way I can prove it.' There was no fear in him now. There was nothing but exhaustion.

Clive said, 'I can get rough again.'

Alcott's gaze met his steadily, and held it.

'It's a strange thing,' Alcott said. 'I don't think it would matter if you did. It isn't the body that's important.'

Clive smiled. 'I believe you.' He picked up the pistol and gave it to Alcott. 'You don't want me to talk to Jane, do you?'

'No. I can't get into the Army, but there must be other things. I'm going to find out, by myself.'

He held out his hand suddenly. 'Thanks,' he said, 'for the beating.' He turned the key and went out.

Clive watched him. 'My God,' he whispered. 'People!' His dark eyes had an unfamiliar softness.

He went upstairs again and told Johnny to put a man on Richard Alcott's tail.

Driving south on Vine, Clive saw that there was still no one following him. Below Sunset he hesitated and then turned down a side street toward Sugar March's apartment. There was a new For Rent sign in front – *Rear Apt., 3 Rms Furn, $27.50. Apply #1*. Clive went up the cracked and settling steps and punched the button.

The hard-faced woman who had watched him and Gaines opened the door. She was still wearing soiled blue pajamas. Her mouth and hair were the same dry terra cotta, and her hands were stained with tobacco smoke.

'Did you want to see the apartment?'

'No,' Clive said. 'I want to talk to you.'

'Yeah? Well I'm busy.'

Clive held the door with his shoulder. 'Don't make it tough for me, sister. I don't give a damn what kind of a place you run. I only want to ask a couple of questions.' He pushed his way in.

She said harshly, 'You get funny and I'll call the cops.'

He laughed. The room looked just like her. It smelled the same, too, smoky and unaired.

She said, 'Law?'

'Private.'

'Private! You got your nerve!'

'I want something. If you've got it I'm willing to pay.'

She dragged nervously on her cigarette. 'How much?'

'Maybe nothing. Depends on what you have.'

'Maybe I don't sell anyhow. I mind my own business.'

'I'm not asking you to stool. All I want to know is who brought Sugar March home the night before she was killed.'

Her eyes opened wide and then blinked shut. She let smoke out of her mouth very slowly. Clive drew a bill from his pocket and began to smooth it lengthwise between his fingers.

She said, 'What do you care about the March kid?'

'I care ten dollars – maybe.'

She laughed, sneeringly. 'Cheap skate.'

'I always scale to size.'

She stared at him for a moment, furious. 'Get out,' she said. 'Get to hell out, you cheap little bastard.'

Clive shrugged. He put the bill away and turned the knob.

'All right, all right! If you want to act like a kike in a hockshop . . .' she screamed.

Clive came back again. She paced up and down in a cloud of smoke.

'Some guy brought her home,' she said. 'The driveway goes right under my bedroom window. I heard 'em talking, and it made me sore because sometimes I get insomnia and I was just drifting off when they came in. I looked out the window. I was gonna tell 'em to shut up, but by that time they were almost back to the garages. The girl sounded pretty sore about something and this guy was kidding her along, like he thought she was right and ought to do something about it. I couldn't hear any words. There's an echo out there. You can hear voices loud, but the words break up.

'Anyway, all of a sudden the March kid laughs, real nasty, like she's got somebody right where she wants him, and the guy laughs and pats her on the shoulder. They go upstairs and he kisses her and she goes in and shuts the door. And he goes away.' She came to Clive and thrust her hand out. 'That's all.'

'What did the man look like?'

'For twenty I might remember.'

Clive smiled. He folded the ten carefully and shut his fingers on it. 'The man was tall. He wore a black coat and a black hat pulled down over his face. And there was no moon so you couldn't have seen what he looked like if he'd been stark naked. Am I right?'

She cursed him.

'Sure,' said Clive wearily. 'Sure. I'm not even very smart. I was just repeating something I heard before.'

He threw the bill on a table and went out. At the corner drugstore he stopped to call his office.

'Johnny, get busy on the phone and find out if anybody at the Skyway Club saw who Sugar March went home with the night before she died.'

Johnny groaned. 'You hand me the sweetest jobs! Got something new?'

'Our pal in the black coat. He was with her when she got home. He still hasn't got a face.'

'Hey, that ties up with the keysmith. But there wasn't any tall guy in black, or anything civilian, near her when she fell.'

'Maybe,' said Clive reasonably, 'he's really two midgets. I'll call you back.'

He bucked traffic at a modest twenty-five down Vine to Rossmore. He was still all by himself. A couple of butterflies began to play tag in his stomach. He thought, Hell, I've been in this game too long. Pretty soon I'll be looking under my bed nights instead of in it.

He stopped at a drive-in and weighed the butterflies down with some solid food. They were still fluttering when he went into the Cardiff Towers to see Mrs. Julia Krebs.

Clive took his clean shirt and expensive tweeds across an acre and a half of deep mulberry carpeting and gave his card to a sleek middle-aged man behind a circular desk.

'I'd like to see Mrs. Julia Krebs.'

The man lifted a telephone, making the diamonds sparkle on his fingers. 'Six-A, please. Six-A? This is the desk calling. There is a Mr. Edmond Clive to see Mrs. Krebs.' He turned to Clive. 'In regard to what did you wish to see her?'

'In regard to a Mr. Michael Hammond.'

He repeated that into the phone. There was a pause. Clive counted the silver-fox coats going in and out. Presently the man said 'Thank you,' and turned again. 'Mrs. Krebs is not in. Will you leave a message?'

Clive said pleasantly, 'Tell the maid to tell Mrs. Krebs – when she comes in – that there is a matter of some correspondence that has become rather urgent. Mr. Hammond is anxious to have it taken care of right away.'

There was further conversation with the telephone. This time the sleek man hung up and gave Clive a peculiar look.

'Mrs. Krebs will see you, sir. Sixth floor, Apartment A. The elevators are on your left.'

'Thank you.' Clive's face was blandly innocent. 'She made a quick trip, didn't she? Modern transportation is a wonderful thing.'

The maid let him in. She wore an ugly uniform, but the loose cut couldn't hide what was underneath. She had no make-up and her hair was drawn tight under an unflattering cap, but even that didn't spoil her much. Brown curls sneaked out anyway, her eyes were lively, and her lips were pink and full. Clive smiled at her when she took his hat. She wanted to answer it, but didn't. He went on in.

The apartment was one of those modernistic movie sets where the newly rich like to bask. White rug, thick square furniture with shaggy upholstery in unpleasant colors, shapeless art pieces, and miles of plate-glass windows. There was a nice view of the golf course. Mrs. Krebs was occupying center stage in front of it.

She fitted the place like a decorator's piece. She wore something flowing and informal in black velvet with a wide gold belt that showed off her perfect corseting. The neck was cut very low. Her black hair was dressed short, her hard, predatory face carefully made up and set off with gold earrings. She had nice hands and called attention to them by carrying a cigarette in a six-inch ivory holder. She wasn't as young as she hoped she looked, but for a certain type of man she would still have a lot of attraction.

Clive wasn't the type. He waited patiently until she got tired of trying to stare him down. Finally she turned to a pale green sofa and laid herself into it cornerwise, so that her long clean lines showed to advantage.

She said coldly, 'I don't believe I understood your cryptic remark, Mr. Clive. I don't believe I liked it.'

Clive sat down in a chair, without being asked. 'May I smoke?' Mrs. Krebs nodded curtly. Clive lighted a cigarette. He seemed to have all the time in the world. She watched him with impenetrable black eyes.

Clive said, with no particular emphasis, 'Persecution, Mrs. Krebs, is a serious offense. The victim can collect quite a sum in damages.'

'Will you please come to the point!'

'Michael Hammond is innocent of the crime with which he is charged. When he's acquitted, he's going to take steps to end a particularly unpleasant type of mental blackmail.'

'I don't understand you!' She rose and faced him accusingly. 'Innocent! Mick Hammond killed that girl and you know it. I remember your name now, Mr. Clive. I know what your game is. Mick needs money for the trial. I imagine his wife isn't going to pay for it! And you've decided that I'm the logical victim.' She made a vicious gesture with the ivory holder. 'The bastard,' she whispered. 'He told me he destroyed those letters. I should have known.'

'You should have known better than to write the ones you've been writing for the past six months.'

She said nothing for a moment, trying to probe Clive's hard eyes. 'What are you trying to do?'

'I've been hired for a certain job, Mrs. Krebs. I'm trying to complete it.'

She wasn't a show piece any longer. She was an angry woman, not very handsome and fairly scared. 'I won't pay blackmail, do you understand? I'll fight you. I'll see that bastard Hammond put where he'll never do any more harm, and you with him. Do you understand that, Mr. Clive?'

Clive smiled with his mouth. 'You have this a little mixed, I think. Hammond is the one who will sue you.'

'Sue me?' She laughed. 'This is a brand-new approach.'

'They found several clear prints on those letters. Will you object to having yours compared?'

'But of course my prints were on them . . . *Who* found them?'

'The police. And a typewriter is as identifiable as handwriting. Where do you keep your Royal, Mrs. Krebs?'

'But I wrote them by hand . . .' She stared at him, running slender red-nailed fingers along the neck of her gown. 'Mick showed them to the police? I don't understand.'

Clive stood up impatiently. 'Let's stop playing games. I don't care about any romantic swill you may have written Mick. I'm talking about the letters you've been sending his wife. You hate Mick. He used you, and that didn't go down very well. You wanted to get back at him. So you hired somebody to check up on his past and started feeding the details to Mrs. Hammond. You even told about yourself. A nice little touch of vengeful masochism there, Mrs. Krebs. You probably thought that would relieve you of all suspicion.' He picked up the phone. 'I think it's time we had some law in on this.'

She gestured sharply. Her white breast lifted hard, and her nostrils were pinched. Clive held his hand over the mouthpiece.

'I didn't write any letters like that,' she said. 'I don't know anything about them. I haven't touched a typewriter in years. I don't own one. If there are prints on the letters they aren't mine. I don't mind having them checked. But I don't want any scandal. Please don't send the call through the switchboard. I'll go with you. I'll be glad to –'

142

'You'll have to do better than that, Mrs. Krebs. You didn't have to write the things yourself. The man who did your snooping for you – your maid – your secretary. The police are very thorough. They have ways of finding out.'

She straightened. Her face was composed again, the shrewd cold face of a woman who knows how to climb up in the world.

'Very well, Mr. Clive. Call the police. I shan't object to anything. I shall only say this: When everyone is quite satisfied that I had nothing to do with those letters I shall sue the police department and you personally for the highest damages my lawyers recommend.'

She turned her back on him, returning to her original position by the windows. Clive laid his finger carefully on the connection lever, holding it down. He spoke into the dead phone, watching her.

'Police headquarters? Clive speaking. Get me Lieutenant Gaines.' He waited. Mrs. Krebs didn't move. Clive put the phone down and laughed softly. 'All right,' he said. 'If you're bluffing, it's good enough to take me this time. I can always come back.'

She didn't look at him. 'Get out.' At the entrance into the hall her voice stopped him again. 'I just want to say this. I'm glad someone sent Mrs. Hammond those letters. I wish I had thought of it myself. I hope that you will never find who did it. And I hope that Mick Hammond will be convicted whether he's guilty or not.'

'Yes,' said Clive quietly. 'I rather thought that was how you'd feel.'

The maid wasn't there. He picked up his hat and went out.

He found the service door down the hall. It let him onto a clean concrete landing with iron stairs running up and down and four white doors facing each other. He rapped on the one marked 6–A. The maid opened it.

She was startled. Clive took the door out of her hand and came inside and closed it.

'Don't be scared, honey. I only want to chat a while.' He removed his hat and let his eyes admire her. She flushed and looked away, patting at her hair.

143

Clive said, 'For Pete's sake, why do you go around hiding under that burlap?'

She jerked her head toward the apartment. '*She* makes me.'

'I'll bet I know why.'

She had lovely teeth, and two dimples. 'You do?'

'Sure. She doesn't want you stealing the scene from her.'

She laughed, bending over a brilliant kettle on the electric range. Clive sat down on a white enamel stool and sniffed at a plate of cookies laid out on a tea tray.

'Have one,' the girl said. 'There's plenty more.'

It was crisp and had lumps of chocolate candy in it. 'Good,' he said. 'Any chance of Her Nibs coming out here?'

'Not her! She wouldn't dirty her feet walking into the kitchen.' The girl banged a cup and saucer down. 'And I happen to know she used to work in a bargain basement in the Bronx!'

Clive picked up another cooky. 'Been with her long?'

'Nearly eight years. Jobs weren't so easy to get for a while. But the way things are now . . .'

Clive let his eyes wander again. 'I'll bet you'd look cute in coveralls, riveting.'

She giggled, passing close to him to set the tray.

He said casually, 'I guess you know a lot about Mrs. Krebs.'

'You bet I do! I . . .' She stopped suddenly and turned on him. 'Who are you? What do you want?'

He slid off the stool, smiling. 'Take it easy, kid. I'm just a little guy with a job to do, and it doesn't have anything to do with tattling to Mrs. Krebs. In fact, I wouldn't blame you if you sneaked all her girdles into the rubber drive.' He pushed the remaining half of his cooky between her pouting lips. 'Right now,' he added, watching her mouth move, 'I'm enjoying my work.'

He leaned over and kissed her, keeping his hands between them. She squealed and colored, fumbling at the neck of her dress.

'Ooh!' she gasped, feeling the crackle of paper money. 'What's that for?'

'Who bought the story of Mrs. Krebs and Michael Hammond from you?'

She stared at him, frightened.

'No one will ever know. I promise.'

She glanced at the dining-room door, and then back again. 'All right,' she said hurriedly. 'He said his name was Bill Kennedy, and he was a private detective. He met me down in the areaway one night and asked a lot of questions, and gave me a hundred dollars.'

'Could you see what he looked like?'

'Well, it was dark, and he kept his hat pulled down. But he was tall, taller than you are a lot, and bigger. I think he was wearing evening clothes. He had a nice voice and – well . . .' She flushed, laughing. 'He had a mustache. I know that.'

Clive laughed, too. 'Dark or light?'

'I could't tell by the feel of it. But I do remember that his skin looked as if it must be awfully dark, because I could see his teeth when he smiled in spite of there being hardly any light.' She frowned, pausing. 'It seems to me I can almost remember *almost* seeing his mustache, once I knew it was there, like it would be lighter than his skin.'

Clive stood for a moment, looking at her and not seeing her. She caught her breath and drew back.

'What is it? What have I . . .'

Clive began to smile, almost caressingly, but not at her. 'Nothing,' he said. Only – you just started to put a face on Murder.'

CHAPTER SEVENTEEN

THE ROAD that Clive had chosen to take to the beach was narrow and not much traveled at this hour. He jammed the throttle down hard. Fields raced by beyond a deep ditch. Plowed land, and long straight rows of green. Presently, from a ramshackle little farmhouse up ahead, an ancient truck wheezed onto the highway with a load of celery.

Clive drove his foot down on the brake and his hand on the horn ring. The old truck didn't move any faster, finishing a left turn. Clive swore and pulled back on the emergency.

He wasn't doing more than twenty-five when the front wheel came off. The car slewed off into the ditch, churning mud with its rear wheels. The celery truck trundled away without stopping. Clive killed his motor and sat still with his eyes shut, gripping the wheel.

Somebody yelled, 'Hey! Hey, there! Are you all right?'

A black sedan had pulled up on the edge of the road. A heavy-set man who looked like an oil-field worker stood at the top of the ditch.

'Yeah, I'm all right.' Clive got out stiffly, holding one arm tight across his middle. The man leaned over and gave him a hand up.

'Lucky for you that truck slowed you down,' he said. 'If you'd throwed that wheel while you was travelin' like you was when you passed me . . .' He whistled.

'Yeah.' Clive looked at his car, and then at the wheel lying fifty feet away in the mud. His mouth twitched. 'Can you take me to Del Rey?'

'Sure, goin' home that way.' He helped Clive in. 'Brother, you're sure lucky! Sure you're okay? You look kinda white around the gills.'

'Knocked my wind out, that's all. Get going.'

'Sure,' said the man in a hurt tone. 'Sure. Only *I* ain't breakin' no speed laws.' He drove thirty-five miles an hour and no faster. He didn't speak again.

Clive loosened up enough to thank him when he reached Del Rey. He called his auto club and arranged a tow, and then got a taxi. He left it at Avenue Thirty-seven and said, 'Wait.' He climbed the steps of the little house where he had gone three nights ago while Dion Beauvais waited in the fog.

The thin young man opened the door. He was still wearing his denim pants and his faded jersey and his cigarette. There was a large mottled bruise on the right side of his forehead.

He stared at Clive. 'Jeez! I thought you was in the hospital.'

'I didn't have time to stay.' Somewhere out back a child was having a tantrum and a woman was yelling in a high, strident voice. The young man grinned.

'Home sweet home. Phooey. Come in?'

'No, thanks. There was just something I wanted to ask. When you fell that night – how did it happen?'

'Well . . .' The young man scowled down at the sandy, oil-stained pavement at the bottom of the steps. 'I ain't just sure. I got down the stairs okay, and then the walk just seemed to yank itself out from under my feet. I went down flat. I must have been stunned, because I seem to remember trying to get up and then it was like somebody hit me from behind.' He turned his head. 'I gotta bruise under the ear. See?'

'Yeah. You didn't see anyone or hear anything?'

'Naw. It was blacker'n the inside of a cat. Hell, it was just one of those things, I guess. I still don't see how I cracked both sides of my bean, but you do funny things when you take a spill. I remember once when I was a kid . . .'

'Sure,' said Clive. 'You used the word "yank." Why?'

'That was what it felt like. Like somebody pulled the sidewalk out from under me.' He shook his head. 'Damned if I can see yet what I tripped on.'

Clive stood for a moment looking hard at nothing. Then he smiled and fished a bill out of his pocket. 'Look, fella – I feel kind of responsible. Buy yourself some headache powders on me.'

'Jeez! I can drown myself in 'em for that. Well, thanks, pal!'

'Forget it. And the next guy that asks you to call the cops for him, boot his teeth in.'

'I ain't sure that would be any healthier! Hey – can't you tell me what goes on here? I mean, being practically in the middle of it, like . . .'

'Read the morning papers in a couple of days. By that time the news can't do you any harm.'

Clive went back to the cab. The child was still screaming. A dog barked savagely somewhere between the faded houses. The sun was bright, the sea smelled clean and strong and sharp with salt, and there were sea gulls crying. None of those things had changed any, in spite of the sprawling black stains on the sand.

He experienced, as always down there, a strange moment of duality. He was two people walking down the street: a boy in overalls who had not seen anything yet but the brightness and the cleanness and the soaring gulls – and a man named Ed Clive, who had.

He looked at the black stains without hostility. They understood each other.

Back in Hollywood, he left the hacker waiting and went up to his office. Jonathan Ladd Jones was nursing the Scotch and brooding at the telephone. He began to speak, slowly and with care.

'I hate Alexander Graham Bell. I hate his father, his mother, and his grandparents. I hate the telephone company. I hate the guys that string the wires on the poles.' He took a deep breath and lifted his gaze to Clive. 'I am getting so I hate you.'

'There seems to be a general swing of opinion that way.' Clive was busy with a cigarette.

Johnny watched the way his hands moved and said, 'What happened?'

'Somebody unscrewed the lugs on a front wheel and piled me in a ditch.' Clive sat on the corner of the desk and picked up the phone. The switchboard girl at his apartment house answered.

'Hello, honey. Clive speaking. Look, will you and Chuck and whoever else happens to be free get busy on something for me? Somebody got into my garage after my car was brought back. . . . Yeah, a little tampering job. Will you find out if any of the tenants who came home late that night happened to see anyone? Thanks. Call me back at my office as quick as you can. If I'm not here I'll get in touch with you later.'

He hung up and began pacing. 'What did you find out, Johnny?'

'Like always. One of the waiters saw Sugar get into a car, but he couldn't see who was driving except that it seemed to be a man in black, like he might have on evening clothes.'

Clive smiled.

Johnny said patiently, 'Okay, Ed. You've got the twitches and you're walking like a tomcat on hot bricks. What gives?'

'I don't know yet.'

'All right, make like a wooden Indian. I just work here. Mrs. Hammond called three times. She found out you'd skipped the hospital and she wants to be sure you're all right. If you can sit

148

still that long, you can call her up. I'm not touching that damn phone again. The next time I do it'll bite me.'

Rather slowly, Clive dialed 0 and gave Jane Hammond's number. Mulligan took the call. Jane came quickly, as though she'd been waiting close by.

'Ed, you shouldn't be out of bed!'

'I'm doing fine, thanks.'

'Well, please be careful! I don't know what we'd do without you.' She paused, and then said so low he could hardly hear, 'Are you going to save him, Ed?'

'Yes. Yes, Jane, I'm going to save him.' He heard her sharp intake of breath, and then the empty humming of the wire. 'Is Vivien there?'

'I – I don't know. Oh, Ed, do you mean that?'

'I mean it. Will you find out if Vivien is there?'

He heard her call to Mulligan, and then she said, 'Why do you want her? Is something wrong?'

'No. Look, Jane. I'd like you and Vivien to stay home tonight. I'm sending Johnny over.'

'Then – you must be afraid of something . . .'

'I don't know. I just don't want to take any chances.'

Clive put another cigarette in his mouth and lighted it from the butt of the last one, moving restlessly within the reach of the phone cord. Presently Mulligan came back and Jane said, 'Vivien is down in the pool. Do you want to speak to her?'

'No, thanks. Just see that she stays there with you. I may have some news, later on.'

Jane whispered, 'We'll wait, Ed. Be careful.'

He hung up. Johnny was getting his hat and coat. He glared.

'Now I know I hate you. Parking me with a couple of dames just when things start breaking. I oughta go on strike!' He jammed his hat on. 'Besides, Ed, I ought to stay with you and you know it.'

Clive smiled briefly. 'I need you right where I'm sending you. Take your gun and make sure it's loaded.'

'Trouble?'

'I don't know. Maybe.'

'Farrar?'

The phone rang. Johnny started back hopefully. Clive said, 'Get the hell out, will you?'

'I know,' said Johnny nastily. 'For what you're going to do you don't want any witnesses.' He slammed the door.

The switchboard girl was on the other end of the line. She was breathless with excitement. 'The Bevises. They came home about two o'clock from a friend's house and picked up a man with their headlights just as they turned into the drive. They almost hit him. He ducked around the corner real quick and went off down the street.'

'Could they see what he looked like?'

'He was a tall man, wearing a black coat and a black felt pulled down. But Mrs. Bevis said she saw the lower part of his face. He seemed to be quite sunburned and had a fair mustache. Does that help you, Mr. Clive?'

'It's just what I wanted. Thanks, honey.' He pressed the lever down and then slowly and deliberately dialed another number.

A feminine voice said, 'Wilshire Crest Apartments.'

'What time does the night clerk – Gibson – come on?'

'At six, sir. Is there a message?'

'No, thanks.' Clive hung up and looked at his watch. It was five thirty-two. He got out the Scotch, noticing as he poured it that his hand shook slightly. Then he locked the office and went down to the waiting cab.

'Wilshire and Fairfax, and fast. I've got a damned important errand before the shops close at six.'

They made it in twelve minutes. Clive shoved a bill at the driver. 'Know any prayers, bud?'

The man stared at him. 'I was brought up Catholic, and I married a Jew. I know all the prayers there are.'

'Well, say 'em for me.'

He walked away, looking at signs on the store fronts. May's Wilshire towered above the crowds waiting for buses on all four corners. The gold clock on its onyx front said five-forty-five. Two blocks up the Boulevard the modernistic windows of the Wilshire Crest burned flame-yellow in the low sunlight.

There were two cleaners-and-dyers in opposite blocks. Clive went into the nearer one. There was a girl about sixteen behind the counter, wearing the inevitable Sloppy Joe and an upswept

150

hair-do trimmed with flowers. She smiled at Clive out of a wide face covered with freckles like rust spots.

Clive said, 'Does a man named Kenneth Farrar bring his cleaning here?'

She kept on smiling. It didn't seem to mean anything. 'I really couldn't say. I'm just helping out here while . . .'

'Could you find out?'

'Well, I don't know. I don't know just where my father keeps his records and everything. You see I'm just helping . . .'

'You said that. Is –'

'Could you come back tomorrow?'

'I could not. Isn't there somebody out back there?'

'Father's just putting some early deliveries in the truck. We're really ready to close . . .'

Clive put his hands flat on the counter. He said carefully, 'Go out and ask your father if he has a customer named Kenneth Farrar. If he has, tell him to come here.'

She stopped smiling.'Now you wait a minute, mister. This is our shop, and if we –'

'This is a homicide investigation. Will you get your father or shall I?'

She let her mouth stay open while she looked at him. Then she whirled around and went out.

When she came back with a stubby, bald, freckled man who held her protectively behind him, the clock on May's Wilshire said five fifty-three. It took the stubby, bald, freckled man exactly three minutes more to go through the *F's* and make sure that he did no cleaning for anyone named Kenneth Farrar. He seemed pleased about it.

Clive went out again.

He had to cross two intersections to get to the other shop. He reached it just as the woman inside turned the hanging sign around to CLOSED. The door was locked. Clive rapped on it. The woman shook her head. She was a small, alert, and very business-like brunette in neat green pants. She started away through the back of the shop.

Clive swore. He knocked again, furiously. The woman looked angrily back and he flashed his illegal badge.

The woman returned and unlocked the door. 'Well?'

151

'Police business. I want to ask you some questions.'

She let him in, reluctantly. 'John,' she called. 'Oh, John.' A big sandy young man came through from the inside room. She said, 'He's a policeman.'

'What do you want? We haven't done anything.'

'Homicide investigation,' Clive said. 'Do you do cleaning for a man named Kenneth Farrar?'

'Homicide!' said the brunette. Her eyes grew very bright. 'Has he committed a murder?'

'Then he does bring his cleaning here?'

'Oh, yes. He's a steady customer. Lives right up here at the Wilshire Crest –'

'Did he bring in a black coat recently?'

'Seems to me he did. . . .'

Clive watched her. The place was hot, choky with steam and chemicals. He was sweating heavily, and the nervous tic pulled his facial muscles at intervals.

'Why, yes,' the woman said. 'I remember. He showed me some grease spots on it. Said he'd had to change a tire on the road and could I get the stuff out.'

'Has it been cleaned yet?'

She looked inquiringly at the sandy young man. He shook his head.

'We're so far behind on our work it isn't even funny. You can't get help these days, I have to do all my own pressing –'

'Sure, sure! May I see the coat, please.'

The young man shrugged and went into the back room. Clive walked up and down, smoking. He didn't look like a man who wanted to talk. The woman kept quiet. After a while the man came back with a black topcoat.

Clive spread it on the counter. There were two or three streaks of grease on the skirts, outside. They might have come from changing a tire, or doing something else to a wheel. He turned it over and looked at the inside.

There were two distinct places where the cloth was bruised and scraped as though from heavy friction. It had been brushed, but the broken fibers showed plainly. There was sand worked deeply into the fabric, and one big smear of oil.

Clive took his hands away and smiled.

152

The woman drew back against the wall. 'My God. You look . . .'

He started, laughed, and began folding the coat. His fingers touched it as though it were the naked skin of some woman he was very fond of.

'Wrap this,' he said. 'Put it in a safe place and don't touch it again. Someone will be around from Headquarters in the morning to pick it up.'

She moved toward it, still staring at Clive. The pleasant excitement had all gone out of her.

The lobby of the Wilshire Crest Apartments was small, expensive, and empty except for the man behind the desk. He was plump and pink and baldish, wearing a very neat conservative dark suit and steel-rimmed spectacles.

'You're Gibson?'

'That's right, sir.'

Clive handed him a card. 'I'm working on the Hammond murder case. I want to talk to you – in private.'

'Oh, yes. Yes, indeed, Mr. Clive! I spoke to you once before, I believe, over the phone.' The same note of thrilled excitement was in his voice again. Middle-aged suburbia whose chief relaxation was reading murder mysteries. 'Has something new come up?'

'Yeah. Where can we talk?'

'The manager's office, right over there. I'll have to call the boy to take over the desk.' Gibson pushed a plunger on the switchboard.

'Is Kenneth Farrar here now?' Clive said.

'He went out not five minutes ago.'

Clive nodded and went across to the door marked *Office*. He paused a moment, studying the lobby. The desk was to the right of the doorway, the elevator and stairway directly opposite, to the left. The elevator was automatic.

The office was a neat, impersonal little room, containing nothing but a desk and three chairs. Clive walked around it restively until Gibson came in.

'Now, Mr. Clive, what can I do for you?'

'Sit down.'

He sat. Clive went on walking.

153

'You told the police that Farrar came in about a quarter to one on the night Laurel Dane was murdered, and didn't go out again.'

'That's right.'

'How do you know it was Farrar?'

'I – why, I just know it was, that's all.'

'Did he come up to the desk?'

Gibson's pink face was beginning to look frightened. 'Why – no, he . . .'

'Did he speak to you?'

'No. He seemed surly – perhaps a trifle, well, under the weather.'

'Did you see his face clearly?'

'Well, yes. That is, I . . .'

'Did you!'

'I . . . he had his hat pulled down over his right eye. He always wears it that way. But I know it was he!'

Gibson was sitting on the edge of his chair, his plump fists clenched on his knees. Clive came and stood over him. His face was impassive, hard with a hardness that Gibson had read about but never seen. He said slowly, 'The man didn't come near you, he didn't speak to you, you didn't see his face, but you know it was Farrar.'

Gibson ran his tongue twice across his lips. 'But it never occurred to me that it could be anyone else.'

'Exactly.' Clive seemed faintly contemptuous. 'I'll tell you what you saw, Mr. Gibson. You saw a tall man, of Farrar's build, dressed in Farrar's clothes. At that hour in the morning – what time do you go off duty?'

'Two o'clock. I live in the building.'

'All right. At a quarter to one your powers of observation are not very alert. You have no reason to suspect that what you're looking at is other than what it seems. You see a man resembling Farrar, wearing his hat and topcoat. You see him walk across the lobby with his back to you, toward the elevator. His hat is pulled down over his face and he is apparently somewhat drunk. Therefore you do not think it strange that he doesn't speak, and any dissimilarity in carriage you automatically put down to the influence of liquor. Am I correct, Mr. Gibson?'

Gibson ran distracted fingers through his thinning hair. 'I don't know. I'm all confused. When you put it that way, I . . .' He glanced up. 'I just know it was Mr. Farrar!'

Clive looked at him sullenly. 'Mr. Gibson!' He leaned across the corner of the desk. It was as though he were the defense attorney and Gibson a witness on the stand.

'Mr. Gibson, this is a murder case. At least three lives have been taken. Attempts have been made to take others. From my own personal knowledge I can say that my client is innocent, and I have definite, concrete proof of Kenneth Farrar's involvement. Your word is all that stands between one man and the gas chamber.'

He bent closer. His voice had an impersonal ruthlessness. 'I'm only a private detective. In the courtroom you will face expert legal men. Can you go honestly into court, knowing that a man's life depends on you, and give your sworn testimony that the man you saw on the night of the murder was Kenneth Farrar?'

He stopped. Silence closed in, very still, pressing silence. Gibson closed his eyes. There were beads of sweat on his bald forehead. After a while he relaxed, with an air of letting go.

'No,' he said quietly. 'I don't suppose I can. And after talking to you I can see that it would do me very little good if I did.'

He rose, looking at Clive with direct and simple dignity. 'I am still sure in my own mind that the man I saw was Kenneth Farrar.'

Clive gave him a smile of surprising gentleness. 'Murder, Mr. Gibson, is only fun to read about – for most people. If it's any consolation, you've saved an innocent man.'

'I hope so. Is there anything else I can do for you?'

'Can you find me some paper and an envelope?'

'I believe there's some in the desk.' He laid it out on the blotter. Clive wrote hurriedly, sealed the envelope, addressed it to Detective-Lieutenant Jordan Gaines, Homicide, put a stamp on it, and handed it to Gibson.

'I noticed a box just outside. Will you drop this in for me?'

'Of course, but . . .'

'I'm leaving by the back way. In case I was seen coming in here, it's a little less public.'

Gibson went rather white. 'You mean . . .'

'Exactly.' he patted the little man kindly on the shoulder. Gibson stared at him as though he were something strange and not quite human.

'Down the hall to your left,' he said flatly.

CHAPTER EIGHTEEN

IT WAS almost dark, with a scatter of huge stars burning on a deep blue sky. There was a broad paved area at the back of the building, with the garages beyond. To the right of the back steps a short flight led down to a door marked *Janitor*. Subdued light spilled out over the pavement from windows set flush with the ground.

Clive went down and rang the bell.

A stocky little man with a tough, good-natured face opened the door. His speech had a definite tang of Billingsgate.

'What'll it be, sir?'

Clive looked past his shoulder. There was a radio playing popular music. From a half-open door across the living room came the usual sounds and smells of dinner cooking. There was no one within hearing. Clive identified himself.

'Gawd!' said the janitor. 'I read the papers. Guess they've got Hammond right where they want him now.'

'They've still got the wrong man. Do you want to help me prove it?'

Bright, shrewd eyes studied him. 'How?'

'I need a passkey.'

'Here, now! I can't . . .'

'Of course not. But people drop things sometimes. I think I just dropped a bill there on the steps. Maybe you dropped the key.'

The janitor grinned slowly. 'Maybe I did,' he said. 'Now maybe I did, at that.'

Clive turned his back. He heard a metallic rattling and then something rang on the concrete near his foot. He picked it up.

'You should get that hole in your pocket fixed. Good night.' He climbed the steps. On the way his shoe pushed a folded bill down into the light. The man laughed.

'I like it better this way. Thanks, and good hunting, pal.'

Clive waited for a couple coming from the garages to precede him into the apartment house, and went unnoticed up the back stairway to the third floor.

There was no one in the hall. There was only the usual murmur of voices, radios, and people moving around. Clive unlocked Farrar's door and locked it carefully again behind him. He didn't turn on the lights. His pocket torch gave him all he needed.

He worked quickly. The apartment was neat with the sterile neatness of a man who kept nothing, not the smallest scrap of paper, except what might be locked away in a safe-deposit box. The only thing Clive found in any of the desk or table drawers was a medium-caliber revolver.

It was the same with the bureau and the dressing table. Even the pockets of the suits hanging in the closet were stripped clean. Farrar was a businessman, and a good one.

Without much hope, Clive dragged a small suitcase out of a corner of the closet and opened it. The things in it had evidently been thrown there in a hurry. He pulled out a pair of soiled blue pajamas, slippers, and a silk dressing gown. There was nothing else. He went through the pockets of the gown. The first one was empty. The second held a handkerchief with a smear of lipstick on it, and a crumpled penny postcard.

It was a commonplace, unimportant thing. Something pocketed for future attention, and then forgotten. Just a form notice from the gas company that the monthly bill was overdue. It had been mailed two days before the death of Laurel Dane, and was addressed to Mr. William Kennedy, on Lookout Mountain Avenue.

Clive's hands began to tremble.

Moving very quickly, he shoved the card in his pocket, put the bag back in the closet, and went to the telephone in the other room. He called a taxi, giving instructions for it to stop on the side street. When he went down the back stairway to meet it he was smiling. His eyes glittered like agates in the light.

He found the cab, parked in heavy shadow under a line of trees. There were several cars along the curb and more half a block away on Wilshire. Any one of them might have had a watcher in it. Apparently no one followed the taxi, but between the darkness and the dimout a car without lights would have been hard to see. Once on Fairfax there was enough traffic to make it impossible to tell.

Clive chain-smoked all the way up Fairfax to Laurel Canyon, and then up a winding narrow road between the hills, climbing Lookout Mountain past little dim cabins clinging to the canyon walls. He had the itch between his shoulders again, as he had that night in the fog, with Beauvais.

The driver stopped high up toward the crest, setting the brake hard.

'That's it, ahead there. The last house on the road. If I go any farther I won't be able to turn around. Want I should wait?'

'Yeah. Turn off your lights.'

The road behind them was a tunnel of solid black twisting down the mountain. There was no other house closer than three hundred feet, and that was deserted. There were no sidewalks, no light but the pale shine of stars with mist across them. The air was cold, sharp with sage and eucalyptus, and it was quiet – the crisp, brittle quiet of a place where little furry things make all the noise there is.

Clive transferred his automatic from the holster to the front of his waistband, leaving his coat open. He walked up toward the crest.

Presently he made out the shape of a low roof and the heavier darkness of shrubs below it. His shoes grated softly on gravel, and then there were steps, rough wood, and a handrail greasy with dampness.

The front of the house was three stories high, with a garage on the bottom and the living room on top, and something with no windows and a padlocked door in between. The lock was rusted far beyond opening.

The front door was locked, too. Clive followed a flagged path back into a small garden. There was nothing but stillness

between the crouching shadows of the plants. He found a rear
door. It was fastened tight, but it was made of glass. Clive used
his gun barrel to smash the small pane by the lock. It made a
hellish racket. He waited. Nothing moved anywhere. He reached
in and turned the key.

Inside there was pitch blackness and stale warm air. Clive
locked the door and put the key in his pocket. The slats of
the Venetian blind were already pulled shut. There was a roller
shade on the one larg window. It was down. Clive flashed the
tiny beam of his torch.

There was a double bed with a spread of red satin pulled
half off and trailing on the floor with a tangle of bedclothes.
The pillows and the lower sheet were rumpled. There was a
thin layer of dust on them. A woman's filmy white negligee lay
on the floor across a pair of satin mules.

Directly opposite him was a door leading into a long, narrow
hallway. Beside it, the wing mirror catching the torch beam in
a maze of reflections, was a low dressing table. There was a
picture on it: Jane Hammond in a silver frame.

Clive went quietly down the hall.

There was a big window with curtains of striped crash drawn
across it in the left-hand wall. On the right were doors to a small
bath and a midget kitchen, and an open arch to a dining alcove.
At the end were two steps leading down into the living room.

It ran the width of the house. Rustic ceiling, knotty pine
walls, wide windows covered with the striped crash, bookcases,
a few pieces of light furniture, and a couch before a huge stone
fireplace. Clive stood listening. There was no sound but his
own breathing.

The front door had a bolt, but he left it undrawn. There
was a string of Persian camel bells on the wall, the horsehair
tassels brilliant turquoise against the wood. He took them down
carefully, so that they gave off only a faint chiming. He hung
them on the handle of the door and tied them there with his
handkerchief. Then he returned to the bedroom.

Jane Hammond's picture threw bright glints at him from
its silver frame. He went through the dressing table. In the
middle drawer were a comb, a brush, a box of powder, and
a lipstick. They seemed unimportant to him and he left them

159

alone. In the lower right-hand drawer, flung in as though in anger and hanging partly outside, was a transparent nightgown of some silky white stuff. There was no laundry mark on it. The label bore the name of a good, but not exclusive, maker. Clive dropped it back and turned away, unconsciously rubbing his hand across his thigh as though he has touched something not quite clean. He picked up the negligee. There was a cleaner's tag on an inside seam. He laid it on the bed and reached for the mules — 5½ M, from an expensive shoe company. Clive put them with the negligee and swung his light around.

A bureau. Nothing on the top, the drawers half open and empty. A closet, also empty. Nothing more anywhere.

Clive folded the negligee, laid the picture on it, put the satin slippers on the picture, and rolled the whole thing into a neat bundle, tucking it under his arm.

In the bath there was only an impersonal collection of soap and toothbrushes. The kitchen had not been used for some time. He went into the living room, snapped off the torch, and stood listening to the crickets singing outside in the brush.

Using the light again, he found a door in the front corner of the room. There seemed to be only an empty closet beyond, until he saw that part of the left-hand wall had been cut away and there were steps going down, like a ship's ladder. The closet floor creaked as he walked over it.

Below was a big unfinished room, to which belonged the door with the rusted padlock. Rough empty shelves, a couch, a scarred table and chair, and a green-shaded lamp hanging from the ceiling. Probably in the beginning it had been a writer's workroom. Clive leaned over the table.

There was nothing on it now but a film of dust. By shining the light obliquely he could see the faint smudges left by the rubber-padded feet of a typewriter. There was a trace of fresh eraser dust in the cracks. Otherwise the place was stripped clean.

Clive went upstairs again. There was no sound in the living room, no faintest chime from the bells. He returned to the bedroom, turned the key noiselessly, pulled the automatic out of his waistband, and stepped into the garden, moving fast and making no more noise than a cat. It was still empty of anything but shadows.

The air struck cold on his skin, with a smell of sea fog under the bitterness of the damp hills. He walked along the path to the front and halted. The roadway below made a blacker streak against the rough ground. He could make out the shrubbery around the steps, and off to the left the lighter blob of the yellow taxi. The driver was smoking. The tiny red coal of his cigarette glowed and paled behind the windshield like a lantern seen at a great distance down a railroad track. The crickets chirped drowsily.

Clive stepped out into the starlight.

The stairway was narrow, long, railed in, and naked. His body made a moving patch of shadow. The light touch of his feet on the treads sounded loud, like a man walking in a church. He reached the bottom, covered with cold sweat.

He crossed the gravel path to the road. The little red glow of the hacker's cigarette dimmed and brightened, dimmed and brightened. Clive gave himself a crooked, self-derisive grin. He let his gun hand drop to his side and walked on down the hill.

The driver flipped his butt away, an arc of fire against the night. The motor snarled, coughed, and settled to an even purring. Clive quickened his pace. The lights blazed on. Bright lights, the big beam, a blinding white glare.

Clive jerked up a startled hand to shield his eyes, and before it could get there the motor roared into gear and the lights were rushing at him.

He yelled. Sheer muscular reflex sent him leaping for the ditch. A tremendous weight struck him glancingly on the hip. He went down in a spurt of stinging gravel and a cloud of exhaust fumes, rolling over on brush and rocks and hard earth.

For a moment everything went away. Then, down at the end of a long spinning funnel of blackness, he saw the taxi again. It rushed backward obliquely down the hill, shining its red tail lights, carrying the white beam of its lamps behind it like a bride's train. It was coming for him, in the shallow ditch.

Clive was still gripping the automatic. He raised it and fired twice through the rear window, so rapidly that the slam of the shots blended into one echoing crack against the sleeping hills. Then he threw himself out of the way.

The taxi swerved and crashed the ditch beside him, so close that the impact jarred him clear to the heart. The motor died. The headlamps blinked and then went on shining, a hard-edged path across the hillside. The crickets had stopped singing.

The door by the driver's seat swung open.

A man came out, slowly, the upper half of him first, sliding face down along the edge of the seat, his knees still under the wheel. His hands slipped over the running board, tightened, and gripped it. There was blood on them. It looked black in the reflected light. The hacker's peaked cap fell off his head. He had fair hair, but the whole left side of his face was black – black, and glistening.

Presently he fell the rest of the way, into the gravel on the edge of the road, and lay still. He was not dead. He breathed, an agonized sound.

Clive stood up. He was very slow about it, but reasonably steady. He took the flashlight out of his pocket and turned the beam full in the man's face.

He must have been twisted around, watching over his shoulder through the rear window, steering with one hand. One of Clive's bullets had taken most of his cheek away.

He was still recognizable as Kenneth Farrar.

Clive flashed the torch into the cab. The hacker lay in the luggage space, his head propped up in the corner under the dash, his knees doubled onto his chest. He didn't mind the discomfort. He didn't mind Clive's light in his eyes. He had bled slightly from the nose and ears.

Clive put the flashlight away. He got a cigarette and lighted it with his left hand, watching Farrar in the reflection of the headlamps.

Farrar began to pull his hands and feet in under him. It took him a long time. He lifted himself up onto the running board finally, leaning back against the seat. He made a vague gesture toward his face, but did not finish it. He seemed not to want to know what had happened there.

Clive said, 'You almost had me.'

Farrar's eyes had a curious bleached pallor, as though the color was running out of them with the blood. They were not so different from the eyes of the dead man behind him. He tried to speak. He didn't go on with it.

Clive said, 'You saw me going into your apartment house.'

Farrar nodded. A lock of blond hair had fallen over his forehead. A handsome, devil-with-the-ladies lock.

'You waited for me. You knew you'd been seen the night you loosened the wheel on my car. You knew I'd know who it was even if I couldn't prove it to the police. You felt me walking up on your heels, Farrar. So you waited. You followed me. And I walked into it. I don't really deserve to be alive.' He paused. 'Too bad you had to kill the hacker. It wasn't his fight.'

He dropped the cigarette and stepped on it. Farrar watched him. There was a cold understanding in his eyes. He tried to speak again.

'I'll tell you,' Clive went on. 'You didn't pay your gas bill. You shoved the card in the pocket of your dressing gown, and then Laurel was killed and you forgot it. Such an unimportant little thing. Bad luck. But you've played in bad luck right along, haven't you? You were seen when the keysmith died. You were seen with Sugar March. No face. Just a tall black shadow. But even a shadow can be traced. I found your coat, Farrar. It hadn't been cleaned yet. The police will have it tomorrow.'

Farrar moved his hands up to his belly. They were half closed and lax, the wrists pressing in. His eyelids had drawn narrow. Clive gestured toward the house.

'She didn't take her things away. She's been too busy.'

Farrar leaned forward. His voice came out, but there was no shape to it. Clive nodded slowly, and smiled. Farrar began to laugh. He laughed until he choked on the blood running down his throat. After that it was still again.

Clive put another cigarette between his lips and lighted it, left-handed. In the quick flame his eyes were steady, dark, without emotion. Farrar's hands crept higher. Clive took the cigarette in his left hand and held it out, butt foremost.

'Smoke?'

Farrar nodded. He raised his right hand and wiped the back of it across the side of his mouth that was still there. Clive leaned over him and placed the cigarette carefully in the corner of his lips.

Farrar's hand dropped down, fast, inside his coat.

Clive let him get the automatic in his palm, clear of the holster, clear of his coat. Then he shot Farrar once through the center of the forehead.

He stepped back.

The body fell slowly forward and lay quietly in the dust. Clive's eyes widened, suddenly hot, with the reddish blaze that brown eyes get at times. Presently he put his gun away and went back to the ditch.

He found the filmy robe and the slippers and the picture where he had scattered them in his fall and wrapped them together again. Walking diagonally up the road to where it ended, he selected a place where rainwater had channeled the hillside and hid the bundle under a pile of dead brush and debris. Then he returned to the house.

The crickets were singing again. Down the road there were two men who didn't hear them. The crickets didn't care. The hills didn't care. Nothing, here, would ever care.

CHAPTER NINETEEN

THE CAMEL bells were back on the wall. The front door stood open to the night, throwing a hard electric glare across the damp shrubs outside. Men with heavy boots tramped on the wooden stairs. Down the road there were lights and voices and men moving around, the white explosions of flash bulbs, a jam of official cars, and the morgue ambulance. There was a cordon across the road, and beyond it a surprising number of people who had followed the sirens up from the main road.

In the living room Edmond Clive sat in the one big chair, smoking. He had his hat pushed back and one leg hung comfortably over the chair arm. Lieutenant Gaines leaned on the edge of a table, looking sullen, suspicious, and annoyed.

'All right,' he said, 'it all checks, and I suppose it's a clear case of self-defense.'

Clive smiled with innocent pleasure.

Gaines sighed. 'You goddam son of a bitch. Okay. Go ahead and draw me a diagram.'

'Sure thing, sonny.' Clive's attitude was kindly. 'There has been from the beginning a tall dark shadow mixed up in everything connected with Laurel's murder. He was around the night the keysmith was killed. He was with Sugar March before she died. There was a distinct odor of him that time at the beach when Beauvais and his pal took me to the wall. Then he had a stroke of bad luck. Up to there he was just a shadow. But he tinkered with my car, and somebody saw him. They put a face on him for me. Farrar's face.'

'You've got witnesses, of course.'

'I'll give you the list tomorrow. I checked the cleaning shops in Farrar's neighborhood and found a coat he had brought in. You can get it in the morning. There's grease on the outside that will check with the grease on the front wheel of my car. On the inside, you'll find something much more interesting.' He paused, glancing up at Gaines. 'I'm afraid you'll have to let Hammond go.'

'For Farrar? He had an alibi.'

'Yeah. *Had* an alibi. Check with Gibson.'

Gaines settled his big body on the table edge. 'All right, Clive,' he said. 'This will have to be good.'

'It's good enough.' Clive leaned back in the chair. He looked drawn and tired, and there was no mockery in his voice now. 'Farrar dropped into the Skyway Club one night and heard Laurel sing. He fell for her, fell hard. He tried his best to make her. But Laurel couldn't see him, and Farrar didn't like that. He was used to getting any dame he wanted. He kept on trying, looking sillier and getting madder. Probably Laurel gave him the rough side of her tongue – she had one. So Farrar decided he was going to break her, or else.

'He paraded as a private dick, and he was a good one, but it was only a professional means to an end. His chief income was from blackmail. I knew it. You knew it. We all did. He was just too damned smart to give us anything to prove it with. He guessed, the same way I did, that Laurel had a past and that she was afraid of someone. He decided to find out about

165

it and use the knowledge to club Laurel into doing what he wanted her to.

'I was out of town all that time, but he must have known he'd have to tangle with me. He was willing to. He'd gone too far to back out without making a fool of himself, and he was no canary. He figured himself for a very hard boy, and he was. Besides, we'd been drifting toward a showdown for a long time.

'He got Laurel's apartment key out of her dressing room, had it duplicated, and then searched her place. He found the same thing Big Fella found – the marriage license and the picture of her and Dion Beauvais. He was all set to put the screws on. Then I got back in town.

'Laurel was scared, not of Farrar, but of Beauvais. She knew her apartment had been searched. Naturally, she connected it with her husband. She wanted my help. Mick Hammond was rung in. Things began to look more complicated. Perhaps Farrar began to get a little nervous.

'He and I boxed our opening round that night at the Skyway Club. After that I have no way of knowing exactly what went on in Farrar's mind, except that he was sore as hell at me and annoyed because his plans had got bitched up. Korsky checked him through several bars – he was dosing his grouch with alcohol, and that never helps much. Maybe he knew then that he was going to kill Laurel. Maybe it had reached the point where he had to have her or kill her. Maybe he wasn't sure what he was going to do. But he was a cautious bastard. He was already closely identified with Laurel, and he had, in an unguarded moment – Farrar was human, he got tight at times, and he had an ugly temper – shot off his face to Sugar March. Probably all he said was that Laurel was too damn snotty and needed taking down, but still it was unfortunate. Whatever the reason was, he fixed himself an alibi, just in case. In case, maybe, that he ran into me and had to do something permanent about it.

'He got some guy, probably a small-time mugg who had done things for him before and could be made to keep his mouth shut, to put on his, Farrar's, hat and coat and go home to the Wilshire Crest. He figured that at one A.M. the clerk would accept any man of his build, wearing his clothes, and appearing slightly drunk, as Kenneth Farrar, if he didn't speak to him or see his face clearly. Then Farrar went up to Laurel's apartment.

'It was dark and quiet. He decided Laurel was alone and tried to get in with his key, but the door was bolted. I got knocked out about then, but Farrar must have waked Laurel by knocking. He forced her to let him in, threatening her with what he knew. She wasn't really frightened. She must have wondered where I was, but she knew I wouldn't leave her. She thought I'd be right back.

'Farrar may not have realized right away that Mick was in the bedroom. He put the squeeze on Laurel. I suppose that first she was angry, and then she began to get scared. I didn't come back, and I had her gun . . .'

Clive's gaunt face tightened. There was a thin film of sweat on his skin.

'She tried to wake Mick, and Farrar hit her with the black-thorn stick, lying so handy on the table. Maybe he didn't mean to kill her. Maybe he just wanted to shut her up. Maybe he was so damned mad at her he didn't care. Anyway, he hit her too hard. It's easy to do, at the base of the skull. She died, and he was there with a murder on his hands.

'But it was a pretty good murder. He'd used Mick's cane. The act didn't look premeditated and he had an alibi. There was nothing to connect him with it except the key he'd had made, and a tottery old guy like the keysmith would be easy to get rid of. He wiped off the stick and the doorknob and went away, leaving Mick framed for the kill.

'It was no trick to push the old man downstairs. Farrar was clean. I might have suspicions, but he could handle me. He was sitting pretty. And then the news broke about the guy in the kitchen.

'That bitched him, right there. He must have sweat blood. He wasn't in any danger from Big Fella, but he couldn't know that. He had to find out who the man was and get rid of him, and that wasn't going to be easy. However, the guy didn't spill over to the police, and that meant to Farrar that he was holding out for blackmail. But nobody approached Farrar. Then it occurred to him that I was the logical one for the mystery man to make a deal with. With my personal involvement I'd be willing to pay him highly, offer him the most protection, and have no motive to bump him off.

'So Farrar started tagging me around. He must have seen Beauvais going into my place. He fixed up your prowl car so it wouldn't interfere, fixed up a couple more so it wouldn't look deliberate – Farrar had a well-developed accident technique – and followed us down to the beach. He knew, of course, that Beauvais was clean, so he was pretty sure we were leading him to the man in the kitchen.

'We did. I'll give Farrar credit for being able to tail us in that fog. The guy was a genius at it. He followed me up to the house where I found out where Big Fella was living, and then another complication came up. He was close, a lot closer than Beauvais, and he heard me tell the young guy to call the cops. He didn't want cops. He didn't want another murder, either – one there couldn't be any reason for. He didn't, above all, want the guy just knocked on the head, which would have made it obvious that somebody besides Beauvais and me was in on the deal. He didn't, of course, have any idea how the business was going to turn out. So he arranged another accident. . . . I wrote you a note about it, in case I got the worst of this game.'

'You gave yourself plenty of time to play it alone.'

'It was black as hell down there. His coat was dark. He laid it down at the bottom of the steps, waited till the young fellow came out, and then pulled it out from under him. He took a nasty fall, and Farrar gave him one under the ear just to make sure – an extra bump he might have got hitting a step or something. You'll find sand, oil, and friction burns on the inside of Farrar's coat. Then he went down to Big Fella's cabin, crawled up close in the fog, and watched the fun.

'Everything worked out swell, for him. Big Fella was playing his own game. All Farrar had to do was ride my car down over Big Fella's neck. Another accident, sweet, clean, and simple. He left Beauvais alive to nail the gas-box shut on Hammond. He didn't know whether I was still kicking or not, but he didn't think it mattered. He supposed even I would be convinced.'

Gaines said, 'What about the horn you heard blowing?'

'As you said.' Clive shrugged. 'Some local wolf having trouble with his girl. Probably that's another reason why Farrar didn't stop to bother with me. He was afraid somebody might come. He was sorry afterwards. I wasn't convinced. And with all the other suspects eliminated, that left Kenneth Farrar sticking out like a beacon in a blackout. His guilty conscience began to work on him. Just the police wouldn't have bothered him so much, because police have to have proof. He knew I didn't have to. He tinkered my car. Somebody saw him, and I didn't get killed. He knew he'd left traces behind. You can't help leaving them. They didn't add up to anything for the cops, but he knew they would to me. He had to get me before I got him, and before I could convince anyone else that he was guilty.

'He had a stroke of luck. He saw me going into his place. He waited for me, followed me up here, and got all set. He wanted me dead by accident. It might look just a little queer if I was murdered. Also, bullets can be traced and there was no ideal place to hit me over the head from behind. Besides, he couldn't afford to have signs of violence around this house – it could be traced to him through the rental agent, who could identify him, and Kennedy is an alias he's used before. That's one reason he had to kill the cabby too, poor bastard.

'He was going to run me down and then put me inside and ride the cab onto some other road and off into a gully. If it didn't catch fire by itself he could always throw a match in the gas tank. Regrettable accident. Poor Eddie, the son of a bitch. I hope he's in hell. You and Farrar could have wept a little on each other's shoulders. And from there on out he was as clean as a whistle. Only it didn't work, quite.'

'Too bad.'

'Yeah.'

Gaines said morosely, 'Why did you think this house might have something to do with Laurel Dane's murder?'

'I didn't. I was just fishing for anything I could get. The coat and the broken alibi were good, but maybe not quite good enough for a jury. The house turned out to be just another love nest, but Farrar convicted himself.'

Gaines fingered the transparent nightgown on the table. 'He must of had some fun up here, at that. What about the March dame?'

'Maybe he was planning to kill her, maybe not. Anyway, she did it for him.'

'Uh-huh. And the nasty letters. They were just a side issue?'

'Yes. Mrs. Hammond can do something more about them or not, as she pleases.'

'I don't suppose Farrar was mixed up with those letters.'

'There doesn't seem to be any evidence one way or the other.'

Gaines shifted his weight slowly onto his feet. 'We'll check all this. Up, down, and backward.'

'Go ahead, kiddie. It's all yours.'

'All right,' Gaines said sourly. 'I guess you hold enough aces to take my hand.'

Clive nodded pleasantly.

Gaines said three words with careful distinctness and turned on his heel. Clive laughed.

'Give my love to Korsky.'

Gaines went out. Clive rose and telephoned the Hammond house. Mulligan answered.

'Everything all right there?'

'Yes, sir. The ladies are with Mr. Jones in the library. Shall I . . . ?'

'No. Just tell them to stay put. I'm coming right over. And Mulligan – you can tell Mrs. Hammond that Mick will be home in the morning.'

Outside there were sounds of breaking up and going away. A plain-clothes man waited impatiently to lock the house. Clive called a taxi, and went out.

The noise, the lights, the cars, and the people drained back down the black funnel of the road. For a few moments he was alone. He threw his head back and struck his fist against the side of the house and laughed.

He got the filmy white bundle out of the brush and walked down to meet the taxi.

CHAPTER TWENTY

JANE HAMMOND said softly, 'So that's how it was.'

She sat in one of the rose-colored library chairs, looking long and slim and lovely in blue. She had a radiance about her that did not come from the lamplight.

Clive nodded. 'That's how it was.'

Jonathan Ladd Jones, hunched up sullenly by the fireplace, turned to glare at him. 'I should have been with you. I told you that. What if you'd been killed?'

'You'd have been out of a job and a quart of free Scotch a day.' Clive stood up, glancing over at Vivien. She was curled in a corner with her feet under her, her face in shadow. She watched him with silent intentness.

Jane said, 'Why were you afraid for us, Ed? You should have had Johnny with you.'

'I had a reason at the time.' He grinned. 'It turned out not to be a very good one. Even a genius like me can make mistakes.'

She rose. 'And Mick's all right. Everything's all right. Oh, Ed . . . God bless you, Ed.' She came into his arms.

He kissed her, drawing her close, very gently. It was a long time before he took his mouth from hers. She drew back a little and looked up into his eyes.

'Ed,' she said softly.

She put her hand up against his cheek. He took it in his own and said with rough good humor, 'Beat it upstairs and cry.'

'Yes. Yes, I can do that now, can't I?'

She smiled at him through a bright mist and went out. Vivien had not moved. Clive went over and put his hand on Johnny's small hard shoulder.

'Time to go home.'

Johnny got up. He opened his mouth, remembered Vivien, closed it again, and breathed harshly through his nose. Clive chuckled.

'You can beat me up tomorrow. I'll sit still for it.' His eyes had no laughter in them.

'Johnny stopped glaring. He frowned. Clive said, 'I'll be in the office sometime after noon.'

Johnny's mouth moved uncertainly. He looked at Vivien and then back at Clive. He said, 'Good night, Ed,' and went out.

Clive stood with his back to Vivien, smoking quietly, until he heard the outer door close and the faint click of Mulligan's heels going back into the service regions. Vivien neither stirred nor spoke. The soft, regular sound of her breathing was the only sound in the room.

Clive said, 'I have something for you, Vivien.'

Her breathing stopped. Not as though she were frightened, or even surprised, but as though she wanted to be sure she heard what he said next.

'I left it down by the pool when I came in.'

Her legs made a rustling against the chair as she unbent them. 'I'll get my coat.' She went past him and up the stairs.

Clive crushed out his cigarette and walked down the hall to the French doors. He stood there, waiting. His face began to twitch, and he put up his hand to stop it.

Presently Vivien came down, wearing the same short camel's-hair coat she had worn that afternoon at the hospital. Clive held the door for her.

They crossed the terrace in a heavy fragrance of stock and roses under salty dew, and then followed the flagstones beside the black look of the hedge. The bitterness of evergreen replaced the cloying flowers. A dim moon hung behind the mist, striking a glint of tarnished silver from the pool. There was no wind, and it was cold in the hollow.

They walked over slippery tile at the water's edge and went into the pavilion beside the dressing house. It was no more than a slanted roof upheld by slender pillars. There were big rough chairs cushioned in canvas and wrought-iron tables supplied with smoking things and magazines. Clive found the small white bundle and spread its contents on a long chair.

'I thought you might want these back.'

She looked at them, her hands thrust deep in her pockets. 'How do you know they're mine?'

172

'With that photograph, it had to be either you or Jane. The negligee is too short for Jane, the slippers are too small. That leaves you. Besides, the bedspread was your color, not hers.' He touched the silver frame. 'A psychologist would be interested in that. Love and hate are so close together, aren't they? It was almost like having Jane there in person to throw your sins at. Homeopathic torture – a nice primitive touch. You're a masochist, Vivien.'

She shrugged, turning away. 'I didn't suppose anyone would find them. I didn't want them any more.'

'No. No, you wouldn't, would you?'

'Don't be cryptic. I hate people being cryptic.'

'All right, I'm answering both statements. You wouldn't suppose anyone would find them because – count me out, I wasn't supposed to live – because no one had any reason to look for the house, or even to think there was one. And as far as you both knew, there was no way to trace it even if anyone did. Farrar just slipped up a little on that postcard. And can you blame him?'

She made a small harsh sound that might have meant anything.

Clive went on, 'And we both know why you wouldn't want the things any more.'

She glanced up at him from under the corners of her lids.

Clive said, with a peculiarly brutal softness, 'It hit you right where you live, didn't it, when he walked out on you for Laurel Dane?'

She studied him silently for a long moment, and then laughed. 'You bully,' she said. 'You cheap little bully.' She sat down, leaning back against the canvas cushions. The moon touched the high surfaces of her face with a chill whiteness. Only her mouth was dark, moist and glistening.

Clive said, 'You don't love me as much as you did this afternoon.'

'No. No, I don't.'

'What changed your mind?'

'I think it was the way you kissed me. Very kindly, as you'd pat a dog on the head, not even your dog that you were fond of, but just any dog. Ed Clive, handing out a favor. God on a mountaintop, being kind to a miserable sinner.'

173

'You must have been sorry then,' Clive said mildly, 'that you saved my life down there at the beach.'

Her lids opened wide. The eyes behind them were cold, shrewd, aware. A little surprised, but even then not afraid. She leaned forward to speak.

'Shut up.' Clive held his voice low, but it was harsh with violent anger. 'God damn you, shut up! I'm talking now. Me, Ed Clive, the guy you and Farrar thought you could use for a football and get away with it.' He bent over her. 'I threw Farrar to the wolves. I wanted it that way. I was going to frame it that way, but I got the breaks and I didn't have to frame it, much. All right. I gave Gaines a story, a good story. It's got holes in it and he's going to worry about them, but it's close enough to the truth so he'll have to take it and like it, because there isn't any evidence to show anything else. And he doesn't have to worry about taking it to court. Farrar isn't going to stand trial. I took care of that. But I held out a little on Gaines. A couple of small items that make a story with no holes in it at all.'

She was unmoved. 'Items like those?' she said, and nodded her head at the long chair. 'So I was living with him. He wasn't the first man, nor the last. So what?'

'So you have guts, Vivien, a damn sight more than I gave you credit for.'

She smiled. 'You're enjoying yourself.'

'Yes.'

'Men never grow up. They're always just little boys, puffing out their chests and showing their muscles.'

'But little girls do, don't they? They go along for years, stamping their feet, pulling their sisters' hair, smashing their dolls, and screaming. And then all of a sudden they find the thing they've always wanted, and they're grown up. They're people, finished, mature, with the door shut forever on the nursery.'

She lay relaxed against the cushions, not even her eyelids moving. Clive laughed. He got cigarettes from a box, lighted one, and passed it to Vivien with an oddly intimate courtesy. Then he lighted one for himself, sitting on the edge of the table, facing her.

'Farrar cleaned up very nicely after the letter-writing. Gaines looked down into the workroom, but he didn't even bother to go

174

in. Your fingerprints are all over the place, of course, but why should Gaines care? One trollop more or less . . . And how could he ever identify them, anyhow? The negligee and slippers might have tempted him . . . and besides, I had another use for them.'

Her mouth twisted, blowing a contemptuous plume of smoke.

'I'm not trying to trap you, Viv. Nothing as childish as that. I know. Bill Kennedy had to ask people about Mick. Some of the people remembered it.'

She stopped smoking, stopped breathing, and then she shrugged.

'All right. I hired Kenneth Farrar to look up Mick's past for me. I loved Mick. I told you that. When he married Jane I thought I couldn't stand it.' She laughed. 'The child, screaming for a toy somebody had stolen. I'd met Ken at some party or other and I thought he'd be a good man for the job. I was rotten enough to know that he was rotten, too.'

Clive nodded. 'You figured that one of two things would happen. Either Mick would kill himself, or Jane would divorce him. This was after the accident, of course, when you knew the marriage would never break up by itself. It was a beautiful way to get revenge, and you weren't taking too much of a chance. Only then you fell in love with Farrar.'

Vivien gestured impatiently. 'All right, you're a brilliant detective. I left a lot of neon signs up there in the cabin and you read them. Once again, so what?'

'So this. Farrar wanted your money, and he was willing to take you too if he had to, to get it. Everything worked out swell until Mick got the idea of going to the Skyway Club after me. Farrar followed Mick, thinking he was on the trail of an especially fresh and nasty story, and incidentally met Laurel. Pretty soon the incident got to be the whole thing, and that left you sitting up on a dark mountain all by yourself. You didn't like that, did you?'

'Would anyone? Did you, when that black-haired bitch took somebody else to bed with her?'

He leaned over and slapped her across the mouth, not hard. Curiously, not hard at all. Her eyes blazed at him.

'God damn you!' Then she laughed, deep in her strong throat. 'You sentimentalist! Because she's dead, she did no wrong and I'm not fit to speak of her. Oh, Ed!'

175

Clive said nothing.

'All right!' She sat forward on the chair. 'Is this any of your business, any of it? You've done your bragging. Now what more do you want?'

'All right, Viv. We'll finish it. Why do you think I held out on Gaines?'

'Not for my sake!'

'No. For Jane's. For Mick's. And for mine.'

'For yours?'

'Yes. I could have taken you and Farrar into court together. But courts are uncertain. Juries are uncertain. Do you know that out of ten thousand murderers every year, only two per cent ever reach the death chamber?'

She straightened up slowly, in withdrawal. Her hands slid back into the deep pockets of her coat.

Clive said, 'That's what Farrar was thinking when he killed the keysmith. It would be awfully hard to pin that murder on him. But if the letter business ever broke in court, he was a dead pigeon. He couldn't have beaten that blackmail rap, nor the other ones that would have followed right on its heels.'

Vivien said carefully, 'I thought Ken killed the old man to cover Laurel's murder.'

'He did.'

'Then you're not talking sense.'

He smiled at her, a strange, intimate smile. His eyes were almost warm.

After a while Vivien whispered, 'You can't scare me, Ed Clive. You can't do it.'

'That's what makes this such a good game. Answer this one, Vivien. What motive did Farrar have to kill Laurel?'

She moved abruptly as though to rise. Clive put his hand out, and she relaxed, with sullen pettishness.

'You told us yourself.'

'It wasn't a very good motive, though, was it? That's the biggest hole Gaines is going to see – not that it'll help him any. With the setup what it was, Farrar would have had a lot more reason to kill me. He might have got around to Laurel later, if she proved stubborn, but not then. Not that night, right off the bat, with that keysmith to identify him and everybody in the

Skyway Club ready to tell the world that he was crazy about her. He was a cold-blooded bastard, Farrar was. He'd have done a better job than that. He wouldn't have left anything to chance, like finding Mick in her apartment. It would have been perfectly planned, with every angle covered in advance. And particularly, and especially, there wouldn't have been Sugar March.'

'What do you mean?'

'Farrar wasn't the type to run off at the mouth, especially to a dame like Sugar. And if he had, all the more reason not to kill Laurel *before* Sugar was taken care of. Loose ends, Viv. Too many of them. Farrar was a tidy person. That's why nobody could ever get anything on him.'

'Then why did he frame that alibi? You're not being –'

'He didn't frame any alibi. Gambler's luck, Viv. I got it, and he didn't.'

Her mouth opened, and then closed again.

Clive said, 'He went home sulking and a little drunk, and he didn't speak or show his face. Farrar wasn't near Laurel that night, after he left the Skyway Club.' He inhaled deeply and let the smoke idle out with his words. 'You want to take it from there, Viv?'

She said, in a peculiarly calm voice, 'You're doing all right. Go on.'

'You're grown up now, but a few days ago you were still a violent, emotional, unbalanced sort of person. You loved Mick enough to want to kill him when he married Jane. You admit the letters.'

She nodded slowly, 'Yes.'

'You admit you fell in love with Farrar, lived with him, and took it pretty hard when he walked out on you, emotionally at least, for Laurel.'

She nodded again.

'You fought Farrar about her, I imagine. You must have suffered. Laurel didn't have anything to offer but herself, and still Farrar preferred her to you and your money. You brooded about it, and probably drank too much, and finally you went down to the Skyway Club to see what you could do about it. But Laurel wasn't there. There was only the hat-check girl. And you blew off.

177

'The landlady heard something of what Sugar and Farrar were saying when he took her home that night. Sugar didn't have anything on Farrar. She had it on me, and what she had was you. Farrar was checking up on her to see whether she remembered and what she was going to do about it. She was going to use it to get me. Only you got her first.'

Vivien said, 'She died by accident. She tripped off the curb.'

'Sure. You tripped her. You were right behind her in the crowd, but you're short and Johnny's short, and he didn't see you. I imagine you weren't wearing that bright red coat. You didn't want Sugar's death to look like murder, of course. Farrar didn't want to risk it, and besides, you wanted the fun of it. I remember how you came home that afternoon and went swimming, like somebody high on dope and dreaming.'

She shivered, a shallow twitching of the skin.

Clive leaned forward and said softly, 'You found something, didn't you, when you killed Laurel Dane? The ultimate sensual thrill, the closest thing to being God. You found your strength, Vivien.'

She stared at him with wide pale eyes. And she smiled. After a long time she said, 'You can't prove any of this.'

'Maybe not. But let's see if I'm right. You stole the key to Laurel's apartment from Farrar. You went up there that night, and woke her, and she let you in – and you made a scene. She started to get Mick, and then you were scared because you didn't want it to come out about the letters. Or maybe you'd have killed her anyway. You picked up the blackthorn stick on the table and hit her with it, and she fell down, and you knew she was dead. And a whole new world opened up for you.

'But you'd put Farrar in a spot. He must have been furious with you. He had to kill the old man to cover himself, and Sugar had to be killed to cover you. And it would have been all right, with Mick taking the fall, only for the man in the kitchen. The man who stood out there in the darkness and watched you kill. And from there on the game got harder and harder, and the more things you and Farrar did to cover up, the more things there were to do.

'But you had fun, didn't you, Vivien? More fun than you ever had with hundred-mile clubs or men. You were discovering your hidden talent. Resourcefulness, turning any little spur-of-the-moment thing to your own advantage. Excitement, playing a secret game and playing it well. And above all – there was murder.'

She was leaning forward now, and she was still smiling.

'You were going through a transition, an emotional coming-of-age. All your life you'd been tortured by a sense of weakness, a lack in yourself, a hatred of the strong and the beautiful and the good because they had something you couldn't find in yourself. Now you stood beside them, feeling the warmth of their flesh, hearing them breathe, and you thought, *I can stop that. With my hands and my brain and the power in me I can stop all that, forever.*'

He tilted her chin, gently, holding her face in the moonlight, and brought his lips close to hers. 'There was only one thing wrong. You fell in love with me.'

He kissed her.

She gave herself. Then she thrust him away and sprang up, trembling. He sat back on the table edge and laughed.

'Jane told you I was still bent on saving Mick. You told Farrar to jimmy my car, but this afternoon you had to come and see me, just the same. I remember so well what you said, Viv. "You've broken everything to pieces. Anybody else wouldn't have mattered, but it had to be you."'

She cursed him, whispering.

'And then I said you could be strong, and you said, "Maybe." And you said you'd found something better than hate.'

He rose suddenly and took her by the shoulders and bent her back, looking into her eyes. 'Does it still frighten you, Vivien – the thing in me that you once said could kill you?'

For a long still moment they stood, and then she said quietly, 'Nothing will ever frighten me again.'

'Because I kissed you this afternoon, and you knew that the world I stand for was gone forever. You crossed over into your own place, and you'll never look back.'

'No.' She moved from under his hands. 'I'll never look back.'

He bowed to her slightly and turned and sat down on the end of the long chair. She laughed.

'I've admitted it, haven't I? All right, Ed. But we made a good run of it, didn't we?'

'Yes. A good run.'

'I did most of the planning. Ken was too methodical, as you said. I thought you must know something when you sent Johnny over, but I couldn't be sure.'

'The letters, plus the timing of the job on my car, plus the emotion pattern of the crimes that didn't fit Farrar's type, added up to either you or Jane. Partners in crime are always having trouble – I didn't know what minute one or the other of you might decide to call it off, permanently. And I wanted both you and Jane pegged down tight so I wouldn't have to watch anybody but Farrar. I think,' he added, 'that it was the way that horn blew down at the beach that first made me think of you.'

'I was quite close, hidden in the fog. I watched them beat you. I loved you very much.'

'The aphrodisiac of pain.'

'I begged Ken to help you. He wouldn't, and I began to blow the horn. It was all I could think of to do.'

'And then you rode my car down over Big Fella.'

She nodded. 'It was the other man who screamed. I thought for a moment he'd seen me. Then I realized the lights were in his eyes. He tried to get up, and then he fainted.'

She leaned back against a white pillar, her hands deep in her pockets. 'All right, I've confessed. But you can't do anything about it now. I'll deny it. Ken's dead, and without him you can't prove any of this.'

'Do you know why I did that?'

'I think so. Partly you wanted to get Ken yourself, but mostly you were thinking of Mick and Jane. You're a sentimentalist, Ed, for all that hard-bitten front you put on. You figure they've suffered enough, and for their sakes you'll cover me. You knew what a nasty scandalous mess all this would make in court. You knew how Jane would feel about it. You knew how it would go on and on, trials and appeals and newspaper stories. Oh, I've thought a good deal about what would happen if I got caught. With a good lawyer, a really good one, and a psychiatrist, I hardly think I'd get the death sentence. Women usually get the balance of sympathy. The first crime was unpremeditated, more or less – they couldn't have proved more than second-degree murder. And I could so easily have blamed the rest on Ken. Sugar March and the big man nobody could ever have proved one way or the other. I might even have wangled myself clear of prison entirely, with a stretch in a sanitarium to correct my tragic psychosis. It's happened before, in crimes of passion. I've made a study.'

'So you think you're pretty safe.'

'I think so. Jane's better off not to have a sister in prison or a mental home. She's stood a lot. I suppose there's a limit.'

'And for the future. You know what happens to a dog when he takes to killing sheep.' Clive got up. 'Do you think you're safe to run?'

Her lips gave a sensual little movement. 'I don't know. Perhaps I won't ever have the need or the desire again. But – I don't know.'

She glanced up at him sideways, under her lashes. 'But you don't have to worry about that, do you? It's all out of your hands, now.' She laughed. 'Poor Eddie! Defeat in a good cause, but still defeat. It doesn't taste nice, does it?'

He turned away sullenly.

'Never mind, Ed. Think of Mick and Jane, lying safe and happy in their little nest. I don't hate them any more. I don't have to. Think of them, Eddie, and you'll feel better. You saved them, singlehanded, all by yourself.'

She walked out into the moonlight, onto the bright moist tile. Clive followed, not speaking. The pool lay flat and still, looking at the sky.

She stopped and turned. 'Ed.'

'Yes?'

She put a hand on his sleeve, blocking his way with her body. A curious softness had come into her face, something of the trembling childish look she had lost.

'Ed, I ... Oh, nothing makes sense, you think you have the pattern and you'll never lose it, and then all of a sudden something won't fit. ...'

He pushed against her, and she gave back a step or two, toward the corner of the pool.

'Ed, please.'

He stopped.

'I don't know why, Ed . . . People don't go on all the time being detectives and murderers. Sometimes they have to stop and be just men and women. Ed, you kissed me this afternoon, and you kissed me just a moment ago. Perhaps I can't explain, but you mean something to me, something I saw when I was a child, perhaps, and could never find. I didn't like either of those kisses, to be all of you I ever had to remember. I mean the inside you, the you I loved – the you I think I'll always love, in some corner of my heart.'

He said slowly, 'I'll be God damned.' He tried to get past, pressing her back on the tile.

'Ed, please . . . just for a minute let's not be Ed Clive and Vivien Alcott, hating each other.' Her hands, her body clung against him, warm and pleading. 'Kiss me just once more, for what I might have been. For what I wanted to be, before it was too late.'

He said somberly, 'I thought you weren't going to look back.'

'This isn't back. This isn't anywhere. It's just now, a little piece of time that doesn't fit, and that I want to keep forever. Kiss me just once – the me that might have had a right to you . . .'

Her hands fell away from him. Her eyelids drooped, leaving an unseeing, dreamy darkness. Clive's face twitched sharply. He put his arms around her. Her breath went into his mouth, and her left hand slid back under his shoulder, drawing him tight. Then, almost shyly, her lips found his.

His left hand dropped downward, a single violent movement.

They stood close together, the touch of their lips not broken. Clive's left hand held her right and twisted it, the strength of his wrist against hers, outward and upward. Her breath panted against his. He could feel her teeth, small and sharp and predatory.

Something fell on the tiles with a flat, hard clatter. A little gun. A lady gun, but big enough.

Clive laughed, without sound.

'I wanted powder burns on you,' she whispered. 'Powder burns, so I could say you attacked me. Did you think I could let you live? Did you think I wanted to let you live?'

He said softly, 'No.'

He held her, the living, furious strength of her. She gave back, one step, two steps, looking up into his face. There was no fear in her.

'It was a good run, Ed. A damn good run.'

He did not answer. In the bleak light his face was without eagerness or cruelty or even hate.

'Your eyes are triangular, Ed. I never noticed that before. A killer's eyes.' She laughed, raising her head on the strong column of her throat. 'Even this won't bring her back, Ed. She's gone. Forever, gone.'

He let her go.

His belly and loins pressed her, no more strongly than with the force of a deep breath drawn in, but enough. Her heels slipped on the wet tile and went over the edge. She did not scream. Her body fell across the angle of the pool and her head struck the hard rim of the corner. He could hear her skull crack. There was no great splash when she went under.

Water came out over the deck almost to Clive's shoes, and drained back again. One great bubble rose and burst, then smaller ones, a string of them, and then nothing. The ripples died. Clive took off his coat and hung it neatly on a chair back. Using his handkerchief, he picked up the little gun and dropped it into his pocket. Then he kicked off his shoes and dived in.

He swam easily and well. It took him some minutes to find the body, in eight feet of water and the darkness of the bottom. When he did he towed it to the shallow end, lifted it up onto the deck, and climbed out. She was quite dead.

He put on his shoes again and hung his coat over his shoulders. He began to shiver in the cold air. He rolled up the bundle of slippers, photograph, and negligee and put it under his arm, hidden by the coat.

He walked away across the dark lawn, and did not look again at Vivien Alcott.

The house was silent. He met no one in the hallway, nor on the stairs, nor in the upper hall. He walked very quietly on the thick carpet. One door had light under the crack, and that was Jane's. He knew where Richard's room was. The second of the other doors he opened proved to be the one to Vivien's room. He went in and turned on a small lamp.

He hung the negligee in the closet, somewhat apart from the other clothes so that it would dry where water from his shirt had soaked it. He placed the mules on the shoe rack and Jane's photograph on a low table. Protecting it with his handkerchief, he laid the little gun in a bureau drawer under a pile of lacy underthings. Then he turned out the lamp.

He went out silently, and silently down the stairs. The darkness of his tanned skin showed through the thin wet fabric of his shirt. He pulled the coat closer around him. Drops of water ran down his face from his dark hair.

Mulligan was waiting at the foot of the stairs.

He looked at Clive, and past him up the steps, and then back again. He said nothing. His face showed no surprise. There was something curiously timeless about his being there.

Clive stopped by the graceful newel post. He said quietly, 'Miss Vivien has had an accident. She slipped at the edge of the pool. She's dead.'

Mulligan looked again up the stairs. Will you tell Miss Jane, or do you wish me to?'

'I'll tell her, after I've phoned.'

Mulligan inclined his head. Clive went past him, out onto the polished floor. Mulligan said with an odd, shrewd softness, 'Perhaps it's the best thing, after all.'

Clive stopped. The set of his head and shoulders was that of a tired man.

He said slowly, 'There's an old saying, Mulligan, that of all things, never to have been born is best.'

He walked on across the hall, to the telephone.

blue murder

☐	LEIGH BRACKETT No Good From A Corpse .	£3.95
☐	The Tiger Among Us	£3.95
☐	GIL BREWER 13 French Street & The Red Scarf	£4.50
☐	DAVID GOODIS The Burglar	£3.50
☐	DAVIS GRUBB The Night of the Hunter	£3.50
☐	DOLORES HITCHENS Sleep With Slander	£3.95
☐	Sleep With Strangers	£3.95
☐	GEOFFREY HOMES Build My Gallows High	£3.95
☐	WILLIAM P. MCGIVERN The Big Heat	£3.50
☐	JOEL TOWNSLEY ROGERS The Red Right Hand	£3.95
☐	NEWTON THORNBURG Cutter and Bone	£3.95
☐	CHARLES WILLIAMS The Diamond Bikini	£3.50
☐	CORNELL WOOLRICH Rear Window and Other Stories	£4.50

All these books are available at your local bookshop or newsagent, or can be ordered direct from the publisher. Just tick the titles you want and fill in the form below.

Prices and availability subject to change without notice.

Blue Murder Paperbacks, P.O. Box 11, Falmouth, Cornwall.

Please send cheque or postal order, and allow the following for postage and packing:

U.K. – 60p for one book, plus 25p for the second book, and 15p for each additional book ordered up to a maximum of £1.90.

Overseas (including EIRE) – £1.25 for the first book, plus 75p for the second, and 28p for each additional book thereafter.

Name ....

Address ....

....

....

....

....